Violet

Hill

Also by Henrietta McKervey
What Becomes of Us
The Heart of Everything

ACKNOWLEDGEMENTS

Many people played a part in bringing *Violet Hill* to life. For her advice and constant support, many thanks to my editor Ciara Considine; also to Joanna Smyth and the team at Hachette, and to Hazel Orme. A big thank you as always to my agent Margaret Halton, whose wise and patient words are always appreciated.

The events in this book are fictional. Although Sir Arthur Conan Doyle's support for spiritualism is well documented, he never had a business manager by the name of James Forrester, nor met a female detective called Violet Hill. Padraig O'Riordan of the Metropolitan Police Super Recogniser Unit explained what life is really like for someone who – literally – never forgets a face, and answered my many questions about super recognition and police procedures with patience and humour – any mistakes are mine, not his.

For reading and commenting on early drafts, many thanks to Sarah Gilmartin, Andrea Carter and Natalie Ryan. Thanks to the Arts Council for a Literature Bursary, and also to the Irish Writers Centre for the Jack Harte Bursary, which enabled Violet and I to spend much-needed time at the Tyrone Guthrie Centre. Thanks also to Kathleen MacMahon.

Love and thanks as always to Feargal, Cal and Rosa.

Violet
Hill

Henrietta McKervey

HACHETTE
BOOKS
IRELAND

First published in 2018 by Hachette Books Ireland
First published in paperback in 2019

A CIP catalogue record for this title is available from the British Library

ISBN 978 1 47368 268 9

Typeset in Cambria and Darwin by redrattledesign.com
Printed and bound in Great Britain by Clays Ltd, Elcograf S.p.A.

Hachette Books Ireland policy is to use papers that are natural, renewable and
recyclable products and made from wood grown in sustainable forests. The logging
and manufacturing processes are expected to conform to the environmental
regulations of the country of origin.

Hachette Books Ireland
8 Castlecourt Centre
Castleknock
Dublin 15, Ireland

A division of Hachette UK Ltd.
Carmelite House
50 Victoria Embankment
London EC47 0DZ

www.hachettebooksireland.ie

For my father,
Tony McKervey

DECEMBER 1918

I

None of us went in search of death. Did he think it or say it aloud? He's not always sure. But so many of them – *us* – are gone, it feels as though they each courted Death, teased and pulled its tail till it reared up and bit them. That's the truth of it. Because death in arms wasn't even in their minds, at the beginning. That was the way of a different generation, those greedy, guzzling old men whose wars were fought in hot, unfamiliar lands and spoken of as something of the past. Governments pick the fights, then leave it to the workers to fight them. So fight he did, and return he did, and where did it leave him? Alone on a pawnbroker's doorstep, that's bloody where.

All day the sky above London has been a swollen tit, desperate to let down its milk onto the streets below. As the first flakes of snow finally begin to fall, he glances up, a bare blink, just enough to check whether the woman is still at the window. Across the road and three floors up, she is a broad shape silhouetted against the glass. A fuzz of untidy blonde hair, a suet pudding of a face.

A newspaper lies open across his lap. 'Visiting Spiritualist J.C. Selbarre Causes Commotion at Society Gathering!' the headline insists. 'Sir Arthur Conan Doyle Leads Rapturous Applause!' The man leans forward slightly. He smiles, then slowly, deliberately, spits a long green gob. 'Selbarre' is covered; the black ink smudges. He folds the newspaper over, looks up from his lap. Gazes first at the feet marching past. Boot after tightly buttoned boot, shoe after scuffed shoe. On and on they go, grinding down the grit and grime of the pavement. He lifts his gaze a little higher. Legs next: striding, strolling, trotting. Each tethered pair carrying its own bag of fear, of want and greed. Then arses, torsos, shoulders, heads. They go past, these ordinary, new-freed people, Christmas parcels dancing in their foolish hands, words frosting around their heads. Spilled thoughts turned to air hang in the gritty London afternoon. The relief that it's all over is clear in some voices; others pulse with a pain that can't end. Wary or weary: that's what he reads in so many faces, even those desperate to cash in on four years of unspent Christmases.

A tall, thin woman, her hair the colour of unpolished brass, passes slowly by, tugging a young boy by the hand. Her exhausted face tells a story as clearly as if she had a placard in her hand. She pauses by the doorway and shoves the child behind her back, transferring him from one cold-reddened hand to the other. She ignores the seated figure as though his presence is no more than empty space for her and her son to pass through.

Christmas Eve 1918, and the city is a wound whose dressing was taken off too soon. Through all these thousands of streets, men are in doorways, their battlefield crump holes exchanged for lost, whiskery corners. Men who are the same as this one on the step, despite their different mutilations. Ghosts, returned to haunt the living.

He watches as the blonde woman at the window moves out of sight, only to return a moment later. She cranes her head around before she looks at him again, as if to pretend her attention lands merely by chance on the doorstep across the way. Does she think she's watching a returned hero or a lucky fool? He's noticed her before, her pal too. It's the friend he's curious about. He's spied her going in the door of number twelve as a woman – pale, slight and frowning, tight brown curls escaping from either side of her hat – only to reappear an hour later wearing a cap, dressed as a man. Missy Yellow-hair doesn't seem to care whether anyone notices how much time she spends pressed against the window, yet the other woman is different, he's decided. More likely to shun attention than court it. He lights another cigarette, curious to know what story she's peddling. Smoke and snow move in a soft, uncertain waltz around his face. With a final twitch of the curtain, Blondie disappears. A few minutes later she slams the street door behind her and is gone. He watches her walk the length of Cleveland Street towards the omnibus.

There is a flash of ghoulish face paint under the gas lamp. A couple of tarts walk past him, arms linked tight as cheap twine. The nearer of the two has a purplish lick of bruises under the rouge of her cheek. She twitches her skirts and puckers her mouth when she sees him looking. 'Fancy a bit, do you?' Her companion's glance is a mean, flickering sort of apology. A scrap, thrown to a dog, to atone only for the loudness of her friend's voice, not her words.

An elderly man walking past pauses and pats his pockets, searching for his watch. He doesn't acknowledge the man on the step, so close beside him as to be almost touching his knee. Davey regards the feeble glow of the cigarette in his hand. *Fucking invisible, am I?* he thinks, angry. Head down, he leans forward a few inches.

War and death are lovers turned mad by desire and desperation. He did not want to die. But he did, a thousand different times. And yet here he is: a man returned to tell the whole sorry tale to these unscathed men, these borrowed-blood women.

Turns out, no one cares to hear it.

'He mithered, but took it anyway.'

The door opens behind him and David Dockery, formerly of the British Army Seventh Infantry Division and, as of this very moment, a former holder of the 1914 Star Medal, rises awkwardly to his feet. Although his left side is closest to the wall, he has to stretch his right hand across his body to steady himself. The two men stand close in the doorway, their broad foreheads nearly touching. Above their heads, three gold balls glow like Christmas baubles.

'I still think you're wrong to pawn your Star. You won it the hard way,' Will says.

Davey shrugs. He knew his brother would be sentimental about it. Medals are precious to Will, relics cast in the flesh of the fallen. For Davey, they are no more than overdue wages. Coins drop into his palm. Their spill is short, far less satisfying than he wanted. He turns the coins over in his hand, then gestures at the tin mask covering Will's face.

'I could have gone in myself for this!' So much for Metcalfe, a tight fucker like all pawnbrokers, parting with more at the sight of his brother's wounds. Davey sees the two curtains of Will's eyelids lower then rise. Will's breath is a foggy slurp through the narrow open mouth of the mask. It gets damp behind the tin, Will told him, where the skin is worst burned. Raw and sore, his cheeks and nose are constantly clammy, and often infected. When Will was a little lad, not even two years old, Davey remembers him sounding out words in his sleep. Davey would be lying in the bed next to him, a scrawny five-year-old, given to sleeplessness, restless even then, and he'd hear Will speak clear as an adult. *Squirrel. Ointment. Charabanc.* Odd, disconnected words that had no bearing on each other. But when he woke up, he'd be talking ba-ba nonsense, same as any other little lad. Will says almost nothing now, unless he has to.

'The money weighs more.' Davey slowly closes his fist over the coins and drops them into his pocket.

Will shrugs again, a goodbye this time. He's due to get the next train back to Sidcup. They hear all about it from the nurses if they're late back. 'At least you *have* ears,' Davey replies, remembering some of the basket cases he'd noticed when he visited Will at the Queen's Hospital the week before. Will says nothing, just walks away. It's impossible to know whether he took offence. As he leaves the pawnbroker's step in favour of Charlotte Street and the Golden Hind, Davey caresses the coins with his fingertips. He feels the soft, cheering clink of gold waiting to be spun into a different gold.

The pub will be noisy and hot, and smoke will swirl above the drinkers' heads like funeral plumes on horses, but by the time the clock over the bar strikes eight, he will decide he must make a toast. A toast that will take in all of London. The young lady beside him, happy to smile at his money, will not be able to hear him and will move closer (though when she does, he sees she's not a lady or especially young). He will barely hear himself over the din of desperate, dizzying celebrations. His toast will be a roar thrown to the bar, the streets. To the sour, unbearable city.

'What's that, lovey?' she will ask. 'What you muttering for?' Muttering? He doesn't know what is noise and what is the incessant gunfire crack of his own thoughts.

He will look straight ahead, saying nothing. He will only hold the glass tight as a lover to his lips, until it too is empty.

As per, Chrissie has made up the fire too strong and turned the lamps high so that the small room is stuffy, the air thinned. Worn out. Shadows creep from the corners and collide with the light shining as sharply on the scuffed furniture as if it was a stage set. Violet sighs. She has two thick vests on under a cambric shirt and is aware of a new bloom of sweat on her skin, an uncomfortable dampness in her armpits. The lining of her coat is padded with folded newspaper. Chrissie pressed the sheets under books that morning, compacting the paper into strong, slim folds. ('For protection, I suppose?' Chrissie asked, the first time Violet showed her how to fold the pages into long strips and pin them the length of the jacket, then tack the lining into place. 'Flatten them to stop them rustling,' was Violet's reply.)

'That poor man ... There's nobody to love him, I'm sure of it.' Chrissie is at the window again. Her head and shoulders are invisible behind the curtain; only her well-upholstered backside protrudes into the room. Violet sighs again, loudly this time. Her supposed assistant spends too much time staring down at Cleveland Street and commenting on what she sees. Every dray's rumble, every clerk's umbrella ... it all warrants a remark. It's unfathomable to Violet: despite everything, Chrissie persists on seeing the world as one sentimental tableau after another, as though life is nothing but a series of chocolate-box wrappers or a seemingly endless variety hall stage being played out just for her, all day long. She's one of the few who seem to have been almost untouched by the war. She lost no one, not really. Chrissie's father died in 1916, but not in battle. He tripped on a loose cobblestone and went under a Hopeworth's delivery horse.

'Drunk, of course,' Chrissie had told her, adding, 'I feel so bad for that poor nag. I hope they didn't send it to the knacker's yard. You can be sure that horse worked harder than he ever did.' Chrissie had been almost embarrassed by the whole business: at last there was a bereavement she could claim as her own, a band to wear on her arm if she chose to, but such a foolish one! How could she lay claim to the death when she wasn't bothered by his life? And all around her women – young women! Younger women! – were in agony from grief all day long, their lives over even as their adult days were still laid out flat ahead of them, fresh as sheets from a mangle.

Violet wonders if Chrissie is in some strange way dissatisfied. Not that she would *choose* to be visited by suffering, more that she has been disregarded by the changes suffering brings. In 1914 Chrissie tossed the coins of her future into the well, and four years later here they are, scooped up in her pail and back in her purse, right down to the last farthing.

'The poor love. Another one just back, I'd say, forced to beg for his supper. I've not seen a single person give him so much as a ha'penny.' Chrissie sighs. 'And so handsome!' She stares at him, three floors below. Watches how he sits so still, looking downwards, ignoring the Christmas shoppers, the jig of parcels parading past his knees. Watches the yellow light falling through the glass-paned door behind him. Why, it's like a halo over his perfect head! Her sigh kisses the cold window. 'I hope he's not too cold. He looks cold. And it's starting to snow.'

'Chrissie, stop gurning out the window. You'll draw attention to us.' Violet is in front of the cheval glass, slowly dirtying her face and neck. Her movements are slow, and with each swipe of her sponge she conceals a little more. 'You're the arse end of a pantomime horse, standing like that.'

A snigger comes from behind the curtain as Chrissie wiggles her bottom from side to side. 'Cheek! But here's an idea! How 'bout if I canter down and see if he'd like a cup of tea?'

'How about if you see would your employer like a cup of tea?'

Chrissie drops the curtain and walks towards the dresser where she keeps their tea things. Violet has a grubby cloth and is beginning to remove some of the dirt she's put on. In her reflection she sees a working man, a man in a hurry to give his grimy face a lick and a promise. She learned early on that a woman standing around on the street will draw all manner of unwanted attention, but as a man with a newspaper and a cigarette, her presence is of no more consequence than a gas lamp.

'Any callers or post when I was out?' Violet has been growing increasingly worried about the state of her finances, and several accounts have been owing for months. Chrissie keeps the books – and does it well, Violet has to allow her that – yet she never seems to consider the implications of the growing disparity between what comes in and what goes out every month. For all that she's good at her sums, Chrissie seems unable to add the two-and-two of business life together.

'Mr MacArthur brought his cheque, so I took it to lodge earlier. He's going to dismiss his cook and gardener as soon as he's been to the employment agency to be sure of replacing them. He said he'd report them to the police for good measure, and I was to give you his thanks for exposing their devilish cheating ways. His words, not mine.'

'The police? There was no need for that – I told him as much. He'll wear his shoes out running for a bobby every time he finds someone with a finger in the larder.'

'But didn't they only rob him cos he paid them so badly?'

'Chrissie! You never said that to him?'

'Course not. I told him all-found staff are hard enough to get these days, so it stands to reason that having a reputation as a good employer makes it easier.'

'Thanks,' Violet says quietly.

'And there's a postcard from a – it's hard to read the writing – James Forrester of Chelsea, it looks like, asking would you call on him. On Boxing Day, if you don't mind.' She holds the card up to the light so Violet can read it, turning it slowly from front to back. 'The address is Cheyne Place. Swanky.' Yet it's an ordinary postcard, one of the *Daily Mirror*'s Canadian Official Series: a horse on a narrow track pulls a large cart holding three wounded men, while another soldier walks beside them, his head turned over his shoulder to stare at the photographer. One of the men has a bandage across his nose, neat as a Boy Scout's badge. *Victorious but Tired* the caption reads. *Tired*? Violet frowns. She has yet to see anyone newly back from the war who fits that description. Tired is what she is, after a long day on her feet, trailing some fool through the city streets, trying to catch a careless spouse with their lover. Tired is the despairing life of the city itself, bloody and bludgeoned after years of war. The same five letters cannot possibly sit around the head of any returned man, considering what they must have seen and heard. What they must have done.

'Oh, silly me, I almost forgot!' Chrissie rushes over to the dresser. 'The new calling cards arrived. They turned out lovely, too.'

'Just leave them. I'll look later, when I've washed my hands.' Violet smiles, turns back to the mirror. 'Your mother would like you back early tonight, wouldn't she, Chrissie? Go now and you'll be home by seven.'

'What about you? I don't understand why you've got to work on Christmas Eve. It can wait a few days, can't it?'

Violet shrugs. 'Work is work.'

But what about her? Her Christmas Eve will be spent walking London's streets. Her voice will be lower, gruffer. It will move miles east, shedding letters as it goes. When she can walk no more, she will go to her room in Kensington, where she will wake alone on Christmas morning and stay so until it's time to work again on Boxing Day. Violet is twenty-nine and has been fending for herself for twelve years. When she moved to London from Witney she had been determined to escape a life that promised only domestic servitude – either through marriage or employment – and held no hope of adventure or even of being *herself*. Violet had realised early in life that the liberty to be the woman she was born would be hard won.

She is used to being alone. But how is the run of her hours

to go? She can already count them off to herself, can predict the windmill of the day, the way time will turn and fold over and over on itself. She will open the present Chrissie gives her (sure to be a twill brooch, the fabric sewn as a spray of violets, the entire thing the size of a penny; there was a hawker at the far end of Cleveland Street just last week with a tray of them – Chrissie won't have been able to resist). She will stay in bed until lunchtime and then go out in search of a café where she will eat alone, a book open and unread on the table in front of her. It's only one day, who's to care? She can be herself for one day, can't she? Boxing Day she'll be back at work. She will be someone else again. A man in a flat cap; a servant, another invisible woman, surplus to the country's needs. Whoever. Violet is everyone. (*Violet*, Violet will fear, during a low, bored moment late in the evening of Christmas Day when she realises she has nothing to do, and no one to tell the thought to, *is no one.*)

Chrissie hands her a small package. 'Happy Christmas, Vi. It's only something small, I'm afraid, but I think you'll like it.'

'That's very good of you, thanks.' Through the newspaper wrapping Violet can feel a small box. Still, a brooch is better than the last gift Chrissie gave her: Mrs Miller's *A Bachelor Girl's Life*. The book's forced chumminess got on Violet's nerves. ('As soon as you rise in the morning, strip your bed and drape the bedclothes over a chair at the foot of the bed before arching the mattress'; 'Tea should never be taken with meat lunches as the tannin within will be sure to act injuriously on a woman's ability to digest meat.') It was like having a bossy teacher permanently perched on her shoulder. Chrissie used to ask her about it: had she cooked any of the recipes, or used the cleaning advice? She stopped asking the day Violet replied, 'I made her potatoes and salt last night. You cook potatoes and put salt on them. Then you eat them, by yourself, in bed in the dark because you've no penny for the meter.' Afterwards she'd felt very mean. But honestly, Chrissie! You could just pinch her, sometimes.

'Your envelope is on the desk, by the letter opener. That box there, that's for you too. Happy Christmas.' Violet had nipped into Boots earlier and bought Chrissie a flash lamp. She wonders if Chrissie will think it a stupid gift, more suited to a small boy than a grown woman. She wishes she'd taken the booklet that came with it, *A Chat about Flash Lamps and Batteries*, out of the package. Will Chrissie think she's being off, or having a dig at her over using too much gas in the office? She should have given her the little bit extra in her envelope and left it at that.

When the sound of the street door tells her Chrissie has finally left, *Merry Christmas* and *You're ever so good* trailing behind her like scent, Violet peeps around the edge of the curtain. Night has come in, low and heavy. The man on the step opposite must be the chap Chrissie was going on about. She was right: there is something curious about him, about the way he's glancing around himself as though he is real but no one else is. Chrissie's got it wrong, Violet thinks. He's not begging. He's the opposite of most beggars who, as they're pan-handling, are wheedling with it, trying to make themselves frailer, needier, even as they put themselves in your path. One hand lies across his knees, the other holds a lit cigarette. She's getting used to seeing men back, walking around the streets. There's a similar cast to them all: either shaken and hollow-looking, or guiltily giddy, jumpy as horses in a lightning storm.

Caught in the yellow shine of the window, each flake floats dizzily, beautifully. She is about to turn away when she notices a man in a heavy tweed overcoat, his umbrella still furled despite the snow, pause in front of Metcalfe's and take out his pocket watch. He stands there as though the step next to him is empty, as though there isn't another human sitting just behind him, level with his knee and close enough to touch it with the smallest movement. The sitting figure slowly leans forward, and extends the lit tip of his cigarette. After the briefest flare, the wool is dark again. The man walks on, oblivious to the fresh burn in his coat.

The door behind the seated figure opens. She gets a glimpse of his profile as he rises from the step and turns, though in this light he's all shadows and angles. A second man wearing one of those horrible tin face masks – poor sod – appears to be giving him money.

Mystery solved. She was right: he wasn't begging, just waiting. She turns away from the window, goes to wash her hands, then sits down at Chrissie's desk.

Black letters spill across the creamy card. Her own name repeated over and over. Hers. A decade earlier, Violet had taken a job as secretary to a private investigator in Russell Square. It was interesting at first, but as time went on she realised that not only did she dislike the repetition of her own job but she could do his better than he ever would. He had no certainty, no sense; every case was no more than a ripped map that needed to be glued back together. What appeared to her to be humanity's obvious motivations – greed, desire, power – bypassed him. She was getting his new calling cards printed one afternoon when she decided *her* name should be on them. It had been that simple: it had to be, else she'd have lost her nerve. She's had that same clear note of pleasure from new cards every time since. She could ill-afford this set, but who knows? Perhaps they will bring her the bit of luck she needs.

Violet Hill Investigations.

12 Cleveland Street, WC.

TN Regent 2820

Specialists in private enquiries of a personal or delicate nature.

'Violet Hill? Where's that, love?' the man at the printer's had asked, when Chrissie spelled out the order, a sliver of silver type quivering in his hand.

'It's not a *where*, it's a *who*,' had been Chrissie's answer. 'She's the only woman detective in London.'

Violet turns a card over in her hand. Fans out a row of them. Her name skips and dances in front of her. It is hers and hers alone. She puts the cards to one side and turns back to the man in the mirror. She smiles at him. He grins back, his face rough and grubby, his eyes staring straight into hers.

Across the room, the fire is burning down to nothing. She locks the office and leaves. Yet, despite what she told Chrissie, she has no trail to follow this evening. There is no case, no client paying for her evening. The time she is spending is her own. Every breath in and out, every thought, her own. Now, her shoulders hunched, hands jammed into her jacket pockets, she is nothing more than a tired labouring man, walking home after a long day's work, glad of the respite of Christmas Day to come. As a man walking alone at night, she is invisible. She can go where she wants, watch whom and what she needs to. But as a woman? She would be supposed to be either up to mischief or in danger of it befalling her.

The two men outside the pawnbroker's have gone. Metcalfe is putting his shutters up. He looks tired. Christmas Eve is always busy. He doesn't see through her disguise, and she doesn't greet him. She puts a hand into her jacket pocket and touches the postcard. *A Mr Forrester of Chelsea*. She shrugs. Might as well. She's walking anyway and it's better to have somewhere to go, even if it's just a garden gate.

A clock strikes a quarter to eight as she passes the walls of the Physic Garden in Chelsea and turns down Cheyne Place. The snow has been falling constantly in the hour she's been walking, and the white space between the pavement and the front door of Mr Forrester's house lies even and untouched. It is big, expensive-looking. That's a good sign. Tall chalk-coloured walls grow from the frozen earth to a red-brick bay window one floor up. All the shutters are closed, and only an uncertain sliver of light slips through from an attic room. She climbs the front steps slowly, stopping halfway. Her route already betrayed by her footsteps in the snow, she decides that two steps away from the door is far enough.

As she turns away, the memory of Gareth Slatten, dead by his own hand on a similarly quiet, snowy night five years earlier, sighs and stirs somewhere deep within her. It was long before Chrissie's time with her and she has never told Chrissie, or anyone else, about him. Even before the war Violet had known many deaths – her own parents had died within eight months of each other when she was seventeen – but somehow his always stood apart. She hadn't even been a year in business when she was commissioned by Hannah Slatten to discover why her husband had been accused of stealing from his employer, Henry Gardiner, Marquess of Denismore. Hannah had once worked in the same household – she was the Gardiner children's nursery maid until her marriage. The accusations were false, she was sure: her Gareth was no thief. Slatten had been arrested a week earlier and placed on remand in Brixton Prison. A week later he had departed his cell a corpse, and was buried in the prison grounds. Violet tried to do right by Hannah, by Slatten's children, but she failed. She doesn't know what has happened to them. It had been her first case that didn't legitimately deserve the word *petty* attached to it somewhere, and she had been determined to solve it, no matter what. Well, she had done as she was asked and found the truth. But it turned out to be an answer Hannah could not bear to hear, or her husband bear to live with. Violet believes in truth. Believes it to be solid and powerful as a cliff. And if that makes it a hard and immovable thing, then it also makes it high and strong. A protector. Facts exist in and of themselves, and can be – must be! – called to account, not so much to determine what is right and wrong, but to *create* it.

One morning early in the war they had been reading the newspaper together when Violet had said to Chrissie, 'Before this all started I knew a man who died, and it was sudden, and so shocking, and I felt that one death everywhere, all around me, for ages. And now, look, every single day, they're all just lists of names. They're only words.'

Chrissie replied, 'If he'd not died then, Vi, he'd be most likely gone by now, when you think about it.'

Violet stayed silent, hating what Chrissie had said, though she knew her intention had been to comfort: *Your grief wasn't wasted: if he wasn't dead then, he'd be dead now.* The city breathes – no, more than that: it moves, grows, trades!

– on the memories of lost lives. The recent dead crowd the air, choking it like soot that crawls inside you and takes up residence in your lungs, becoming part of your body.

The truth of what had led Gareth Slatten to Brixton Prison was not hers to tamper with, yet she can't help but wonder: would he still be alive had she acted differently? And what of Henry Gardiner, a man so completely convinced of his rights over his servants that he saw no responsibility towards them? She hates her memory of him. How cold and unyielding in his power he was! How dismissive of another man's family, of their very humanity. Violet had done her best, hadn't she? Yet the dark of her heart whispers Hannah Slatten's name. Asks her where those three children are. Two men had power over Hannah, over the lives of her children, and both of those men, in different ways, had cast the family into poverty. Hannah would have been better off a war widow with a pension, because her husband's death had left her without a penny. As it was, she had pawned clothes and furniture for the deposit on Violet's hire.

The streets are quiet. Behind the walls and doors, the city puts its young to bed. Yawning and fretful, wishing another day done. She pictures everyone but her at home, protected from the street by bricks and mortar, by fear and need and hope. The clock strikes eight as she backs down the steps and turns for home, treading only in the marks her feet had already left in the snow. She moves swiftly, smudging her earlier footprints, imagining a diminutive Mrs Miller perched on her shoulder, arms folded tight and high under her shelf of a bosom, briskly advising: 'Walk along swiftly and convey a sense of purpose; a cold stare will usually put a stop to any annoyance.' She walks as though she could unmake her route, as though her journey was a row of knitting she could unravel back onto the ball.

'Blast it!' she mutters. She's left Chrissie's present in the office. She'll have nothing to open tomorrow, after all.

II

The first stroke of midnight shouts, peals, whimpers across London. War is over, but the peace has yet to begin. It's an impossible state of nothing, of un-being, though equally impossible is the idea that there can ever be peace again. All the hate that had been stoppered up, held back by a dam of privilege and money, had poured out in a violent torrent over every city, town and village. And as the bells sound, people are still crying, talking, laughing. The cheap mattress of Armistice Day continues to be turned over. In rooms throughout the city, as on that night six weeks before, women are lifting their skirts, men dropping their braces.

In Chiswick, an exhausted officer holds a service revolver in his hand. It's heavy, but smooth, cool to his touch. He handles it gently, for he is about to blow his brains out. His wife and child will find him in the morning alongside the Christmas tree. His little daughter will wake up early, excited to open her present, and slip downstairs. She will see his feet first, soles upright and, laughing at the great game Papa is playing, will drop to her knees to crawl under the tree and hug him. The white gleam of his exposed skull, a pinkish mass that will make her think first of blancmange, will stay with her for the rest of her life, which will be long and, because of what she will see in six hours' time, lonely and muddled.

Across the city in Thorburn Square, an elderly man, four sons dead and not a single body to bury, his wife in an asylum and in such a state from the grief as to be dead to him too, closes the door on the bedroom he shared with her for thirty years. He walked the noisy streets all day, a final pilgrimage to the city in which he reared his sons, yet the firm *click* of the lock is the loudest sound he has ever heard. On the twelfth stroke, he will suck a rubber tube fastened to the gas jet. The char who finds him two days later will take his good wool overcoat for her trouble. There's a cigarette burn by the hem at the back but a coat's a coat.

At the bottom end of Regent Street, two men pay each other no attention as they pass in opposite directions. Violet Hill is one. She is finally fatigued and, now that the turn into Christmas Day has begun, allows that it's time to go home. She is lightheaded from walking, but happy, too, from the hours of being free, being someone else, being no more than an ordinary man, walking alone, unencumbered and unaccosted. The second man is drunk. Within hours Davey Dockery will sober back into a profound depression, a sensation he recognises as of his life now, never of his life before. For good or ill, what is done is done, whether in madness or in love makes no odds. The only way to shove this new blackness from him is to seek out distraction. *Life*, as he thinks of it. *I just want some life.* Unsure how to animate this sensation, he drinks in the hope he may find out.

He lifts his head to the sky. The snow clouds have cleared and stars glint through, as though obligated to do so because of the day that's in it. His Star is gone, squandered in a single evening. Davey's wounds aren't worth much. Only three weeks earlier, he'd thought that he and Will were lucky because they were among the first to leave the army, even if Will had been sent to live in a hospital. At the demob camp they'd been given railway coupons, a clothes allowance, a ration book and promise of a pension of thirty-eight shillings a week for twenty weeks. For those with serious injuries, there was more money to be had. Davey's injured left hand didn't earn him much – the money was less for a left than a right – but he's better off than Will, because there is no extra allowance for wounds from the neck up. The army put no value on their brains. Brawn was all they were ever paid for.

Davey needs a piss. He stumbles down a lane, his arm and shoulder still aching, wrenched and sore. Those fuckers in the Golden Hind! He'll not be going back there again. A rat scuffles alongside his feet. More than one, probably, though it's hard to see properly. Rats in the trenches got fat white faces from eating dead bodies: human flesh made their faces bloated and strangely luminous, he doesn't know why. They were fearless, an army of greasy ghosts. He leans against the wall and kicks out, hard. His foot connects with something soft, something that struggles. Got you, bastard. He stamps his boot down. There is a brief resistance, a stiffening under his foot, before the rat goes limp. He steadies himself and looks down. Only a small one, but he pisses on it anyway. He reloads his foot and takes fire. The carcass arcs through the air and thuds into a gutter on Regent Street.

The bells fall still. Wait! He stops, turns his face to the sky:

is that singing he can hear? A choir singing Christmas carols. Course it's fucking not. *You stupid cunt, Davey*. He sniggers to himself, imagining himself dropped into a postcard, *A Soldier's Christmas of Peace*, a picture-book choir singing in the snow to a delighted group of limbless men. He decides he needs to make his toast again. Loudly this time, so the entire city can hear him. The snow is turning to slush, yet he can still see the steps of the evening cross-hatched in the street. A human palimpsest of wishes and desires. He walks to the middle of Regent Street and raises his arms to salute the drained snow clouds, the dead, the living.

'Happy fucking Christmas, London,' he roars.

December 2017

I carried the fear inside me all Christmas. Heavy and lumpen, it was the hard swallow in my throat, the melancholy weight in my stomach. That case was worse than usual for some reason (not that we ever had a *usual*). Three sexual assaults in seven weeks, each one in a public place. The perpetrator – or what I'd been able to see of him from the hundreds of hours of grainy, poorly lit CCTV footage I'd viewed so far – haunted me. I hadn't seen his complete face, just flashes of features: a flicker of an ear and a high, wide cheekbone, a crescent of pale chin protruding from under an umbrella. It was as though he knew where the cameras were that recorded the unvoiced stories of the streets, and was taunting us. No, not us. *Me*.

I scanned footage collated from dozens of recordings. As he approached each victim he carried an open umbrella – black, unbranded – in one hand and a large bunch of flowers in the other. The bouquet was always wrapped in clear cellophane with no visible florist's sticker. And though such props made him easier to locate, the coverage they gave his face meant isolating his features became so much harder each time I found him. Three times I had watched him stop a woman in the street. Always between seven and half past on a dark wet winter evening. Always close to where a Tube station waited to swallow the last late office workers. Each of the women was young, and looked distracted. Vulnerable and slight and tired, as though the high-heeled urgency of that morning's commute had drained away in the drudge of a day's work.

I watched him greet his third victim as though they knew each other well. Watched him spinning all the hapless charm of a grainy, soundless rom-com, as he launched into a smiling grovel from behind the bouquet. He put the flowers into her hands before she had a chance to realise what he was doing, all the while talking non-stop, distracting her, as he gently moved her to one side and slightly backwards, as though he was embarrassed at having to plead in public, and needed privacy for her to capitulate, to laugh, to admit that her confusion or annoyance was feigned. The umbrella, too, was clever: it made it harder for any passer-by to remember him, and because he immediately tilted it over the woman as well as himself, he took possession of the very ground she stood on, an explorer roughly staking his claim over an island. Onlookers saw a handsome, well-dressed man, cravenly begging his lover's forgiveness with a bouquet.

Three women, each approached within ten feet of a smaller, much quieter space: the mouth of a lane, a poorly lit entrance, a dead-end. The most recent assault had taken place not far from where I lived, in a passageway near Chalk Farm station where scaffolding and tarpaulins covering a building renovation between an office block and a small grocery had almost entirely concealed an already-narrow lane. He never panicked, never raised his voice. How could that be threatening? A passer-by who was later interviewed as a potential witness to the second assault shrugged, 'But I thought he was shielding her from the rain.'

My working life was spent looking at images taken from CCTV footage and connecting faces from different recordings, as though London was a vast join-the-dots puzzle. There could be months, years, of a time gap between sightings, but I would remember a person. *Snapping*, we called it, when we recognised an individual across a number of recordings linking them to what had previously been considered unrelated crimes. But in the Super-Recogniser Unit, you are only ever as good as your last snap: when my boss had assigned me to this identification on top of a heavy caseload a week earlier I had promised myself I'd have an ident for him before the Christmas break. Only I hadn't. I was confident I'd got all available footage of the assaults, yet I knew I didn't have the full story. He wouldn't have chosen a random street, a random woman. Men like him never do. Stage settings, such as the flowers, the dark, rainy evening, the umbrella, told me that much. He was a planner, a preparer. He must have staked out territory for weeks, possibly even months. *That* was the version of him I was looking for: unguarded, eyes-about. A figure snooping around odd, interstitial gaps on every busy street, the dim, quiet spaces that go unheard in the undersong of the city.

Frustrated at my failure to snap this stranger, I called a colleague to my desk and replayed some of the collated footage. Last year, 80 per cent of the idents in London had been made by six police officers. And 30 per cent of the 80 per cent – more than five hundred individual identifications – had been made by a softly spoken former UK judo champ from Tenby. Leon was our top snapper, holder of a long-standing record of twenty-five idents for one criminal, which had led to convictions for thirty separate offences. His technique for recognising people was different from mine. For me, it was more of a pinhole camera, like looking from a negative to white paper and watching it develop instantaneously. Leon had worked as a computer programmer before he joined the Met, and to him faces were complex circuit diagrams. He'd look for signature moves, the tilt of a head, say, or a particular posture, then link them together. Back when he was on the beat he had arrested a guy for being drunk and disorderly. Then, from the way the man twisted his earlobe between his fingers, Leon had recognised him as the teenager who'd nicked his lunch money seventeen years earlier.

Silently we watched the man walk into shot from the left, his back to the camera, then reappear moments later via a second, differently angled, camera. I paused the screen: 'Look how he holds the flowers up close to his face when he meets her, so she's confused at first as to whether or not she actually knows him. A second later he's by her side and has the umbrella tilted over her head, so again it's hard for her to see his entire face.' I didn't need to tell Leon what had happened next – they'd moved out of sight of a camera, the man now behind her, firmly nudging her along. We watched the woman's jerky movements. In those seconds I hated knowing what she still didn't: that she wouldn't see his face again. That he would push her head against a wall, that he would assault her from behind, wordlessly, the closed umbrella pressing against her neck until she was afraid her throat would close in on itself. That in less than a minute she would be battling for each breath.

The descriptions I'd collated from witness statements and

the victims' recorded interviews were vague: early thirties; 'Neutral accent,' said one, 'Posh voice,' said another; pale complexion; blue eyes. Navy coat; black scarf wrapped high. No scars or visible tattoos, nothing particularly distinguishing. He could have been one of the thousands of white men I saw on screen every day. 'My first thought was how attractive he was,' the second victim said. 'A good-looking bloke calling to me on the street. *Lucky me*, I thought. But only seconds later I realised I didn't know him at all.' A long pause in the recording was broken by the sound of her crying, alone, and then she said, 'Only by then his hand was on my neck . . . and I was in the alley and it was dark.'

I knew what it was to be grabbed from behind. It paralyses and terrifies all at once. You suddenly become aware of the very edges of your body as every synapse fires, screaming, *No, no, not me*, desperate to deny the moment its urgency, to push beyond the outlines of your skin and escape.

No one stopped him. No one saw a terrified woman being tugged towards a dark space by a stranger: the few passers-by who took any notice saw a man trying desperately to win over a hard-to-persuade, make-him-suffer-for-it girlfriend. The flowers, the neatly anonymous appearance, the calm voice beseeching her, speaking over her protests. It took confidence – crimes committed by sane people do – but there was more to it than that. It worked because his technique traded on a clever insight into the casual, glancing assumptions everyone makes about what's going on around them. Three women sexually assaulted because passers-by took one well-groomed smiling man at face value and didn't realise – or didn't want to – that the narrative he was visually peddling didn't add up. We watched the relentless movement on the street in silence. Leon drew a blank on him. 'Fuck's sake, what's wrong with people?' He frowned. 'If he'd been trolling women online there'd have been plenty weighing in to have a go at him.'

Behind us, our colleagues were shutting up shop for Christmas. It was unusual to hear the sound of the room winding down, chairs squeaking, the click and sigh of screens switching off. Six of us usually worked full-time at the unit in Lambeth, though two were temporarily deployed offsite, JD to counter-terrorism, Jessica to the gangs unit in Hackney. Our official hours were eight to four, but we all put in much longer days. There was invariably someone around when I arrived each morning, and though I usually aimed to leave by six I was often first to go home, wiped from tiredness. A visiting journalist once expressed surprise that so much of the unit's work was done by people, because mapping faces against each other seemed such a computer-perfect job. And though we did use technology, it hadn't got close to matching what we could do. When we reviewed a crowd scene, we weren't merely making predictions based on the history of the criminal being tracked, we were also seeing patterns of behaviour based on motivation.

Because most of what we viewed at work was grainy, speeded-up recordings, a full day spent watching strangers' lives playing out at speed often left me with a bumbling, slightly giddy sensation. We watched thousands of messy, plotless true-life movies every day, but never in real time. Disorienting, too, was that so few of the thousands of people we saw every day made any sort of eye contact with the cameras. I regularly felt as though I'd spent an entire day in someone else's dream, wandering around a frustratingly vague landscape in which the hinterland perpetually rolled away, hazy and incomplete.

Our office was a large room and supposedly hot-desking, but we'd all ferreted out corners we liked and would gravitate towards. As I closed the window beside 'my' desk, a glittering string of red tinsel fell from the blind onto my chair. Irritated, I flicked it into the bin. The air was cold, suffused with a whiff of hospital-grade soup from the vent outside the basement canteen.

'Time to go, Susanna. I think you need a drink.' Leon leaned over and switched off the large double-screen monitor mounted over my computer. The man, the umbrella, the flowers froze, then disappeared. In my last sight of him, the side of his head was dipping down, as if nodding in agreement. 'Whoever he is,' he added, 'he'll still be there after Christmas.'

I picked up my coat and bag. 'That's exactly what I'm afraid of.'

The Windjammer was noisy and hot, and reeked of Christmas lunches stretched out into the early evening, endurance tests of booze. I hated that enforced party spirit, the crazed, sweaty dance of it. The room was heaving, but we got lucky and nabbed a table as a pissed-up office crowd left in a farting cloud of Santa hats and sweat. I squashed in next to the window, Leon beside me. Outside, I noticed an elderly couple pause under a streetlight. The woman crouched to tie the man's shoelace. Beads of rain on her plastic hat sparkled, as if she was being lit for a stage. He stared over her head as though he didn't know she was there. His thick white hair was brushed high off his forehead, almost into a quiff. His face meant nothing to me. He held a Bob the Builder toy phone to his ear. The yellow plastic glowed. 'Hello?' he said, and then again, his tone unchanging, 'Hello, hello?' Awkwardly, she manoeuvred herself upright and I got a proper look at her face. I had seen her a couple of times before, maybe a year or so earlier. Without saying anything, she took the phone from his hand and slipped it into the pocket of her coat. She held out her arm for him to lean on and they moved off down the road.

'That's love for you,' Leon said, over my shoulder, as we watched them walk slowly away, her head bent low, as if scanning the pavement for change. Was it? I wondered what he saw in them that I couldn't. To me, it looked like duty.

'Fuck's sake,' I said, to myself rather than him, 'her hat is wet.' I wriggled out from behind the table ('Sorry, sorry, I'll catch up with you later') and through the crowd to the door.

The temperature in the office had fallen in the half-hour I'd been gone. Even though a radiator clanked and groaned in the hallway outside, it was cold. I didn't bother putting on the overhead lights, just my desk lamp. It was gloomy, the corners jittery with shadows. I heard the pad of a security guard's footsteps on deserted corridors, but never saw him. From a desk across the room came the small, soft tick of a clock. I'd never noticed it before. Twice I got up to check the door was closed. To be sure I really was alone.

In the CCTV recordings taken from the third assault scene, it was raining. But when he appeared in the footage on Haverstock Hill, diagonally across the road and about ten yards from the station, his umbrella was barely wet. I cursed myself for not noticing it earlier. He must have put it up just before he approached her, which meant that even though the footage showed him walking down Haverstock Hill towards the Tube, he might have just *exited* the station, crossed the road and put his umbrella up, as if appearing on the scene for the first time. I made a note to investigate the electronic readers in the stations closest to the assault locations in case I could isolate one fare card that had been used at all three, then began to scan the footage taken from the area again, this time looking for a man without an umbrella.

Just over an hour later, a freeze-frame face stared back at me. 'Got you,' I said, my voice oddly nervous. I didn't need to compare it to the slivers of his features I'd isolated earlier to be sure that I had him. Grainy and incomplete, but more than enough. His eyes appeared to stare straight into mine as he left the station twelve minutes before the assault had taken place. I couldn't see any flowers, but could just make out the swing of a plastic bag in his far hand, which may have contained them. He wasn't on file, I had no name, yet I'd finally seen enough of him to know that, from now on, I would recognise him anywhere. I picked up a single strand of tinsel that had fallen on my desk. It glistened blood-red as I twisted it between my fingers. 'Got you,' I whispered again.

Snap, snap, snap.

2

For the previous three years we'd gone to the funfair on Primrose Hill on New Year's Day. My boyfriend loved all the horrible fling-you-around rides, but for me the fair was a far more sedate experience. It was about winning teddies, cheap hot dogs, the sugary scratch of candyfloss.

'Absolutely not. *No* way,' I said, when Alec spotted a new addition and nudged me. The Stratox was a huge rotating drum that used centripetal acceleration to pin riders to the inside wall. It looked terrifying. Seeking out fear, even the ersatz sort, in the name of pleasure bewildered me because I've felt real fear. That plummeting I'm-going-to-die-here terror, the micro-second that lasts a lifetime before flight or fight kicks in. And it's horrible. Terror recalibrates the world, turns a single event into *before* and *after*. I refuse to simulate it. 'I'll meet you afterwards in the Hall of Mirrors.' That was my favourite. I liked its whiff of Victorian quaintness, of dislocation: because everyone's features were equally distorted, equally unrepresented, my brain could switch off for a minute. How could I recognise anyone when we were all unrecognisable?

I turned away. It was a winter-perfect afternoon, clear and chilly. To my right, the snaking queue for another ride shuffled forward. And in the gap, clearly, perfectly, framed . . . that face. So pixelated and grainy on screen, now in living, breathing colour – and no more than, what, ten, fifteen feet away? Pale and dark-haired. High cheekbones, clean-shaven. Wide but not full lips. He was alone, standing on the far side of the queue. Behind him was a clump of tall trees and, beyond, the hedge bordering the park railings. A narrow pedestrian gate opened onto Primrose Hill Road. His hands were clenched, his eyes roaming, scanning the crowd. Everyone in my peripheral vision, the sounds and smells of the fair, they all fell away to nothing. I concentrated only on his face. I walked quickly towards him, taking out my mobile to call in the sighting without dropping my focus from his face. I always kept handcuffs in my bag. 'Shit,' I muttered, as my thick gloves fumbled with the screen. Just as I slowed to take them off the queue moved forward again, and for a second I lost sight of him. I began to run, pushing through the crowd, aware of a woman's 'What the fuck?' as I shoved past her, still stupidly tugging at my gloves. I grabbed his upper arm. He turned, startled, his face only inches away from mine. He smelt of cedar and oak moss.

'No flowers today?' I said, and then, my voice low and controlled, 'Police. You're under arrest.'

Then: whack.

Pain.

Nothing.

I came to splayed out on the cold ground, Alec kneeling on the grass next to me, people crowding behind him. I'd been unconscious for a couple of minutes, he reckoned. 'Shit,' Alec was saying, over and over, and 'What the fuck?'

A woman, large as a lagged boiler in a padded coat, stared over Alec's shoulders, spilling out on either side of him as if she would swallow him whole. Beside her was a child, his mouth a slack, wet circle. I was dimly aware of the flash of camera phones, a series of blank rectangles staring, recording me. I was aware, too, of a second pain, one that wasn't in my head. The sensation down my left arm was of cold and burning all at once. Alec leaned over me, one hand on either side of my arms. For a weird second I wondered if he was going to straddle me, there, on the grass on Primrose Hill, in the smelly shadow of a generator. 'Suze? You okay, Suze?' he whispered, and I was glad of it, comforted by the softness in my name as it slipped from his lips.

'What happened?' It came out a rough crackle, hardly recognisable as my voice.

'You got hit on the head.'

I was aware suddenly of a ticking noise, and turned my head slightly to the left. A silver watch lay beside me on the ground, its face looking back at me, sweet as a lover. Blood had dripped onto the metal tiles of the strap. My blood. I could smell it, ferrous and sharp. I took a deep breath and immediately wished I hadn't. The soil was thick with dampness, brackish and heavy as a freshly dug grave. I felt as though I was going to suffocate, that an unknown force was tugging me backwards, pinning me by the throat to the earth.

'I've called an ambulance – you'll be okay.' Alec ran his thumbs across my cheeks, traced the line of my jaw. His fingers were icy. He'd left the Stratox, he said, and noticed people crowding around someone on the ground. 'And the fucking fright I got, Suze, when it was *you*!' He folded his hoodie and pressed it to my head. A zippy nip-nip ran up my cheekbone, but when I tried to lift my left hand to push it aside, my arm wouldn't work properly.

'Girlie, what a belt you got! You whirled around, then down like a tree in a hurricane,' the woman in the padded coat said. Then, all defensive, as if she expected us not to believe her, 'That watch, it simply fell out of the sky.'

I recalled a sudden flash across the low winter sun. An object, something silver, swift, knife-sharp. An impact. But what had distracted me from spotting it in time? There had been a big queue, I could remember that much . . . and a face, yes, a face had suddenly appeared in the gap. Of course! It wasn't a *what*, it was a *who*.

'A man, I saw a man.' I waited for my usual immediate recall of the man's face, but nothing happened. I blinked, if that would somehow reset the motion, restart the automatic swell-and-release in my unconscious I was so used to. Inside, my head felt chaotic, as though every thought was backed up, trapped inside a long, airless tunnel. Where the interminable click, click, click of shutters of recognition would normally summon up the face I wanted – plus every other instance in which I had ever seen that particular person – there was . . . *nothing*. I had no memory of him other than that I'd been looking for someone. Looking *at* someone.

The woman shook her head, licked her front teeth. 'No, girlie, there weren't no man with you. You was alone till this guy showed up.'

I stared at the strangers around me. All I could see were faces.

Just faces.

I thought the thought again, slowly. Felt the strangeness of it, the panicky, sandpapery rub: *Just faces.*

Shit.

Something inside my brain had gone seriously wrong. Carefully as I could, I turned my head to look at Alec's face and then around, at the people still gawping at me, like I was a monkey pissing through the bars of a cage onto its keeper's hat. The rubberneckers were nothing more than random strangers. Collections of features, forgettable and alike.

'Where is he?' I said. 'Where's he gone?' I tried to roll onto my right side and force myself upright.

Alec put out a hand to stop me. 'Suze, you're confused. There's no *he*. Please don't try to sit up. Just wait for the ambulance.'

I closed my eyes again, ignoring the nausea and dizziness, while Alec told the last few people to go away, that there was nothing to fucking see.

'Is this where it landed?' A new voice. Geordie. He paused for breath, panting. 'Oh, Christ, is she all reet? It just went flying and what was I to do, like? The ride didn't stop for ages!' The voice moved closer until I could tell he was crouched beside my left temple. I knew if I opened my eyes I'd try to process his face, but what if I couldn't? What if I couldn't remember his face afterwards either? Better to say I didn't see him than to have to admit later that I couldn't ID my own accidental assailant.

'Christmas present from the missus. She'd have killed me if I'd lost it the first week,' he said, as if that explained everything. 'There's blood on it!' he exclaimed. Alec muttered something, I couldn't hear what, and the man added, 'Yeah, okay, sorry.'

'Susanna?' Something in Alec's whisper told me it was safe to open my eyes. 'That guy, he was on the Extreme – you know, the upside-down twirling one I went on last year? – and his watch fell off and hit you.' The Extreme was sixty metres off the ground, and about a hundred metres away from the Stratox. As accidents go, getting hit from that height and distance sounds so implausible, yet it was what had happened. And after the best part of eight years in the Metropolitan Police, I know the implausible can *easily* be what really happens.

'And guess what, Susanna?' He imitated the man's accent. 'It's still working! That's Casio for you, reet, pet?'

The pain had bedded down and was shooting red-hot shards into my left hand and arm. 'My wrist,' I whispered, trying to concentrate on something else: Pharrell Williams blaring through cheap speakers; shrieks of excitement and terror; the drone of the generators. I watched the sky darkening over my head, the day reduced to a few slate-blue clouds streaked with orange and purple vapour trails and the flash of a police helicopter searchlight. All around us the funfair went about its business of taking punters' money in order to terrify them. People queued and laughed and selfied, bickered and boasted and pushed past each other. My story was already over, processed into a nugget of random news – 'Two inches to the left and it would have got you instead, wouldn't it, love?'; 'That's a reet good watch. It didn't lose a second!'; 'I'd sue! I'd sue the bloody lot of 'em!' – ready to be handed on, a source of LOLs for strangers. A woman carrying a grubby tote with the slogan *Pain is temporary . . . Internet results last for ever* stepped over my feet and barely looked at me.

The ambulance had parked on a tarmacked area close to the entrance to the funfair, but our path to it was partially blocked by a passing crocodile of older people, most of whom wore high-vis vests with *Dunease Court* on the back. The majority were walking; a few used frames or were in wheelchairs. Dunease Court was a private retirement and care home just off Sharples Hall Street. Alec and I used to walk around Regent's Park most weekends, evenings too, during the summer, so I'd seen this gang on their travels plenty of times before. The paramedics seemed happy to wait and let them all file past, which reassured me. 'At least I'm not a disco case,' I whispered to Alec.

'A what?'

'Nee-nah.' I leaned against Alec's arm, dizzy from the effort of walking. 'A siren-and-flashing-lights emergency.'

'Look,' he said, nodding towards a woman at the end of the crocodile. 'There's your pal.' She wore yellow trainers with glossy beige tights and hugged a vast mink coat around her, its collar turned up. Her thick white bobbed hair fell over her cheeks, obscuring half her face. I didn't know her name or anything about her, but she was such a stylish, quirky old bird that the sight of her always made me smile.

The staff chivvied their charges along as though they were hard of thinking, or cranky children or, in some cases, both. At the sight of the ambulance and its soon-to-be-occupant one man stopped so suddenly that the wheelchair coming up behind him slammed into the back of his knees. He lurched forward. 'Ouch,' Alec winced, 'that's got to hurt.'

We watched the news being passed back through the group, a game of Chinese whispers played through a loudhailer at half speed. 'There's been an accident!'

'A *what*, George?'

'An accident, I said!'

'Are you hurt, George? Is Kelvin?'

'No, no, not us, that girl, up there.'

'*What?*'

'Know what that was?' Alec said, as the last stragglers moved out of our way. He was trying not to laugh, or at least trying not to be caught laughing. 'That was a meme, circa 1960.'

'That there, Alec Lewis, is your livelihood,' I replied.

From behind us, Pharrell Williams was once more asserting how happy he was, and Alec was trying to make me laugh, and the paramedics were being very kind, and I appreciated the effort they were making but, really, all I felt was pain. Pain, and something far worse. Fear.

JANUARY 1919

I

Wigmore Hall has been full to bursting for ages, and the scramble for any last square of seat continues. People are desperate to find a place to jam themselves into. Violet is in the third-to-front row, squashed between a squat, elderly woman wearing a fox stole with one eye missing, and a florid, sweating man. The woman reeks. Violet's nose twitches. Mothballs. There are other scents too. She sniffs discreetly. Vinegar. And something else – sweet, yet a bit off . . . burned, even. Treacle, she decides. People are using all manner of remedies to ward off Spanish flu. The woman's full-skirted black dress is shiny with wear, the inky sheen of a bluebottle.

Exactly as Mr Forrester had told her to, Violet had arrived an hour early (and she wasn't the first, even then). The crowd is expectant, anxious; the sense in the room is that of restless animals before a storm. When the man beside her tugs a handkerchief from his pocket, his elbow jabs her ribs.

'Do you mind?' she says, the second time. He ignores her and continues wiping his forehead. The third time it happens, she pokes him back. When she glances to her left, a single beady glass eye meets her own in a relentless, dead stare. Her nose twitches at the old-dog smell of rain-sodden wool.

A man in the row ahead sneezes violently and people around him stir, skittish. Violet notices a young couple nearby look nervously at each other. A moment later the same man lets loose a relentless bark of a cough. The lady directly in front of him jumps up from her chair and pushes her way out, her route to the aisle hindered by an older woman using her umbrella to stake a claim to the empty seat. Whatever she's hoping to see, it's clearly worth risking her health for.

Violet remembers being at a concert here once. She's not sure when, though it was still the Bechstein Hall so it must have been years before. But more than the name of the building has changed. Even the air, which she remembered as cool and clean – a room where the very light that danced against the marble and alabaster walls seemed to hum summery and sweet with the music – feels different.

Exactly half an hour later than billed, the lights drop to nothing. The crowd, grown restless and noisy with the wait, gasps, as though darkness is somehow unbelievable at five o'clock on a sooty January day. Violet feels the sudden absence of light as a sack dropped over their heads, suffocating and leaden. A child shrieks and is angrily hushed by more than its mother. The blackness persists until the crowd falls quiet, stifled.

Suddenly a single figure is illuminated, standing completely still in the middle of the stage. He is planted there so firmly, it's as if he was there all the time, only no one had noticed, though several will swear afterwards he was on the stage as the room was filling, but with the power to render himself invisible. *Yes*, they will nod. *When he's seen, it's by his own choice.*

'Be under no confusion, ladies and gentlemen. Let there be no misunderstandings within these walls. Despite what you may think, not a single one of you made the decision to be here.' Selbarre's voice is low and soft, yet so powerful as to silence the last few rustles from the back of the hall. This must be what an American accent is like, Violet thinks, all smooth curves and polish. A spotlight is shining on him. Obviously that's all it is – she can see it with her own two eyes, for Heaven's sake! – so why does it seem as though the light is emanating from within him? Why does it appear to be generated by his voice, his very presence?

'No. The decision has been made for you, by those who are here but whom you cannot see,' he continues. 'Those who love you, who have lost you, who have slipped away from this earth plane and into that other room, the room of the spirit. It is *they* who have demanded your presence here, who have brought you here. Be under no illusion that it was your own mortal volition that led you – hundreds of you! – here today—' He breaks off as a woman just a few seats ahead of Violet wails loudly, a raw, broken cry.

Selbarre looks at the woman, his change of expression as swift as to flash on and off, like a code. 'Yes, madam, find comfort in the truth. You have been led here today by one who continues to watch over you!' He raises his arms slowly upward, and continues, 'Every single one of you in this room is here today because you understand the power of the truth. Yes, *truth*. Because what is the world of the spirit but that same land shared by science and investigation? Truth, because what is the world of the spirit but that of philosophy and the study of nature? Truth, because what is the world of the spirit but that which complies with the rules of nature – and who has the right to determine those other than God Himself? I commend you. Yes, ladies and gentlemen, the world of the spirit is God's world – his very laboratory of souls! – and those who discredit it are pouring scorn on our Lord Himself.'

His arms still wide and high, he turns slightly at the waist from side to side. There is a loud *thunk* as the stage lights come on. A gasp goes up across the entire hall as hundreds of pairs of eyes see the same thing at the same time. Sitting next to him. Right next to him, by his knee! Was she there the whole time? Upright in a chair, the girl's hands lie frail and empty, unwanted in her lap. Brown skin and brown eyes and black hair pulled as tight against her head as if it was sewn to her scalp, like an asylum lunatic. Her dress, the same colour as her skin, is so ordinary a style as to be almost indescribable. Violet looks her up and down. Her feet are bare! It's so unexpected as to be shocking. Splayed flat, the toes fatter than you'd think, judging by the rest of her, a fleshy promise of the complete nakedness that beats underneath the mud-coloured gown. A suggestion of a different version of her, whoever she is. Does it feel cold, where her foot meets the bare wood of the stage? Violet imagines the touch of the floorboards against the girl's skin, the planks gone dirty soft, the surface furred by years of wear. The only sign that she is alive is the slight rise and fall in the bodice of her dress. Her heart must be thumping, despite her stillness.

'Mademoiselle DuFerge is a native, from French Equatorial Africa,' he says, and then, 'She knows no English.' A murmur goes up from the crowd. For many, he may as well have described her as hailing from the moon. 'She is a powerful channel for spirit operators, and has no control over who visits *en rapport* through her mediumship. She is a trustee of the spirits, the conduit by which they will contact *you*, for that is their heart's desire. Remember what I say: she does not understand our language. What you may hear has no meaning for her, it is for *you*.' He hasn't looked at the girl once.

'I ask four of you – any four – to rise and walk to me now,' Selbarre says, his voice neutral. 'Four honest men and women, whose testimony will show the truth of what you will all see if the spirits are willing to join us. No!' He lifts a hand high above his head to halt a man who has jumped up from the front row. 'No! Not you, sir. You believe, I know you do. I can see the understanding in your face. I want the doubters at the back of the room. Those who skulk and lurk in the shadows, desperate to denounce what is known to be true. Yes! You!' His long arm points straight down the central aisle. Heads turn to see who he's indicating.

'Me?' comes a shout from the back of the hall. Violet turns to look behind her but can't see who spoke.

'Do you volunteer, sir?'

'Go on, then, I will! Prove yourself to *me*, if you dare.'

Selbarre merely gestures with a wide sweep of his arm and the man walks slowly up the far aisle towards the stage, the trip-trap of his boots on the tiles sending faint echoes of their own footsteps before and after him.

Violet's head turns this way and that, trying to take everything in, without knowing exactly why she's there, or what she's meant to do. ('Go and watch Selbarre's performance,' was all Forrester told her. 'And meet me afterwards, by which time what I need should be abundantly clear to any detective worth their fee.')

'And who will join this man?' Selbarre continues. 'You, madam?' He points again. 'And, yes, you, and you. Are you of sound mind? Strong of faculty? You must be.' The woman, halfway to the stage, falters. 'No, madam, no,' he says. 'The spirits are already guiding you – why else would you do something so out of character? I'm right, aren't I? To put yourself on display in this way is not in your nature?' This second woman gulps, falters. 'Then you must listen to the spirits and trust their judgement.' She returns to her seat and he indicates another woman, already standing with one arm raised.

Under Selbarre's direction, the four volunteers circle the seated figure on the stage. The lights have changed again, and are concentrated on the girl. By contrast the volunteers are no more than flitting shadows around her. She makes no move to look at or acknowledge them, even as he directs one of the men to lift her arms and examine the sleeves of her costume. He bends over and touches her foot, the white of his fingers harsh against her skin. And still she doesn't blink or twitch. It's as though she is alone in a room, asleep with her eyes open. Selbarre positions each of the four in a different quadrant of the stage, and once more the lights fall away to nothing. Violet can't see him, can't see the girl, can't see anyone up there, yet she can picture them, moving, circling each other. She imagines them creeping forward in the blackness. Imagines their hands wrapping around the girl's ankle, tethering her to the worn boards of the stage.

Silence. Selbarre, low and controlled, speaks to the girl. He doesn't use her name or look at her. 'The world beyond our world, come,' he says in English, then murmurs something inaudible (Violet's neighbour nudges her in the ribs: 'That's Africanese he's talking!'), but still does not look down at her.

'Lost ones, come. Your guide is here, she is open. Come to her.'

Silence. A single spotlight again, on the girl this time, who remains stock still in her seat as the voice continues to purr unseen next to her. The rapid rise and fall of her chest gives way to slower, deeper breaths. 'I can feel the approach,' he says, louder now. 'Don't be afraid to return to us. We are here, waiting for you. You are loved. You are missed. Come, your altar is ready.'

Silence.

Suddenly loud music spills from an unseen gramophone. *Roses of Picardy* pours through the room. The tenor's voice lingers on the last words, then silence falls once more.

And then! A howl. Loud and horrifying. The crowd shrieks, jumps. It is the shriek of a dying animal. The woman on Violet's left clutches her arm, gasping. Her fur brushes the side of Violet's face, its dry snout landing a camphorous kiss on her cheek. She tugs her arm back, picturing the single eye just inches away, its gluttonous gaze fixed on her.

The light on the girl's face grows stronger as she begins to speak. But the voice that comes from her mouth isn't hers. It's a man's. He speaks low and angry, his words roughened on the banks of the Thames estuary.

'Ma!' says the voice. 'Ma, it's me. Told you I'd be back for you and for Gran. Didn't I tell you?'

'Timothy?' shouts a woman's voice from the back of the hall. The love and heartache with which she says his name breaks the single word in three parts. *Tim-oh-theee*. But Timothy has gone. The girl's mouth opens again, in song. High-pitched and repetitive, a lullaby sung in an unknown language.

The girl drops her head to her chest as a white, gelatinous substance appears from her mouth and spills down her chest.

From her seat three rows back Violet is aware of a rank, sulphurous smell. 'Ectoplasm!' Violet's neighbour is ecstatic. In a discordant and unnatural chorus, the word is picked up and muttered all around the room. The girl raises her head once more and beads of sweat on her forehead catch the light as person after person begins to speak through her mouth. A dead soldier with a message of illicit love; a child stolen by the waves on a summer beach; a vanished sister, her words weighted by an illegitimate secret. Kind, recalcitrant, angry . . . The knocks and taps echo from the wooden floor of the stage at her unmoving feet. And never once does she look to her side, to where Selbarre must be standing, though they are so close as to feel the heat of each other's body. A strange, crackling energy builds up inside the room.

Violet's eyes are strained from staring at the stage as the light on the girl begins to fade. Her face is dimming, turning to shadow. She drops her head back to her chest. There is a long pause in which nothing happens. Violet can hear her own breathing. Her neighbour takes his handkerchief out again and mops his face, over and over. Everyone is staring at the girl. The silence is heavy as darkness, time slowed to a halt. The ectoplasm thins and begins to recede, somehow reabsorbed into the girl's body like a drink magically trickling back into a bottle, waiting to be stoppered again.

Without moving her arms, the girl slides to the floor. It is as though a draught blew her from her seat. Her mud-brown skirts briefly puff out, then slowly deflate, the way a puddle drains into the gutter. Selbarre moves forward and stands in front of her prostrate form. He doesn't help her. Doesn't even look at her! She lies on the stage.

'Come!' Selbarre turns to each of the four volunteers in turn. 'Witness her trance. Come forward as you must and attest that there are no wires. No strings, no hidden gramophone. There is no falsity to be found here, in this room of souls!'

They move around the prostrate girl briefly. The women are more hesitant to touch her. One of the men lifts her feet and runs his hands around her ankles. The brim of his hat shades his face, making it impossible to see his expression. Violet shifts in her seat. He's familiar, but she can't get a good enough look at his face to decide where she recognises him from. The girl looks like she'd break in his hands, but he puts her feet down gently enough.

The volunteers move back into the shadows.

'Nothing!' The older man admits himself baffled.

'Every word he says is the truth!' one of the women adds. Selbarre dismisses them with a wave.

Once more the room falls dark. The lights come up and the stage is deserted. But there was no scrape of chair or shoe, no sly shuffle to the wings. No soft pad of bare, brown flesh against wood. Violet stands up and pushes through the crowd, needing to get out. To get away from the heat and the excitement flowing around her, strong and perilous as a sea current. She feels wretched, despairing and stirred up all at once.

It is over.

From across the hall one of the four volunteers, unseen by her, notices her weave her way to the door. *Well, well, just look who it is*, he thinks. He moves quickly to follow her outside. *You're a turn-up for the books, lady . . . I wonder where you're off to next.*

II

Mr Forrester sits alone at the back of the café, tucked right into the corner where the booth meets the wall. The table is set for four. The spirit lamp under the teapot flickers. Her head is still full of the girl who was on stage with Selbarre, and she feels suddenly open – exposed, even – to whatever lies invisible around her. She experiences a momentary confusion at the scene: are there other guests with him, all unseen to her? She imagines the café as Selbarre's girl might experience it: full of flesh and blood, yes, but also – what? Spirits? The undead? Violet has a sudden mental image of the room doubly, triply crowded, bodies scattered in every corner. 'Don't be an idiot, Violet,' she mutters.

Mr Forrester looks older here than he did at his home the previous week: older and more tired. He is pressed back in the seat, his head leaning against the wood of the partition. Over his right shoulder the wallpaper is patterned with purplish birds peering out through dense, choked ivy. The café is busy, noisy with the hiss of the gas boiler, the shrill rise and fall of voices. The windows have steamed up and the place is stuffy, the air overused, heavy with smoke. Tobacco kills the flu germ, Chrissie told her, swearing blind it was true, and hadn't she heard no less than a doctor say so? It doesn't seem very likely to Violet.

It takes her a minute or so to make her way across the room, but he doesn't seem to notice her approaching. She's glad she hasn't had to meet his eye and watch him monitor her halting progress around the tables. She knows she'd have felt as though she needed to apologise for her speed, and would have been annoyed with herself for feeling it. He struck her as the unforgiving sort, particularly for that which is no fault of others. His thinning white hair is pomaded back from a broad, lined forehead. Despite the overheated room, his coat is buttoned up, his scarf neatly tied. There is something resolute about him, the way the shoreline so indefinably owns a landscape, as though the land repels the sea, rather than being under slow and constant siege.

'At last.' There is a slight pause before he half rises from his seat. Does such a desultory effort at politeness imply he considers himself too busy for manners or her too undeserving of them? A cup of tea sits untouched on the table in front of him. It has the grey scum of old dishwater. The other cups are the same, she can see now. So much for it being a ghostly tea party: he must have walked in and sat at a dirty table. In her experience of cafés such as this, the waitresses tend to punish a lack of etiquette by leaving you to stew in the mess for a while.

'You don't want tea or anything, do you?'

She does, desperately, but shakes her head, unnerved

by the display of disinterest from a man who is paying for her time. She feels oddly exhausted after the . . . the *what*? She's not even sure what to call it. Show? Performance? Witnessing? It was as though a church service had been held on a variety hall stage.

'Well?' he adds.

Speech must be money to him. She pictures the inside of his head as a bank vault, and him a miser in a cap inside it, adding and subtracting each sentence, set on making as tight a marriage contract of coins and words as he can. 'So, Miss Hill? What of it, eh? This spiritism, spiritualism, whatever you choose to call it, is nonsense. And, mark my words, you can be sure that what you saw today was nothing compared to the scoundrel's private sessions.'

'It was very . . .' She pauses to be sure her voice doesn't betray her. She can't let herself be swayed by his tone, his conviction. '. . . impressive.'

'Please don't tell me his ridiculous charade took you in. The man is a mountebank. Greed exploiting weakness, that's his business.'

'I didn't say whether or not I believed anything, Mr Forrester.' *Pompous fool*, she thinks. 'Whatever I may believe about Mr Selbarre's claims – or that young woman's abilities – what I witnessed was an impressive display. Having seen it, I can understand why so many people are choosing to accept everything he says. That is not to say I believe in Mr Selbarre himself, or his methods.'

'I see,' he says, his tone suggesting that he sees only stupidity. 'Perhaps you are not the person I need, after all. If you haven't the wit to apprehend fakery when it's clear as the nose on your face, I shall find myself an investigator who can. There is a man in Muswell Hill who, I'm told, has a remarkable track record.'

But, with so many dead, can he really not understand the *need* to believe? Violet has an awful image of hundreds, thousands of soldiers rising from their muddy, rat-infested graves and walking across the battlefields, desperate for the smell of home, the sight and touch of their families. To feel once more the ordinary dull embrace of their ordinary dull lives. Only recently Chrissie had told her about a neighbour who'd put her dead husband's blood-stained uniform on a tailor's dummy. 'You must have it wrong,' Violet had said, disbelieving.

Chrissie's eyes were wide. 'True to God, Vi, the poor woman puts it in the bed next to her every night!'

Between Forrester's rudeness and the fact that he still hasn't properly explained what he might want her for, she's already half wishing he would tell her to forget the matter and leave. Business is bad enough without her wasting time on this rude man.

'The quality of my sleuthing isn't at issue here, Mr Forrester. Neither are my private beliefs. And if you can't appreciate that distinction, then, yes, you should find yourself a different investigator.'

His expression turns thunderous and he grabs his gloves as though about to leave. That's torn it, she thinks. *You fool, Violet!* Twenty guineas was the sum he had mentioned at his house on Boxing Day. 'Twenty guineas for a swift and successful conclusion.' Put that in your pipe and smoke it, Mrs Miller! With twenty guineas in her pocket, she'd be able to stop worrying about money for a while. The lack of regular, dependable money coming into Violet Hill Investigations nags at her constantly. But James Forrester strikes her as an influential man: with his fee and a couple more like it, she could afford to move out of her bed-sitting room. She regrets ever allowing herself to daydream about giving notice. Hundreds of times over the last week she's pictured herself packing her few bits and leaving the curling wallpaper, the leaking window, moving somewhere small – even in daydreams, Violet is practical – but so bright! Maybe even one of the new mansion blocks up by Regent's Park! Why not? She can do what she likes in her imagination, can't she? She has pictured long, high windows overlooking the park with beautiful voile curtains that flutter in a summer breeze, and the scent of sweet peas, not camphor. A place where furniture is sparse and painted in pale colours, not the creaking brown lumps she's used to.

The booth is small and his knees are jammed under the table, so he is slow to rise. He drops the gloves again and places both palms down to push the table away from him. As he struggles, she watches the imaginary curtain fall still, all the life sucked out of it. She hasn't had a visitor for three months. She leaves home every morning knowing it will be exactly the same that evening. And the next day and the one after that. The thought falls black and heavy as a wet woollen cape around her.

Twenty guineas, Violet!

She puts out one hand, not to restrain his arm but to hover above it.

'Mr Forrester,' she says, regretting her earlier sharpness, 'shall I tell you why you shouldn't hire him or anyone like him? Because I'm a woman. That's why you wrote to me in the first instance, wasn't it? As well as I do, you know what that means: no one will look twice at me at a séance or mesmerist meeting . . . or anywhere else, for that matter. You hired me because I'm invisible. Go out into the street now and find yourself a man with my *track record*, as you call it, who can walk in and out of places, as I did today, without drawing a moment's attention, and you're welcome to him.'

Wigmore Hall had been a sea of women. She had been just another pinched face, just another aching mother, sister, wife, fiancée. Just another woman, alone in a world full of lone women. 'And, yes, it quite possibly is all fakery. And possibly it's not. But my job – any investigator's job – isn't to find confirmation of what *you* believe. It's to find out what's true. And, at this minute, neither of us knows the truth of who Selbarre is or what he and that girl are doing.' She waves to a waitress for a cup of tea, leans back in her seat and waits. Her hands are clasped together under the table, her nails digging hard into her skin.

When he puts down his gloves, the air begins to slip back out of her mouth. He drums his fingers on the table top, then leans back in his seat.

'You're familiar with Sir Arthur Conan Doyle?' he asks.

He might as well have asked if she has ever heard of an omnibus, or what a bolster is for. Sir Arthur Conan Doyle features regularly in the papers and magazines, in company with some of the most famous names of them all. She nods. The voile curtain flutters once more, and through the polished glass of her imaginary window comes the sweet, high trill of birds in the park below.

'His support for spiritualism is well known. For him, the world is merely the forcing ground for spirits.'

She nods again.

'I am Sir Arthur's business manager, as I have been for

fifteen years. I have been concerned for some time that his level of interest in this world is unhealthy for a man of medicine, of such rationality. He has been dabbling in this nonsense for far too long. I blame Lady Conan Doyle's nanny, Lily. She has Lady Conan Doyle quite enmeshed in her own beliefs. But now, because of what happened . . .'

'His son?' she asks. Kingsley Conan Doyle has been dead a matter of months; she remembers it from the newspaper. He'd been badly injured in the very first day of battle at the Somme more than two years before, though what had finally taken him the previous October was Spanish flu. Aged twenty-four when he died, he was old by the standards of those who filled the *Death by Wounds* columns that day.

'Among others, yes. Sir Arthur has lost many members of his family.'

An image of Chrissie floats into her mind: Chrissie looking out the window, commenting on the world; Chrissie watching the war unfold as if it was playing out on a stage while she leaned back in her seat and sucked liquorice.

'And I can't stand by and see him played for a fool any longer. I've known him too long and care for his peace of mind too deeply.'

This is a surprise. So, too, is his expression; he looks upset, genuinely concerned on his employer's behalf. She had begun to suppose him the cold, old-fashioned sort, the type of man who believed it his duty to send younger men out to the fray while he sat in a club, smoking cigars and pronouncing his verdict on the world he had sent them into.

'I will pay you to prove that Selbarre is the fraud I know him to be. No good can come of this man, and Sir Arthur must stop believing in these spurious messages, but he won't. He will hear no dispute on it at all.' He runs his hand across his hair. 'Have you read his stories, Miss Hill?'

'Some, yes.'

'So you understand how rational he can be. How literal. In his writing he insists on taking a point and following an unbroken line to its conclusion, regardless of where that conclusion may be. He is not behaving in that manner now, not at all. But I know that rationality is the part of his mind I can appeal to when I tell him Selbarre is a fake.'

'But if . . .' she feels she hasn't said it strongly enough so she repeats '. . . *if* Selbarre is a fraud, all you have proved is that *he* is. There may be others who are genuine.'

He shakes his head. 'Rationality will come to my aid, Miss Hill. If the line leads to one fraud, how can Sir Arthur trust it to lead to the truth elsewhere? I have seen these . . .' he pauses '. . . infatuations with various proponents of these ridiculous arts before. A medium some years ago proved most vexatious . . . but he and Lady Conan Doyle are already taken by Selbarre to a much greater extent than I have observed prior to this. The very extent of their regard for his supposed powers means that Selbarre will have the furthest to fall. Finding Selbarre's weakness is all it will take to bring down the ridiculous charade, I'm sure of it.'

'Does anyone else know of your . . . intentions? Lady Conan Doyle, for instance?'

'Of course not.'

So it's not, as her cases so often are, one man's story against another's, a matter of distinguishing fact from fiction. It's deeper. *Belief* is the problem: belief, shaded by fear, instinct and grief.

He leans his head back against the partition behind him and briefly closes his eyes. He looks pale suddenly, boxed in by the wood around him, and she experiences the same brief confusion as when she saw him from the door.

'I fear for his sanity, Miss Hill. That's the truth of it.'

January 2018

1

I was kept in hospital for three nights because my wrist needed a screw ('Don't we all?' Alec murmured, and the nurse sniggered). The surgeon reckoned that when the watch hit my head I'd spun back and around, then must have stumbled and landed badly on my left arm. 'Could be worse. You might have ended up with a broken humerus,' he said cheerfully. He mimed plucking off the top of his elbow. 'You'd know about it then!'

'I know all about it now!' I retorted.

I was dreaming about music as I woke up from the operation. Music, and a man with black hair, but a frustratingly blank face. Because of the anaesthetic I felt even groggier than I had when I'd fallen the previous afternoon. Alec was sitting by the bed, listening to music on his phone. I didn't recognise the song, though the fact of it explained my dream. Do hospitals still have radio stations? When I was seven I caught glandular fever, complicated by severe anaemia, and spent nearly two months in Queen Mary's in Sidcup, and music is always associated with those memories: Sinitta and Jason Donovan, The Bangles and The Beatles. (During one of my parents' twice-daily visits Soul II Soul's 'Back To Life' blasted out over the radio. 'That's a bit much in here, isn't it?' Dad remarked. 'Gav-*in*!' Mum replied. She had a way of turning a person's name into a remonstration, complaint and target neatly packaged in a single word.)

My tongue felt huge, a dried-out sandbar in my mouth. I focused on the mole running across the tip of Alec's nose and over his left nostril, dark brown on brown. It's a rough rectangle, elongated at the top and bottom. I closed one eye, then the other. The mole shifted slightly. It looks like Trinidad, I thought, the words pinballing around my head. How had I never noticed that before? He needs to know, I decided, and opened my mouth, but the words were already lost.

'Are you winking really, really slowly?' he asked. He always paused before he smiled, and I had learned to wait, to trust that the smile was coming. He never reacted hastily, good or bad. I often thought he'd have made a better police officer than me.

'Don't think so,' I said, my voice sticky. 'I was . . . I was trying to blink.'

'Traditionally, that's more of a two-eyes-at-once thing,' he said, demonstrating. 'Are you okay? Shall I get a nurse?'

'No, no . . . give me a minute.' I gave it another go and my eyelids responded better, less of a relay race.

'You know how people use the word *literally*, then go on to say something not remotely literal? Well, I am literally the bearer of bad news.' He turned the phone screen to me. The BBC London Live headline, *Local police officer injured at Primrose Hill funfair by high-flying watch*, was sandwiched between an appeal for witnesses to yet another violent street robbery in Hackney, and an article about people watching porn on public transport. I was on Twitter, too: someone who had been filming the ferris wheel had put up footage of me with the watch beside me on the grass tagged #MetsGotToHurt! In a second tweet I was lying on the grass, blood trickling down my temple. Whoever @echochamber21 was, they had helpfully ringed the watch in red. A close-up taken from over Alec's shoulder was tagged #happynewEAR! The angle would match the woman in the padded coat, but I couldn't recall seeing a phone in her hand. 'You're in the *Standard* as well. Do you want to see it?' I shook my head, pissed off that the article mentioned my name and job, already anticipating the slagging I'd get at work.

'You *what?*' my boss, Detective Chief Inspector Colin Kingsley, said, when I called him before going into the operating theatre to explain why I wouldn't be at work that week (and then some). 'Are you having a laugh?' He was right: it *was* a joke injury. All the *is* in fact: ignominious, inconceivable, injurious ... Can you have an injurious injury? I guessed so. My head, my wrist, I could have whatever I wanted.

I couldn't wait to get out of the hospital. The doctor on duty wanted me to stay another night because I had a temperature but I said I'd discharge myself if she didn't let me go home, so she reluctantly agreed. Busy wards are the least restful places to recover, and I had barely slept since the operation. Alec had forgotten to bring any clothes for me to change into, so I had to put on my grass-stained jeans and possibly-shit-stained coat. Bloody dogs. My scarf was ripped and neither of us had a clue what had happened to the fancy leather gloves his stepmother, Chantelle, had given me for Christmas. Two weeks off work because of the concussion and stitches, the doctor reckoned, plus another month after that with a cast from hand to elbow. I told the doctor discharging me that I was a police officer and she assumed I meant on the beat – okay, I let her assume that: it suited me to let her assume that – so she said I could get certified sick until the cast came off. I'm not on the beat, though: I'm at a desk pretty much all day every day. Once my fingers could manage the keyboard, I could probably have done the job with two broken wrists. But my head wasn't working. Every new face I saw was just another person, another random collection of features, so I nodded, scared, and told her, yeah, I'd definitely need the certificate. That gave me six weeks. Six weeks to turn the stranger who looked like me into *me*.

2

Back home, Alec shoved the furniture around a bit so that the sofa still faced the TV but also had a partial view out the window and onto the street below. He had taken down the tree and decorations. It was a relief not to find the stale breath of Christmas waiting for me when I got home.

'I've got to go in a minute,' he said, loading our duvet and pillows onto the sofa. 'We're busy this afternoon and Joey can't cover for me again today.' Alec worked at Winterson's Undertakers, an old family business in Camden. He had been good friends with Geoffrey Winterson, the founder's great-grandson, since they were kids. Alec had left school young and had a few lost years behind him – nothing serious, just stoned, stupid teenage stuff that got him a couple of cautions – but when he was twenty-two he realised if he didn't get his act together his life would go horribly wrong. Slowly, maybe, but wrong nevertheless. Geoffrey's dad offered him some dogsbody work while he got himself sorted, and to everyone's surprise – mainly his own – he loved it.

We'd met at Winterson's, at the funeral of a former police

colleague of mine four years earlier. 'An *under*taker?' my dad had said, when I told him about my new boyfriend. And again, 'An under*taker*?' as though a change of emphasis would flush away the unlikeliness of his occupation. Watching Alec at the service that day, I had wondered what undertakers think about during funerals. Presumably their ordinary everyday lives were playing through their minds, the usual round of what'll-I-have-for-dinner, and God-I'm-bored-will-they-please-just-get-on-with-it. On one of our first dates I asked him why he'd stayed with the one firm for so long, and he'd shrugged, smiled. He liked a job where he'd never have to take his work home, he said, adding, 'The dead don't let you down, Susanna.'

'Tell Joey thanks from me, will you? It was kind of him to give up the last day of his holidays.' Joey, Alec and Nancy, the receptionist, were the only three staff not born or married into the Winterson family. Joey had moved to London from a small town outside Cork because being an undertaker in rural Ireland meant that come Saturday night he'd no chance of copping off at the local disco. Death was, he said, the ultimate passion-killer: all the girls knew him as the guy who'd buried Nana.

'He said the last few days were fairly quiet. Today's should be the biggest since before Christmas.'

'Bells and whistles?' They were my favourites, if it's okay to have a favourite type of funeral. Winterson's were just the right side of old-fashioned, with horse-drawn hearses, all plumes and greatcoats – bells and whistles – as well as electric ones and the ordinary, traditional kind.

'No, electric, at half three. After that, I have to organise two services for next Monday.' He bent down and tucked the duvet around me, then took my hands and wrapped them in his own.

'Thanks.' I sniffled, feeling sorry for myself. 'You're so good to me, thanks.'

'Listen to me,' he said. 'You're not to do anything about work, or think about work, or worry about work, right?'

'But I can't remember what was happening when the watch hit me.' I felt the familiar mutinous ache in my cheeks and forehead as I tried not to cry. 'There was a man there, I'm sure of it. And I'd been looking for him for some reason. So, it must be to do with work, right? I mean, why else would I be looking for someone if it wasn't to do with a case?' Every single new face I had seen since the accident meant nothing to me, like watching a programme with the sound turned down. People I *already* knew, I recognised perfectly. But with new faces, I couldn't tell if I had ever seen them before.

'But you're *always* looking for someone. Lots of someones. It's what you do. So, yeah, of course your brain is going to be full of faces. There wasn't anyone with you when I got there, and that woman said you were alone when you fell. You look at thousands of people every day, so doesn't it makes sense that if you were *thinking* about a case as you got hit, the last thing you'd remember would be a man's face? You've got concussion, Susanna! You know "concussion" is doctor talk for brain injury, don't you?'

I nodded.

'Sweetheart,' he added, 'you're going to be fine. Give it time.'

I had tried to describe it to the emergency doctor who admitted me, but because I was groggy and confused, I made frustratingly little sense. 'Do you mean you don't know people you don't know?' he said, scribbling on a chart, already halfway out of the cubicle. 'Well, um . . . Detective Constable Tenant . . . neither do I.' How was I to explain that the noise of reordering, the interminable, exhausting cross-referencing and archiving of faces that had gone on in my mind every single waking moment for as long as I could remember had been suddenly silenced? An imposter was trapped in my body and I desperately wanted, needed, to get rid of them.

'Remember how worn out you were before Christmas?' Alec said. 'The extra time off will do you good so, please, just relax and give yourself a chance to get better.' He straightened the duvet over my lap and patted it gently around my feet and up my legs, like a child carefully burying an adult on a beach.

'Look at you and your hospital corners,' I said. 'Matron Lewis.'

'I'll be back by seven for your bed bath.' He grinned. He left the room, reappearing minutes later in a black suit. 'Right. North London,' he said, 'bring out your dead. I'm ready for you.' I rarely saw Alec in his undertaker's gear – he usually left home after me and was back before me. The pin-sharp white shirt collar made the wool of the jacket seem denser, his face darker. He straightened his sleeves, pulling his cuffs down as far as he could over the tatty teenage tattoos that ran the length of his arms and onto his wrists. A rough serpent slipped away, nothing more than a haughty blue-black tail disappearing under a rip-curl of white cotton.

'You look very . . .' I paused, immediately wishing I hadn't spoken.

'Very what?'

'Smart.' But I was really thinking *funereal*.

I turned my head to look out the window. Our flat was on the top floor of an early Victorian terrace at the Regent's Park end of Cranford Crescent. It belonged to Alec's father, Haynes, the well-known jazz musician. Haynes had moved to London from Trinidad with a band in the early seventies and met

Alec's mother Lainey at a club in Soho. She was the cloakroom girl. 'She claimed she was a model,' Alec once told me, 'but I reckon the only modelling she did was trying on the punters' coats while they weren't looking.' Lainey lived in Sidmouth now, with her third husband. The day Haynes had moved in with Chantelle he had tossed Alec the key with the words 'Have fun, son.' The flat wasn't very big, but I wasn't complaining. Haynes asked for only half the going rate in rent, and without his generosity there was no way we could have afforded to live in the area on our salaries.

The sitting room had a glass door leading to a tiny step-out that we called the terrace. I loved the view from there, the way it laid out the city rooftops like a magic carpet for me to walk, run, fly across. On warm evenings we would take two small chairs outside – they just about fitted – and sit there drinking beer, enjoying the knowledge that all of London, for good and bad, was playing somewhere below us, intent on its own roaring dance, while we were quiet and happy and alone, with a view of the green blanket of Regent's Park. We had the comfort of knowing that the city's daily symphony continued yet couldn't be deafened by it.

It was a soggy January morning, but after three days in a painfully bright and windowless cubicle on a ward, to me the sky looked beautiful: a vast colour chart of soft greys and blues. In the distance over the park a flock of birds, no more than a series of sooty smudges from where I was lying, swooped and swirled. I had a good look into the top floors of the houses opposite then leaned over the back of the sofa to peer down at the street. It was spitting rain and the road was quiet. Out of sight, a baby's wail was abruptly halted by the slam of a car door. Across the road a skinny woman, head to toe in neon

Lycra, jogged past. Her arms were bunched up tight against her sides, her feet lifted show-pony high, toes pointed. A man strode quickly down the pavement opposite, an umbrella low over his head. My insides constricted. I leaned back, cursing myself for taking painkillers on an empty stomach.

'Susanna?' Alec was watching from the door. 'Promise you won't go all *Rear Window* on me?'

3

When you're born a particular way, you assume everyone is pretty much the same as you, that even differences have commonality, such as being left-handed instead of right. So, before I learned not to, I would greet people simply because I recognised them. Strangers were familiar because every face I saw registered with me.

At school they called me a freak.

'But we don't know those people, do we?' Packing the week's grocery shop into the boot of the car, Dad would exchange looks with my mother.

'Well, no, but leave her, Gavin, she's a friendly little thing, that's all.' Then she'd lean down to me and add, 'But don't *talk* to strangers, sure you won't?'

'No, Mum,' I'd say. But I kept greeting them until I learned not to, shortly after my eighth birthday. We had moved to Upton that January from a dreary no-near-neighbours cottage five miles outside Sidcup, and I suppose, in their delight at their newly acquired suburban life, my parents didn't believe anything bad could happen so close to their middle-class oh-so-very-des res. The street outside was almost an extension of the house, an invisibly cordoned space, sheltered by our neighbours. That this attitude to public space contradicted the *don't talk to strangers* rule didn't occur to them: it didn't apply here, at home.

As childhood rites of passage go, being allowed to walk alone to the local shop is a big one, and when we moved to the new house it hadn't taken much pleading on my part. In my mother's defence, the shop was literally on the corner of our street (a keen-eyed prosecution would be quick to note that Rutland Street is long, and the witnesses' house could be accurately described as at the opposite end of the road to the mini-market). Some afternoons she'd send me to the shop three or four times. She used her shopping list as a way of keeping me occupied.

That day, I'd already been for cigarettes, then milk and, finally, a packet of Angel Delight, our big Friday treat. Unusually for me, I was reluctant to keep doing trip after trip, because I'd fallen in school that afternoon and cut my knee. It was sore, and I was aware of the suck and drag of freshly scabbing skin against my tights. But I'd bought the wrong flavour – vanilla, when she wanted butterscotch – so I had to go back. It was later than I'd ever gone to the shop alone before, and as I left the house I noticed the first orange glow tempering to yellow as the streetlights came on. It had turned cold, even for October, and the usual clutches of kids who'd been outside earlier had gone.

How could it ever have occurred to my mother that, to any opportunist watching the shop hoping to snatch a child, my constant solo visits were making it terrifyingly easy?

Dad told me years later that when it came out in court that

the man had been there on and off during the week, parked across the road from the mini-market in a van with a *Plumber on Call* sticker, my mother wept. Ciggies, ham, fish fingers, bread, more ciggies ... she had given him chance after chance to take her daughter. In that moment she believed herself a traitor to me. A colluder in his crime. She cried too, Dad said, when it was mentioned in court that he had a stepdaughter the same age as me.

My first few years in the Met were spent on the beat. I've been punched, spat at, kicked, had clumps of hair pulled out, and been abused verbally over and over again. Yet I was more terrified outside the mini-market that afternoon than at any other time in my life.

I was still a couple of houses away from the shop when the door of a van parked across the road opened. 'Hi there,' the driver called, as he got out. He smiled and waved. I had never seen him before. 'D'you know which house is the Jacksons'?' He crossed the road diagonally towards me, leaving the van door open behind him. I don't think I was clued in enough to pick up on that being odd, but there was something not right about him. Children can sense trouble – I've noticed that at work. They're often far more perceptive than adults.

'No,' I said, and shook my head. I hurried on. A few more steps and I'd have been at the shop door. I could even see Mr Patel behind the counter, his head bent over a magazine, shoulders shrugging in time with whatever song was playing on the little transistor he kept on the shelf beside the cigarettes.

A hand swallowed my mouth and chin. An arm lifted me from the ground and tugged me backwards. My feet were only inches from the pavement, yet the sensation of not being able to touch the ground was terrifying. The only thing connecting me to my street – to my entire world – was the stranger's hand on my face, the arm clamped around my chest and pushing hard against my ribcage. I felt a rip on my knee as the wool that had dried onto my cut was pulled away. Bizarrely, considering I was being attacked by a stranger, that moment registered with me most: the betrayal of my own flesh as it tore against my tights. Me failing to protect myself.

He dragged me across the road, one arm around my chest, holding me close. He smelt cloying and damp, like a garden in winter. When we got to the van he paused for a second, and I flailed my legs. It was a fluke, but my foot kicked the door shut, so he had to loosen his grip on me to open it again. And, though I'm still not sure exactly how I did it – although I often relived the moment in dreams for years afterwards – I managed to wriggle around so that I was facing him.

As paper cuts go, it was a beauty.

'You little bitch,' he cried, lifting his hands instinctively to cover his eye. There had been no strength behind my fist when I'd shoved the only thing in my hand into his face, yet the thin edge of the Angel Delight packet sliced straight across his right eyeball.

I manoeuvred around him and across the road. He'd caught me again before I'd got to the door, but Mr Patel, stretching up to the top shelf to put the magazine back, chanced to look out. He was outside, shouting and shoving, in what felt like a second. My attacker dropped me again, jumped into his van and was gone. All I can remember about those few seconds before Mr Patel shepherded me inside the shop is that I stood outside in the dark, staring in, panting, desperate for the normality of the mini-market. Needing to see the open fridges, the crisps boxes, the cracks in the lino made by my mum and all the mums like her queuing for the till. The paper boys' delivery bags were full, lined up by the door, like sentries on guard. Mr Patel's magazine lay on the floor. A topless woman with a huge perm and a startled expression on her pale face stared up at me from the cover. She held her breasts in her hands, offering them to me like two wobbling, cherry-topped desserts.

Six months later we went on a family outing to B&Q to pick new wallpaper for the living room. While my parents tried to talk each other into their own preferences – 'Let's get flock!' 'Where do you think we live, the Queen Vic?' 'What about Laura Ashley?' 'Laura *Ashley*?' – I stood to one side, bored, flicking through the strips of paint colours I'd filched from the displays. I liked the names more than the colours: Orchard Cream, Blossom Haze, Fringes of Gold. Through an archway leading into a covered garden display a man was heaving bags of soil-enricher into a wheelbarrow. He glanced up but didn't notice me. I froze.

At first, my parents were reluctant to believe me: I was still so young, how could I really be sure? It was months after the incident, and I'd seen his face only briefly because he had grabbed me from behind. But I insisted. His face was filed in my head, along with those of pretty much everyone else I had ever seen. They were used to me recognising actors between one TV programme and another, even in tiny or non-speaking parts. The day before the B&Q trip I had pointed out an extra in *Charlie's Angels* from a movie we'd watched a year earlier. 'You didn't see him,' I told them. 'So why are you saying it's *not* him?' Perhaps that's why they believed me. Or maybe they didn't, but felt they needed to show faith.

'Okay,' Dad said. 'Yeah, okay.' We went to a payphone and called the police.

It was him.

Mr Patel had got two digits from the number plate as the van drove off, and various neighbours had noticed the van at the time, but no one had been able to describe the driver well enough for the police to do a photofit. Unlike now, there weren't CCTV cameras everywhere. Walk around today and you're filmed all the time; there is no route through central London that isn't under continual CCTV surveillance. (Complaints about CCTV cameras creating a Big Brother society always surprised me because people willingly offer up their entire lives online: personal information, fingerprints, profiles, everyone is constantly recording and recorded.)

His van matched Mr Patel's description. What's more, he'd had a caution the previous year for hanging around the gates of a primary school.

The police, my family – even Mr Patel – all found it difficult to believe that I'd recognised him again. My parents were worried I'd been so traumatised by the attempted kidnapping that his face was burned into my memory for ever, but that wasn't it. He pleaded guilty, so I was spared the trauma of giving evidence. The police said afterwards it had helped that I had never once wavered from my identification. 'It's him. I remembered his face,' was all I said, no matter how many times I was asked. When pressed, I added, 'I keep my eyes open for people,' but that was as far as I could explain it. Because it wasn't that I didn't forget faces, more that I *couldn't*.

One thing changed after *the event*, as I preferred to think of it – I needed a neutral expression rather than 'attack' or 'kidnap', which suggested a victim: I decided to keep quiet about my ability. It didn't matter that it had been proved I wasn't just being a 'friendly little thing'. I stopped pointing out the women on buses who'd been in the library last year, and kept quiet when I recognised the same pretty extra in a month's worth of Saturday afternoon black-and-white movies.

The freak who was almost abducted: who wants to be *that* girl?

I joined the police in 2010, spent three years as a response officer, then was transferred to a plainclothes robbery squad. At some point, my superintendent realised that whenever we reviewed CCTV footage, I would always say, 'I've seen that face before.' A lad I might have seen once, briefly, nervously tugging at his baseball cap as he hovered close to the till in Argos at Marble Arch, I would recognise months later outside a Costa in King's Cross. Or I'd be walking past a staff noticeboard with a selection of new *Caught on Camera* images and I'd spot one, two, even more, of the grainy faces. It became a private daily challenge to see how many I'd recall. Whether it was a day, week or year between sightings didn't make any difference. Over and over, I kept making idents. My boss sent me for tests, after which I was transferred to the Super-Recogniser Unit, a new section established to collect and review images on a CCTV database. CCTV was originally intended only as a deterrent: the fact of the cameras being visible was supposed to be enough to put criminals off. But the images being recorded became a treasure trove for people like me, who looked for serious and persistent offenders, most of whom had never been identified before.

Most people can recognise 20 per cent of faces, but super-recognisers clock up 80, 90, even 95 per cent. My fusiform gyrus responds to faces and facial features in a way that's different to most people's, I don't know why. Everyone in the unit had to pass a series of tests, one of which revealed that although we all had remarkable recognition of *faces*, the same ability didn't necessarily apply to anything else. That made perfect sense to me. Even very young babies can recognise their mothers, so our brains know that recalling faces above all else is vital for survival. Prosopagnosics are at the other end of the spectrum: people with face blindness. That must be worse: the uncertainty, wondering if everyone thinks you're rude or arrogant because you don't say hello. Not knowing whether you know. It must be crippling. Although I often had to remind myself not to let on that I'd recognised a stranger in the street in case I came across as a stalker, I'd rather have too much information logged in my brain than too little.

The way some forensic scientists talked, you'd think we were using ESP or a strange hypnotic skill. The attitude that it was trickery – that it could never compete with DNA or fingerprints – rather than natural hyper-awareness always irritated me. There are no tricks in super-recognition. I just have a weirdly focused memory and I put it to work – hard. My idents weren't fluke after fluke, they were the result of honest human brainpower. But because our brains were incessantly processing faces the flipside was that most of us in the Super-Recogniser Unit had poor short-term memory. The week before Christmas Leon had offered to do a lunchtime shop for the office. On the way to the supermarket he spotted thirteen strangers he knew he'd seen before, his mind automatically cataloguing them in his version of the internal shorthand we had all adopted – *druggie, assault victim, childhood neighbour, barman, druggie-dipper* – but when he got to the shop he remembered only three of the sandwiches he'd been asked to get.

When Chantelle first heard what I did for a living she was very excited. What a cool job, she reckoned. How intriguing. 'So you literally *never* forget a face?' she asked. 'Wow, that's amazing.'

'I think you're reading too much into "super",' Alec said. And while part of me thought, *Hey, don't piss on my parade*, he was right. The reality of spending an entire day poring over grainy CCTV footage was mundane. And, of course, it was faces only. I could recognise someone, make the most remarkable ident, which might even impress the other super-recognisers (we were extremely competitive: we'd have new *Caught on Camera* footage every morning, and the room would remain silent until the first shout of 'Got one'), but I might not have that person's name. Discovering it was often a long, tedious process. Being a super-recogniser could be oddly ordinary. Yet, as a way to live, it was the exact opposite.

But now, lying on the sofa, my lunchtime pills sticky on my tongue and an itch inside my cast driving me crazy, I was scared. How was I to exist if I couldn't be me? I felt as though I was disappearing.

Perhaps the kids at school were right. Perhaps I was a freak after all.

4

I spent the first twenty-four hours on the sofa or in bed, alternating between watching TV, napping and mooching about online. It was as though I was retreating from myself, almost in a trance. Too much of it, and I knew I wouldn't want to leave the flat. The quietly confined space, the winter sun in the window stirring the dust motes, even the childlike, powerless feeling of being at home on a weekday hypnotised me into immobility. Heat was radiating out from the laptop on my blanket; the fan was whirring. That was how I usually felt after a tough day at work, that my brain was an overheated computer. Alec had two funerals that day and wasn't due back till late. The worst types, he'd said: a teenage suicide, and a young woman who'd been hit by a speeding truck. (You might think working surrounded by grief would be an occupational hazard for an undertaker, and that the development of an emotional calcification was necessary to survive without being flayed raw by it, but in fact the opposite is true. Funerals don't necessarily bring out the sadness in people, Alec used to say. Often it's the madness.) Afterwards, he was meeting a man who wanted to arrange his service in advance. He had quite a few of those: Winterson's had a pre-pay package. Most pre-payers – that afternoon's chap included – were terminally ill and wanted to have everything organised in advance, usually to save someone else the trouble later. Surprisingly few were simply practical people preparing for the inevitable. Death comes to us all, yet not many of us want to acknowledge the fact with the full fee up front.

Colin had left two messages asking how I was doing but I replied by text each time. I didn't want to talk, to lie about how strange I felt, how dulled and foggy my head was. Until then my job had been a source of pride to me, but now the very idea of having to sit at my desk, with thousands of images backed up and waiting to be analysed, frightened me. Yet the three sexual assault cases were still raw and on my mind so I texted Leon to ask if there had been any developments. We didn't have one continuous piece of footage of the third victim, only a general time sequence recovered from different angles. What was happening in the moments I *couldn't* see was haunting me, as though in those gaps I had somehow let her down. She was small and slight, and watching the footage had felt like spying on a guileless child dressed up as an adult. *Leave it, Suze*, was Leon's reply. *JD is back 2 cover for u. Everything is in hand.*

The intercom at the door to our flat buzzed. Then a second, fainter buzz and another that was weaker still, an echo travelling down the building, losing force as it moved away. With such short pauses between the sounds, whoever it was couldn't have been looking for any resident in particular. The random pattern continued: our buzzer, then the basement, then the middle floors. An oddly satisfying symmetry to the sound tuned the entire building into a single unified instrument, though its song spoke of emptiness, of lonely rooms.

'Yes?' I said finally, dizzy from the tablets and standing up too quickly.

'You home, love?' His voice was a crackle.

'You tell me. You just buzzed every door in the building. What do you want?'

'I've a plaque to install. English Heritage.'

The duvet still wrapped around me, I shuffled over to the window. Sure enough, an English Heritage-branded van was parked directly below, a ladder sticking out of the open back door. A man waved up, gesturing to me to wait. He vanished inside the van before reappearing with a circular blue plaque. Buildings all over London have them to commemorate a former occupant. There were quite a few in our area. Just before Christmas I'd noticed new ones for the movie star Margaret Warner – my dad and granddad both had crushes on her – and Sylvia Plath.

Buzz.

'See? Got a plaque for you.'

'But I didn't order one.'

'That's not how it works. It's for the building – there'd have been a letter.'

'I didn't see any letter.'

His sigh was a soft, broken wave of static breathed up from the ground. 'No, you wouldn't have. It's sent to the management company or whoever owns the building. That ain't you, is it?'

'No.'

'Thought not. Look, love, I'm not asking you to hold my ladder, I just need someone to sign for it.'

By the time I opened the street door he was tapping his foot against the step, the plaque tucked under his armpit.

HENRY GARDINER
3rd MARQUESS of DENISMORE
1872–1916
Scientist, Soldier
lived here 1903–1916

'Who on earth was he?' I said, disappointed by the unfamiliar name.

'Haven't a clue. I just put 'em up.'

'Aren't you a bit late? Like, by about two years?'

'Huh?'

I pointed at the date of death on the inscription.

'Dunno.' He shrugged. 'Guess nobody asked for him till now. Look, love, it *was* due to go up a couple of weeks ago, but you know how it is with Christmas and all that. Just found him in the van this morning, to be honest.' He passed me a docket and a pen. 'You'd never sign it as December the thirtieth, would you? Twenty-ninth'd be better again.'

'No, I wouldn't.' I sat on the step and tried to squiggle my name. The end of his biro was chewed into shards, and smelt of hash.

'What's that say?' He looked incredulous.

'Susanna Tenant.' I sounded defensive, but he had a point. I nodded at the cast. 'I'm left-handed.'

He shoved the docket into his folder. 'I can't hang about arguing the toss. I've got to be in Croydon for two.'

'Who's getting a plaque there?'

He shook his head. 'Replacement. Arthur Conan Doyle's is cracked.'

Back upstairs, with the sound of a drill from three floors below for company, I googled *Henry Gardiner 33 Cranford Crescent*. I didn't find much, mainly small references on sites recording scientific milestones. Almost all of it was about the contribution he'd made to what is now accepted as the correct order of the Periodic Table, but I couldn't quite follow it. He didn't strike me as a particularly interesting character, toff by birth, scientist by vocation, soldier by death. I could see why English Heritage had waited so long to commemorate Henry Gardiner. He died 'a gallant officer, a virtuous commander of men', according to *The Times* obituary archive, but I was more curious about him as an inhabitant of the same building as myself than as a military leader. Quite a few of the houses in the Crescent are in single occupancy, and whenever I passed, I always had a good look in their windows. The more extravagant the décor, the more likely the curtains were to be open. Our building was divided into three, though I'd never been inside the other flats. It must have been stunning as a single home. I pictured it all stucco and silk, the nut-brown floors polished to within an inch of their lives by servants.

The obituary said the marquess had died at the Battle of the Somme, leaving a wife and three children, the youngest of whom – his heir, Henry Alfred Gardiner – was only nine. This family had walked up and down the same stairs as I did. For three years I had been retracing their long-gone footsteps without knowing anything about them. His children had come through their door one day with a father, and gone out the next without one. How long would it have taken the news to reach his family? Would he have been days or weeks dead when they heard? Days, I presumed, what with him being upper class.

Our flat would once have been the servants' rooms. I looked at our blocked-off grate, imagining the crackle of a long-dead fire, and tried to picture our small lounge as an Edwardian bedroom. What I came up with – single beds, faded rag rugs over gappy floors, water jugs on heavy wooden stands – probably owed more to *Downton Abbey* than reality.

A century earlier, other lives had walked under the same sky. Had breathed into these walls, had shed their skin, hair, clothes. I looked at all four corners of the room in turn. They suddenly felt as unfamiliar as if they belonged to someone else, and I was squatting, stealing their space. Ghosts, sighing in corners, their invisible hands pushing me away. It made me feel uncomfortable, as though I wasn't alone, after all, and hadn't been for a long time. A door slammed somewhere in the building, and I jumped.

'Get a grip,' I muttered.

My arm was aching. I don't know whether it was the painkillers or a poke of concussion, but I fell asleep almost immediately. I dreamed that a telegraph boy on a bike called. I heard the thick click of a latch on a gate. He rang the bell, over and over again. I never saw him, yet knew his face was blank, featureless. Then I was downstairs in the hallway with my back to the front door. A lemonade-coloured sun poured through the fanlight over my head and spilled stickily over a tiled floor that stretched out to infinity in front of me. I kept my back pressed against the door and refused to open it. Outside a large dog was barking and wouldn't stop.

The front-door buzzer woke me. It was just after five. The room had turned to night. Shadows stretched their hands out from the corners, scrabbling for me. For a moment I had no idea where I was. I sat up on the sofa, bewildered and nervy. The buzzer sounded again, two, three times. I stumbled over to the door. 'Yes?'

I could hear breathing. Regular, calm. 'Alec? Did you forget your key again?'

Silence. My mobile beeped from my pocket. *Sorry running late. Home 6.30. x.*

I turned back to the intercom. 'Who is this?' I asked. 'Who's there?' But there was only breath, soft and hypnotic. I ran over to the glass door, unlocked it and stood on the terrace, pushing a plant pot to one side to lean over the balcony. The doorstep was empty. My heart was thumping. Whoever had been at the front door was gone. A delivery, I decided, and Mrs Gore-Kirwin, whose apartment included the basement and ground floor, must have buzzed it in just as I went onto our terrace to look down. She was always on the look out for what was happening in the building.

A wind was getting up. Trees rustled long and thin-limbed under the streetlamps. I stood out there for a minute, scanning the street below. It was as dark as it ever gets in the city, the inky murk shot through with shining points of red and white. Tiny lights – planes, stars, satellites – slipped across the sky. The pavements were quiet. A man cycled past, his hi-vis helmet glowing. On the doorstep of the house across the road a young woman, with two small boys in uniform, was struggling to get her keys out of her handbag. Weighed down by schoolbags, hockey sticks and coats, she was a Buckaroo toy ready to pop. One of the kids saw me and waved. From where he was standing, I must have looked as though I was a shadow on a parapet, and entirely alone.

JANUARY 1919

I

He's copped her looking! She's scarlet. The curtain could have been on fire, she lets it drop that quickly. She ducks back against the wall, out of sight. Violet would go for her, if she was here. Lucky then, isn't it, that she's not?

But now she *can't* see him! He's been standing outside the pawnbroker's opposite for an hour. Waiting for his friend again, most like, same as Christmas Eve. That's nearly a month ago now and this is only the third time he's been back since, as far as she's aware. Not that she's counting, mind. Chrissie doesn't want him to catch her watching – the embarrassment! – but she hates not being able to look at him. She leans sideways again, and nudges the curtain to one side. Only ever so slightly. Nothing wrong with that, is there? A girl's entitled to stand at the window of her own place of work, isn't she?

He's definitely looking up. At her! He must be stiff with cold, standing outside so long on such a cold day. The morning frost that crackled under her feet when she left the house surrendered when the sun began to shine, but though it's bright – the brightest day for months, Chrissie reckons – it's that funny sort of sun, where your eyes sting from the light yet you're still shivering. Violet's favourite weather, but Chrissie's not so sure. Sun should warm you up. Stands to reason.

He's not wearing an overcoat, just the same demob suit as last time. No one seems to know who they were cut to fit – she'd swear she's not seen a man wearing the right size yet. The ones with the tacked-up trouser legs or sleeves are the worst, though: she hates to see the new fabric turned up and sewn shut like that. Might as well be taunting them, poor souls. She's noticed plenty sewn up high, well over the knee. It's cruel, isn't it, not to tailor them proper suits to fit? As if a single chalk outline was supposed to do everyone, that they're all come back the same. The tailor across the landing from their office has said his feet are run off – which was a careless way to put it, all things considered, Chrissie thought – with all the adjustments the demob boys need. Violet reckons that Tanner leaves his door open to suck in a bit of the heat from the fire she's paying for, and ever since Christmas there's been a loud and uneven march up and down the stairs to his room. He's got a foul mouth, Tanner. Violet gave him a piece of her mind when he made a comment about the smell coming off a man who'd only one arm. 'Can't wipe proper, know what I mean?' Tanner had said. He wore his measuring tape around his neck, like a boa, tugged it forward and back, side to side, like he was in a cheap chorus line. 'Some of 'em, they're not men at all any more, if you gets my meaning.'

'I'll take your scissors to you if I hear you talk like that again,' Violet snapped, slamming first his door, then ('And pay for your own bloody coal!') their own.

'It's not right, Violet, sure it's not?' Chrissie had asked. 'All the papers saying what heroes they are for coming home, and then they get given clothes that don't fit right?'

'What's not right is anyone having to pay a bastard like Tanner who sticks his fat nose up at them.'

'Shouldn't the army be helping more? Fixing them up proper or whatever?'

But Violet had shrugged. 'That's just the practicalities of the business, I'd say. Soldiers are always treated as if they're identical. For good or bad, that's how it works. How can the army start treating them all as separate now?'

Sometimes there was simply no working her out.

Over the last few weeks more and more men have appeared on the streets, looking as though they've not a jot to do but wander around all day. Turned out of their houses every morning like dogs. At first, she'd assumed it would balance everything out again. Only it hasn't. Not as far as Chrissie is concerned anyway. During the war proper, when it was just women and kiddies everywhere, or old lads, or men who didn't look injured – though you weren't sure if you just couldn't see what was wrong, or if they were conchies who'd refused to join up – the city had looked off its axis to her. The order of the world, the way that things had been since time immemorial, it was still all askew. At the beginning, she'd been sure the fighting would get her a beau: some nice lad who'd be glad of a loyal sweetheart to keep his home fire burning. She has plenty of chums who got themselves engaged to chaps they hardly knew, as if call-up papers came with a ring glued to them. But not her. The whole four years and not a sniff (Tanner's words come back to her, and her lips fold in distaste) of a proper boyfriend. She's not been asked out, even for a cup of tea, in a year.

She's not much to look at, she knows. Mam tells her often enough that she must work hard to make the most of herself. And she does! It's exhausting, always being ready, always having a glad eye for a possible suitor. It's like she's on parade all day long, smiling at men in the omnibus queue, for God's sake, even the postman – and the state of him, must be sixty to her twenty-three if he's a day, no matter that he's said to have a lovely house in Tooting from the insurance policy that paid out after his wife died. Her lack of a brother counts as a real loss to Chrissie. She has plenty of pals who had brothers and lost them to the war. She envies them these flesh-and-blood dead brothers, she does. She's never had one to lose, never had one to mourn.

Violet doesn't seem to care twopence, which is madness. No, that's not it. She *does* care – she's happy. It doesn't bother her to be 'surplus', as Chrissie's magazine has begun calling women like her. Spinsters. Maiden aunts. Those bossy articles about earning a living in the 'New Woman' style, and considering a future alone, or how best to manage the household accounts when you set up with a pal. *Bachelor Girls Be Warned! Even the Greatest Friendship Can Be Lost over Trifling Matters!* The noise they sound in Chrissie's ears is that of warning sirens. A dull melancholy settles on her when she sees bulging younger women pushing perambulators. And it's not as though she wants to get married just to leave her job. She likes working for Violet, really she does, no matter that the money's not much and it's quite boring because she's by herself such a lot of the time. It's fetching and carrying mostly. She always said she'd never go into service but sometimes she wonders if she isn't much more than a maid now, and if *secretary* is just another type of servant. She enjoys telling people about it, stories of the cases they – well, Violet – solve. But she doesn't want to be stuck in a job for her whole life. What woman on earth would want that? She wants to get married, have kiddies and a home. Why else was she put on God's earth if not to have what everyone knows is theirs by right? She's not asking for much, just that the ordinary run of the world will take her from baptism to funeral via the best day of all, her wedding. Her baptism was probably a plain enough affair, and she's not bothered considering her funeral – she'll be in God's hands then so let Him worry about it – but her *wedding*! Orange blossom and organza. A smiling groom with neat, clean hands that he'll never raise in anger to her, and all her friends and neighbours there, every last one of them pink with envy. And her serene face that of a queen at her coronation.

But it's all gone wrong. The scrabble to find a man is like bloody musical chairs! And if she's not careful the tune will end and she'll be left standing against the bare wall, but for good this time. Who's to know but it might already have stopped? Her entire future might be sewn shut. That's what scares her most. That's the thought that wakes her at dead of night, when the only sound in the bedroom comes from the brass clock on top of the chest of drawers, its tick-tock sounding a warning: *what-then, what-then, what-then.* In the middle of the night she can't see its shiny face, just the dense shape of the chest it sits on.

Oh, Lord, the man in the doorway is waving! While she's been wool-gathering she must have been staring at him the whole time. He's caught her bang to rights now! Blushing, she raises one hand slowly, like a stupid child at lessons. He tips his hat to her, then bends over in a joking bow. When he straightens up again he's grinning. Tall, with broad shoulders . . . The suit is better on him than most, there's no denying that. She drops the curtain again and crosses to the mirror. She's blushing for sure, any fool could see it. It suits her, though, having a bit of colour in her cheeks. Nothing wrong with popping down and offering a returned soldier a cup of tea, is there? But her hair! It's so springy – she hates how it jumps up any old way. She pats it down with some water and shoves in another hairpin. Her heart lifts, thumps.

'Caught your eye, did I?' He holds out a hand and mimes watching something fall *plop!* into it. 'Got it!' His smile is all cheekbones and teeth. He's gorgeous. Suit excepting, he might as well have climbed out of the screen in the Pleasureland. She shivers, which he notices. 'You're good to come down, miss, but you shouldn't have. You'll catch your death and it'll be on my conscience!'

'You'll catch your own death, stood out here all morning.'

'I'm waiting for my brother. He comes up from Sidcup on the train and he must have got delayed.'

'I've seen you both here.'

'Have you?'

She flushes. Does he think she was making a sly remark about them going in and out of the pawnbroker's?

He smiles again. 'It's a good place for us to meet, halfway between the station and my digs. I don't mind having to wait for him. Will needs my help. I'm fine, though thanks for coming down to check. You're a good sort, I can tell. I knew it the first time I saw you at the window. Your pal not with you today?'

'She's out. At work.'

'So that's where you live, then?' He gestures across the road. 'I thought this part of the street was just offices and shops.'

'No, I mean, yes. I mean, it's where we work, but she's busy. Out on a case.'

'A case? You're never a pair of doctors, are you?'

'Doctors!' Chrissie titters. Her hand moves to her hair, palming it flat again. 'You'll never guess, I bet, what our jobs are.' She doesn't give him a chance to reply but blurts out, 'Private investigations!'

'Never! You're a real detective? A *woman*?' He whistles, low and soft.

Chrissie feels a surge of pride and excitement. 'Well, she is. She's ever so clever. I'm her assistant.'

He sounded so impressed that she hears herself add, 'Some of our cases . . . well the stories would give Miss Braddon's books a run for their money, let me tell you. I think they should get written up for a magazine!' Oh dear, does she sound like some silly kid, caught out in boasting? She's flustered. 'But I can't talk about it really. Client confidences and that.'

'Course you can't! It's people's private business, isn't it? That's only reasonable.'

She smiles, grateful that he understands. He's so nice! She's a good judge of character is Chrissie, no matter what Mam might say.

'What an interesting occupation! Aren't you and your Violet quite the pair?'

She didn't realise she'd told him Violet's name. She's not even said her own yet! 'There's plenty say detectives don't belong in skirts.'

'Well, I certainly ain't one of them. And if the detective in the skirt is as pretty as you, even better for it, eh?'

He's got some patter right enough, but she finds herself blushing again. 'Um, I thought you might like a cup of tea.' She glances down, as though she'd had a tray clutched in her hands the whole time. And she would have brought it with her, only it might have seemed too forward. If she'd known how nice he'd be, though, she should just have gone and done it. Lucky, too, that she'd brought those few slices of cake in. They're meant to be for her and Violet, but Violet's not to know, is she? Especially seeing as how she's hardly ever there.

'That would be so kind of you, it really would.' He moves forward, and begins to cross the road towards the street door. But that's not what she meant. She was going to bring it down to him, not have him come up to the office. She feels nervous suddenly. Violet doesn't like strangers in the office. What would she say if she knew? A yard ahead, he pauses and turns back to face her. That gorgeous grin again! 'You, miss, are very kind indeed.' His breath puffs towards her in the cold air, the cloud of his words as soft against her forehead as if he'd leaned down to kiss her. 'It's so cold out here. You were right about that.'

'Oh, yes, but I can't . . . I mean, what about your brother?'

'I'll keep an eye open for him.' He does that mime again, long arm outstretched, his fist snapping over nothing. 'Just like you did me!'

Chrissie does a little run-jump to catch up with him as he strides towards her door. There is a slope to his left side – she can see it now. Just slight, you'd hardly notice it. Not really. His gait is long and fast: he's halfway up the first flight by the time she's closed the door behind her. It's so bright outside today that shutting the front door is like extinguishing a light. The stairwell is gloomy, inky-black the whole way up. The electric light hardly ever works, and when all the office doors are shut it reminds her of walking up that long staircase on the Northern Line. The feeling that you're very slowly tunnelling up from under the earth. Plenty of her friends refuse to use it, but Chrissie quite likes the Underground railway. Being on a train moving about in the earth far below the city streets never troubles her. It's the walk to the surface she hates. She always imagines herself climbing up through time itself, as though different dead versions of London were broken up and buried all higgledy-piggledy on top of each other, people and animals and houses piled any which way just on the other side of the tiles. She can never get from the stuffy, smoky steps onto the street above fast enough to escape the feeling that she'll be dragged behind the walls of the Underground and into the earth itself.

She puffs along after him, wishing Violet hadn't snapped at Tanner that time because Tanner's door is never left open now, and it used to let more light into the hallway.

But, more than that, she really hopes Violet doesn't get back early.

He sits down behind Violet's desk. She didn't tell him to: he just puts himself there. He pushes the seat back and stretches out his long legs, touching the edge of the fireplace. She leans down – she's almost next to him! – to build up the coals. When she straightens, he's staring at her. She touches her cheeks. They're flaming! Perhaps he'll think it's the fire, not *him*. The queer thing about seeing him – a man! – sitting in Violet's seat is that it suits him. Now that Chrissie looks at it, the desk could be that of a man. Violet has none of the bits and bobs that Chrissie keeps on her own desk: the pin-cushion and library books waiting to go back, the magazines and teacups. Violet's desk has just notebooks, a few neat stacks of paper, a flashlight, pen tray and blotter.

'I bet you're the best investigators in the city. I can just imagine a neat figure like yours slipping in and out of windows, chasing burglars all over London!'

'Oh, I don't do much of that sort of thing. My job is to keep things ticking over here. Violet is out and about nearly every day.'

'Well, you keep this place lovely, you really do,' he says, lifting the papers on Violet's desk and fanning them out as if to demonstrate how neat everything is. 'You must be a clever one to be left in charge here, keeping track of everything.'

Chrissie flushes again. He's right, though, isn't he? Well, maybe not about the clever bit, but she does work hard, and Violet is good to her and all, but it's not like she ever properly notices how much Chrissie does, or all the to-ing and fro-ing, all the visits to the bank and the post office, or the hanging around on the street to watch someone go into a tea shop and wait for them to come out again in case they're not alone after all, and all the time pretending to be staring at the same bloody hat in the window next door. And she'd never say it aloud, but one of the best things about working for a woman is knowing that she'll never bother her in that way. Before she'd met Violet, Chrissie had worked as a typist in an insurance firm. On her very first morning the supervisor told her she'd be fine, that her looks weren't the type the boss had an eye for. 'And it's more than an eye, you can be sure!' she added. Chrissie had been relieved, but aggrieved, too, at the assumption that the face she was born with didn't warrant even unwanted attention.

'She's a lucky lady, your boss, to have someone so diligent working for her – I'm sure the cases you work on must be serious. Life and death, even.'

They talk for the best part of an hour. He's so interesting! Asking all about her, about Violet. Where they're from, how they met – she even hears herself tell him about her father and the dray horse. She is surprised at the words coming out of her own mouth, that it is all right to be telling this man what she thinks. What she *feels*. And he doesn't snigger. Just nods, like he's taking it all in. Like she matters. She's not used to having someone look at her so intently, or listen to her answers as though it's the very fact of her talking, of it being *her* voice that's speaking out, no matter what it might be she's talking about. And he's so easy to chat to. But is she nattering on too much? No, she can't be, can she, seeing as how intently he's listening and nodding? Laughing, even. He has three cups of tea and two slices of cake, his feet up on the desk all the time. He has a solid power about him, as though he'd be there for ever, strong and good and true.

A door slams. He sits upright, dropping his feet to the floor. The chair squeaks against the side of the desk as he jumps up and walks to the window. 'That your boss back?'

'No, it was Mr Tanner's door.'

'There's my brother just arrived!' He's pointing down, across the road. 'I'd stay talking to you all day if I could, Miss Bullman, but I'd best be off.'

'Call me Chrissie.'

'Chrissie.' He smiles. 'Anyway, I don't want to cause you

trouble. Sounds like your boss doesn't put up with any nonsense!'

Did she tell him that? It's not as if Violet is easy to understand, and she does leave Chrissie here by herself a lot, but, still, Chrissie would never be disloyal to her. She joins him at the window. The street is empty. Does Davey mean his brother is in the pawnbroker's? She doesn't like to ask in case it sounds rude, as if she's wondering whether he's short of money. Metcalfe's doesn't look open: the inside lights are dimmed. 'Where is he?'

'You just missed him, he's nipped into a shop on this side. He'll be doing the rounds looking for me, that's what.' He puts his hat on. When he turns to face her, his back blocks the light from the narrow window. It's like turning a corner and suddenly finding yourself in the shadow of a gable.

'Goodbye, Chrissie. I do hope I see you again. I've enjoyed our conversation so much. It's done me a power of good. It really has.'

And then he's gone and the world is airless once more. She washes the cups. Then – because Violet will notice the extra one and the plate to go with it – she dries them and puts them away. But! She told Violet she would bring cake today and she might wonder where it's gone, so she puts a single plate and cup back on the draining board. She's worn out and excited all at once, like a child after an outing. It's as though she's been waiting for years for something – someone! – exciting to appear around the corner, but now it has and she's not sure what to do about it. All that time wasted in the waiting, and no thought given to how to act when it was over. She's reminded suddenly of a set of wax crayons she was given one Christmas. She would draw a picture using the colours, cover the entire thing in black crayon, and then scrape the black away to reveal the colours underneath. Only she'd often have forgotten what was where, and the pictures never ended up as she had imagined they would. Everything would be out of kilter, the flowers where the sky was meant to be, with no way of righting it.

She sits down at her desk and opens Violet's ledger. Today she has the end-of-month accounts to send out, as well as the reminders to those who haven't paid since last month (or the one before or more). Chrissie looks up and down the rows of figures. Lives turned into pounds, shillings and pence by her own careful hand. Against the name Mrs Johnson, 146 Albemarle Street, Chiswick, is: *Fee three pounds, expenses two and six.* It's owing six months now. Says she can't pay but Chrissie knows it's *won't*. She hired Violet to prove that Mr Johnson had a ladyfriend in Putney. Turned out he did, but there was a kiddie, too, that barren Mrs Johnson had known nothing about. When Violet told her – and she told her as kindly as she could – Mrs Johnson cut up very rough and sad about the whole business and refused to pay her account.

'The truth will out, Chrissie. That's the sorry rub of it,' Violet said. 'Mrs Johnson thought she was asking me to prove something but in fact she really wanted me to *disprove* it. And how could I do that? I had to be honest with her, didn't I?'

The rest of the day passes slowly. The accounts, the post office. It's not as boring as some days, when Chrissie has nothing to do at all. On such days she often reads through Violet's old cardboard boxes and the books marked *Case Notes, Private*. Violet has carefully recorded every case she ever worked on, and some are such interesting stories, better than anything in the illustrated papers. They go back quite six years, before Chrissie's time: she began working for Violet in 1914. She's never told Violet she does this, though she's not sure *why* exactly. It's not as though Violet has ever said she ought to read them, but she's never said not to either. Still, though, Violet makes such a fuss about keeping clients' confidences that Chrissie decided it was probably safest never to mention it.

Violet appears and almost immediately disappears again. She can be quite the vanishing act when she wants to be. She's busy these days: that spiritualist fellow, two pilfering cases – one domestic, one in an office – and a demobbed soldier who suspects his wife has another man. But his case is just the sort, as she says herself, that takes 'plenty of legwork and hanging around, and won't earn much'. Chrissie had been worried that Violet would just know, fee-fi-fo-fum, that someone had been in the office while she was gone. That a man had been sitting at her desk, his hands touching her things. But she didn't. Barely spoke, in fact, just asked if there had been any callers or messages, gobbled the bread and cheese Chrissie made for her and went out again. For all his manliness, Davey Dockery had left no tell-tale trace.

Waiting for the omnibus that evening, Chrissie is still running through the morning, thinking about *Him*, as she already considers Davey: she has turned this man to *Him* in her mind (as well as to *hers*). How the cold that came from him gradually dissipated, vanishing into the air of the room. His tread, steady and strong when he walked up the stairs. His breathing, low and unhurried. His smell as they paused, pushed close together – the heat off him! – in the tiny, shadowy vestibule while she fumbled for the key, hoping he wouldn't see that her hand was shaking. She extracts nuance from each syllable he said. Each word that fell from those lips! Wide, not really red, more pinkish, and full. She shivers hot and cold just remembering how those lips had curled back to smile at her. Such a lovely name, too. Davey Dockery: solid as he is himself.

For the last week, two chaps have set up selling matches in the doorway of the bakery at the corner of Carburton Street. All day every day they've stood there, suited and booted. The smaller one is always coughing, his face that horrible yellow colour, worse around the mouth.

'Matches, miss?' She'd bought some the first evening, to be civil like, but now they ask her every day. She doesn't want to meet the man's eyes and have to tell him to sling his hook, so instead finds herself staring at his neat row of medals. They're pinned high, almost up at his left shoulder, like they're trying to climb over him and escape down his back. He must shine them every day, she decides, and the thought makes her feel even worse for him.

'Well? Do you, love?' The smaller match man is talking to her again.

'No! I mean, no, thanks, I've no use for 'em again today,' she says. The poor man, but still, Lord above, how many boxes of matches does he think she needs?

She turns away, grateful that her Davey is so clearly a cut above all that.

January 2018

The following morning Alec said, 'You look like you need some air. And that's coming from someone who spends a lot of time with dead people.'

'I've been on the terrace,' I said.

'Proper outside. Moving-about outside. I know you're still tired and in pain, but you've been home for four days. It's time to go outside, even for half an hour.'

'Tomorrow . . .' I paused '. . . maybe.'

'Today,' he said, and despite my resentment at being told what to do, I knew he was right. My days were beginning to divide into those in which I decided to shove the tiny bits of food waste down the plughole, and those in which I dutifully scooped them out of the sink and put them into the bin. I was still panicked by my inability to know whether I'd seen new faces before. Stay calm, Alec told me. It would be okay: hadn't the doctor told me post-concussion syndrome could easily last ten days or longer? 'Now you know what life is like for the rest of us,' he added. 'This is the boring, ordinary world you've missed out on all these years.'

'But,' I said, panicking, 'you hear of people with concussion losing their sense of smell or taste. And what about those cases where someone gets a head injury and starts speaking French or, I don't know, Klingon or something, though they'd never learned a word of it? What if my ... ability, whatever you want to call it, is just *gone*?'

'Hmm, yes,' he said. 'In that case I think we're probably looking at bionic implants.'

'Take me seriously, Alec!' I snapped. 'Please!'

'I am! Honestly I am. A head injury like yours can't change the essence of how your mind works. It's not that different from your wrist, if you think about it. Your head is broken but time will fix it. All the way back to normal – *your* normal.'

He couldn't convince me. Just as he was leaving for work, clearly exasperated by my constant what-ifs, he said, 'Look, maybe you should talk to someone about it.'

'But I'm talking to you,' I wailed.

After the stillness of the flat, the traffic sounded aggressive, agitated. I tried to shrug off a disjointed angst as I walked slowly towards the high street, yet I had the strangest feeling that I wasn't alone. It was as though a shadow was stitched to me, a sensation I attributed to the days I'd spent alone indoors, constrained by four walls. I couldn't remember the last time I'd mooched around the shops on a work day. Clearly Primrose Hill belonged to other people between Monday and Friday than those of us who made occasional appearances at weekends: I was intruding on the territory of delivery drivers, of toned women in skin-tight workout gear and a gangly sprawl of teenagers in uniform.

As I waited at the pedestrian lights at the top of the high

street, a young guy sitting on the ground reached out to me. 'Oi!' he said, his pale hand touching my coat. I started in fright, immediately cursing myself when he added, 'Sorry, love, any chance of a quid?' A driver waiting for the lights to turn green noticed him, then very obviously locked her car door. She saw him see her do it too, the cow. I gave him two pounds, wishing I was in police uniform, so I could have stopped her on some pretext. Forcing an annoying pause into her day would at least have lodged a minor credit against such callousness.

I paused outside Claire Voyante's opticians, trying to decide how much further I should go – I knew Alec would ask – before stopping at a café. The morning was grizzly, grey and cold, and the further I wandered from home, the more uncomfortable, almost uneasy, I became. A huge white sticker in the shape of a pair of sunglasses spanned the width of Claire Voyante's window, its lenses cut-outs in the shape of daisies. The only way to see into the shop was to look through the clear centre of the flowers.

Through one lens, I could see the shop assistant behind the counter, mobile held between ear and shoulder as she scribbled something. The second lens framed her only customer: the woman in the fur coat from Dunease Court, looking as stylishly eccentric as she had that afternoon on Primrose Hill. She wasn't facing the window but to one side. I took my phone out and held it in my hand, so that if she happened to look through the giant daisies I would be just another person pausing to check their screen. Covertly, I watched her work her way slowly down a display of sunglasses, picking up pair after pair, trying them on, then putting them back into the display at random. She didn't use the little mirrors mounted on the racks, which was odd. The fur gave her a slightly fuzzy quality, as though her edges weren't defined. With a pair of glasses in each hand, she turned back to the display. One pair went onto the stand but the other vanished up her left sleeve. Her hand was in and out of her pocket in seconds.

Fuck's sake, I thought. *Her?* The assistant, still on the phone, had seen nothing. I watched her mouth move but couldn't figure out what she was saying. She dropped her pen and ran a hand through her hair, then glanced at her customer for the first time. Her expression didn't change – she saw only an old woman fiddling for a tissue in her pocket. Older people browsing in shops were regularly ignored, their presence registering as benign at best and not at all at worst. The Grey Pass, we called it. It's an odd form of age discrimination particular to retail. A few years earlier I caught an elderly man with more than a thousand quid's worth of clothes from Debenhams, and the store manager had been genuinely surprised that an eighty-year-old could be such a prolific shoplifter. During my time on a robbery squad I had come across highly skilled dippers, trained since childhood by being forced to practise on pockets containing razor blades, and this woman was as slick as any of them. The coat was genius too: not only was the glossy fur code for 'I'm loaded' but its slight burr made the pocket slits almost impossible to spot, shielding her hand as she slid it in and out.

She moved to another display, one closer to the assistant. But when she finished her phone call and – finally – turned her attention to her customer, the woman had already stepped to one side, about to leave. I walked from the window to a bus stop a few feet away.

Recognising wanted criminals when we were off duty happened to all super-recognisers from time to time. JD had been late for his best mate's wedding because he'd spotted a man around the corner from the church and decided to go after him rather than wait. I started to scroll through my phone for the number of the local station: she'd be an easy body for them to deal with. Our rough rule of thumb for deciding to intervene was: *What might happen in the next twenty-four hours if I do nothing now?* Sod all in this case, I reasoned, but I knew I ought to phone it in. Yet I hesitated. My surprise that she was a dipper had made me even more curious about her: what harm could it do just to go with it for a while? Anyway, I could call the station later. I knew where she lived.

After Claire Voyante's she – or, rather, we – went to Camille's to nick a hair slide and to Primrose Pharmacy for a bar of fancy soap. Then she led her parade of one across the road to Pavement Books, where she lifted something from the second-hand poetry section – I couldn't make out what it was from where I had shelved myself in Classic Crime. Each time she stayed calm, got her bearings yet didn't linger too long. It was impressive, I had to admit: she could have given a master class in shoplifting. She walked past Carphone Warehouse, then paused. Ah, no, not here, I thought. Really? I'd have to intervene before she started taking pricey handsets.

I stopped, obscured from her view by a young couple pointing through the window. 'The K2? What you looking at that old crap for?' the guy said.

'It's cool,' his girlfriend replied. 'I like it.'

He shook his head. 'No, you don't.'

Having someone else dictate my route was unexpectedly calming. She moved on, crossing the road to a newish coffee shop, Gordon's Kitchen. I'd never been there, so waited a minute before following her. It was mid-morning busy, and because the windows were steamed up, I couldn't see where she was sitting until I opened the door. An old-fashioned bell broadcast my entrance to the entire café, but no one took any notice. Though I kept my head down, as though aiming straight for the counter, my eyes flicked from side to side.

'Won't you sit down?' a voice called. She was sitting in a small recess beside the front window, shielded from the door. Stupid of me not to have sussed that out. 'Or do you prefer only to accompany me from a distance?' Her voice was deep, languid, her words curling over on themselves.

How long had she known I was there? (Since the optician, it turned out.)

'I've never had a bodyguard before,' she said, one hand waving me towards the seat facing her. She was looking down towards the table rather than at me. The café was stuffy yet the collar of the mink was up around her ears, her hair over her face. 'Well,' she added, 'not one who is unknown to me.'

'Oh, right, um, sorry,' I said, momentarily thrown by her disregard for being caught as much as her comment about the bodyguard. Why on earth was I apologising to her? She had just lifted about three hundred quid's worth of stock. 'No,' I said, regaining my footing, 'I'm not sorry. I've been watching you steal your way up and down the street. I could be the police for all you know. I mean –' flustered again '– I *am* the police.'

'Are you sure?' she said, her arm still extended towards the chair. 'You don't sound sure. But, please, won't you join me? I'd love to hear all about it.'

I was exhausted and my head was sore. My shoulder ached, and my arm was a dead weight inside the sling. What the hell? I thought, and sat, leaning back against the padded seat, my right hand and forearm supporting my left as though I was holding a baby. She waved at the barista. 'I think you have to order at the counter,' I said weakly. Every word she said had me stretching higher, a snake charmed by the music in her voice. 'There's a sign there, by the till.'

'Ready for another espresso, Mrs Hartigan?' Apparently everyone *but* her had to order at the counter. He turned to me. 'Hi?' He sounded Australian: everything was a question. Especially the questions. 'What can I get you?'

'Um . . . tea, please,' I said.

'Tea is the dog of the drinks world, don't you think?' she said, her head turned slightly to the side, away from me. Her bobbed hair was thick and sleek, the ends bracketing her chin. Her fringe just touched her eyebrows. Her eyes were a curious violet-blue. 'Paws up, tongue out, desperate to be liked, at all costs.' She spoke like a character in a black-and-white film: the sultry vamp, not to be trusted. Her words chased each other before slowing down unexpectedly, every sentence a game of catch-me-have-me.

'Does that make coffee the cat?'

'Yes.' She moved her head slowly to her right and tilted it upwards slightly, so that her hair fell back from her face. It was deliberate, I realised afterwards. 'I rather suppose it does.'

I stared, I know I did. But I couldn't help myself. Scars ran down the side of her face from her left eye to her chin. Thin white lines, pools of puckered red skin with paler, creamier outlines. Yet the previous hour in her almost-company had been so surreal that this revelation didn't seem strange. Only when I saw her face properly, fully, did I realise the extent of the mismatch between both sides. Automatically, work-me was curious to know if I would have been able to identify the right side of her face had I only ever seen the left.

'You're wondering why I don't cover it up,' she said, gesturing towards her face.

'No.' I shook my head. 'You're so distinctive, I was wondering why you haven't been caught.'

Her smile reached further on the right than the left. 'Phyllida Hartigan,' she replied, and held out her hand.

When I said I'd seen her around the area for a while, she nodded. 'Yes, I know.' She had been at Dunease Court for five years, she said, without mentioning where she had lived before. 'It's such a tedious place. All those old people.' She stirred her coffee but didn't drink it. 'It would be far better named Done-in Court.'

'You must return the items you stole,' I said, trying to sound official. 'I may not be on duty, but I am a police officer, so I can't – I won't – ignore what you did.'

'You do it for me.' She reached into her bag and put the sunglasses, hairclip and soap on the table. The book seemed to be the only item she was reluctant to hand over.

'Are you German?' I asked, looking at the title: *German Poets of the Great War.*

'Oh, I'm a bit of everything,' she said. 'A mongrel, same as any tea-drinking cur.' A damp whiff stuttered across the table as she flicked through the pages. I remembered various bits of First World War poetry from school, and what with all the centenary stuff in the previous few years, the more famous poets had been hard to avoid, yet I couldn't remember coming across anything written from the enemy side.

She frowned. 'There is no *enemy side* in poetry,' she said. 'These men's hearts . . .' she paused, her fingers resting on the stained red cover '. . . were no different from our own. That's the tragedy of it. Language is a mirror. Blackened, certainly . . .

but always a reflection. Did you ever consider the words that were never written? The poetry that men carried, locked inside them, at their death? My father fought in that war. I remember him remarking many times on the ideas that died on the battlefields, on the beauty we shall never know. "Your future lost in a handful of years," he told me. Of course, as a child I didn't understand. Wasn't the future inevitable, something that would happen despite us rather than because of us? But later I understood what he meant. Perhaps he was right, and my generation's inheritance was rather second-rate. I know he believed as much.' She pushed the book abruptly towards me and turned to the window. 'I presume you're familiar with the little gingerbread man,' she added.

'Huh?' Keeping up with her train of thought was like fact-checking a suspect's dream.

'Of course you are.' Her spoon tapped out a rhythm against the table. '"Run, run as fast as you can, you can't catch me, I'm the gingerbread man."'

'Oh, him. Yes,' I said, bewildered.

'You were following me, so who was following you?'

'What? No one. No one was following me.' But my voice was high, uncertain.

A shadow fell on our table as two women with buggies the size of quad bikes stopped on the pavement directly outside the window. Both wore expensive-looking padded coats and knitted hats with oversized fur pom-poms. We watched through the glass as one reached into her buggy and prised open her toddler's mouth, nodding to the second woman to lean in and take a look. The toddler seemed shocked, then mutinous.

'He should bite her hand,' she remarked.

Alec would have said exactly the same. Phyllida Hartigan was crazy, I decided, watching her observing the tableau outside. Wasn't she? Some sort of dementia, maybe. Or, at the very least, an eccentric with money enough to indulge her Grey Gardens whims. Yet neither assessment – such as they were – sat right with me. I shivered. I was so tired, and my head ached more than ever. It was time to leave. I scooped her haul into my bag. I'd use my ID to return them to the shops with a story about stolen goods being discarded on a park bench or something.

'You are good,' she murmured, smiling.

'Believe me, Mrs Hartigan, this is definitely a one-off. Please do not shoplift again, because you will be caught.' I hoped I sounded more certain than I felt. Despite myself, I realised I was childishly pleased to be on the receiving end of her bewitching, lopsided smile.

Alone outside Gordon's Kitchen, I stared up and down the road. The world looked as it should. No one was acting suspiciously, apart from me. Her stream-of-consciousness nonsense about who-was-following-whom was just that: nonsense. I was seriously out of sorts since the accident, but not so much that I'd suddenly forget years of training, of experience. Yet I couldn't shake off the uneasy feeling that I'd wandered onto a film set by mistake and the terraces of houses and shops on either side of me were backdrops, the passers-by paid extras. Nobody was real; every new face meant nothing. The café was on a corner of a small cul-de-sac. An SUV, one of those big, brutish cars that on small city streets look like the school bullies of the traffic around them, turned sharply at the corner just feet from where I was standing, then roared off in the direction of Regent's Park. As I stumbled back in fright, I whacked my shoulder against a lamppost. I doubled over in pain, and when I straightened up again the car was gone. Embarrassed that Phyllida Hartigan might have been watching the floorshow, I took a last peep through the plate-glass window. She sat alone, her face turned slightly away from me, her fingers splayed on the table in front of her as if stilled while playing an invisible piano. The diamond solitaire on her left hand flashed orange and blue in the sun. She looked impossibly beautiful, her scars a silver trail down her face, telling a story in a language I couldn't understand.

Once again, I slept for most of the afternoon, pursued by anxious, feverish dreams that would leave me confused and out of sorts for the rest of the day. I had just enough time to get sort-of washed and dressed before Alec got home. 'You saw who?' he interrupted, as I began to tell him about my outing.

'The mink-coat woman. From Dunease Court.'

He flicked on the TV. 'What about her?'

I opened my mouth to tell him, but realised: who would I make her out to be? Because no matter how much I had turned it over in my mind, or tried to cast her in different roles, one after another – she was mentally ill; she was a career criminal; she had some sort of progressive brain disease that turned a straight-out-of-the-box Home Counties dowager into a kleptomaniac – nothing felt like the right fit. It reminded me of scanning hundreds of hours of CCTV footage for a particular face in a huge crowd. Occasionally I'd spot a feature so close to what I was searching for that, out of frustration, I'd try to convince myself, *Yes, that's it!* and allow my internal counter to notch up another score. But the smallest push against the thought and certainty would pop, like a balloon, forcing my imaginary scoreboard backwards. My conversation with Phyllida Hartigan hadn't been a long one, yet I was aware of feeling awkwardly recalibrated by it. It was as if she had taken me by the shoulders and turned me ever so slightly, distorting the angle and the intensity from which I viewed the world. I couldn't really explain it. Neither, I realised then, did I want to tell Alec I'd taken stolen goods from her rather than done my job and called the station.

'Oh, nothing, really. Just that I saw her on the high street again, by herself.'

He looked at me curiously. I wasn't sure whether he thought I was lying or going a bit crazy. We lay on the sofa together for a while, my cast propped on a cushion between us.

He watched *Game of Thrones* while I flicked through my Twitter timeline. The term 'timeline' never sat comfortably with me: it made the world sound as though we are all, for good or ill, on a trajectory, that there are markers we will hit – unlike real life, which is uncontrolled, messy. I was still tired, and my attention span was so short that if the first few words didn't halt my hovering finger I moved on. All the news in the world was there, in my lap, and I wanted none of it. There was too much even as there was too little, and it all felt like lies and gaslighting, a vicious oscillation between outrage and entitlement. At work, evil had a defined, well-understood identity – *attacker, abuser, stalker* – but online the terminology was soft-focus, infantilised: *troll, ghost, unfriend*.

I put my phone away. Phyllida Hartigan's comment about the gingerbread man was playing on my mind. I lay there on the sofa and thought of her, and him. And of how, in the end, he gets eaten.

FEBRUARY 1919

I

More ordinary than she had expected, the home of the London Spiritualist Association is announced by a simple brass plaque on its black door. It is a private organisation, for members only, but a painted sign tied to the railings proclaims that the Reading Room is open to the public on Monday and Wednesday mornings. She rings the bell but there is no answer, so she pushes the front door. It's unlocked. The desk in the entrance hall is abandoned. Probably just as well, she decides, spying a large, leather-bound visitors' ledger: she doesn't want to put her name in any book that Selbarre might see. The Gathering Room is to her left. She tries the handle, but the door is locked. An ornate sign for the Reading Room – gold lettering wrapped around an imperious, pointing finger – directs her upstairs.

The only sound to be heard is the tap of her boots against the steps. Over the last few weeks, Violet has seen table-turning and palmistry, spirit photography and levitation, mentalists and mind-readers. The fakes, she believes, have been easy to spot by their hesitations. By restless feet under tables and barely suppressed gagging as muslin is coughed up, by the quick and uneasy looks exchanged between mediums and their managers. She has been glad of the frauds: there is comfort to be found in such carelessness, such common trickery. Violet is at home with duplicity and con artists of one sort or another: she earns her living from them, after all. But she has seen others whose performances have left her at best genuinely baffled and at worst cold from fear. Not that she'd ever have let Forrester goad her into admitting it, but although she wasn't as sceptical of spiritualism – mesmerism, Pelmanism and all the rest of it – as he was, her suspicions had always been that it was almost entirely a business made for selling penny papers. No matter what famous society names were avowing it, so much of what she's seen is variety hall entertainment at best. And, at worst, it's dishonest: the exploitation of misery made gullible by grief, desperate to find any voice in the silence.

The Reading Room is long, rather than wide – it must run the length of the house. Two walls are floor-to-ceiling shelves. Every shelf is full, books and magazines jammed in together, tight as stays. Three old-fashioned readers' tables run in a line down the middle of the room. A scatter of papers, a teacup resting like a paperweight on top, covers the table nearest the front window. The other two are empty.

'Hello?' she calls. 'Is anyone there?' She smiles at her choice of words. There is no reply, so she tours the room, scanning the shelves. *There Can Be No Death*, *A Shilling's Worth of Spiritualism*, *A Key to Physic and the Occult Sciences*, title after title proudly justifying its place. Square cards tacked to each shelf explain contents and time period; there are publications dating back well over a hundred years. A poster tacked to a shelf advertises the London Spiritualist Association Ouija board, on sale for only ten shillings. 'Forewarn and Prefigure!' commands the headline, adding that the board is nicely finished, 'with a felt-tipped table'. She has no idea what she's searching for but, as she regularly says to Chrissie, it's not ignorance that makes a search worthless, it's sloppiness.

Ebony-trimmed glass-fronted cabinets line a third wall. Framed photographs fill these shelves, the sitters identified by the same square typed cards. The Fox sisters are famous: she recognises them straight away. Nervous eyes, narrow mouths. Both wear their hair parted in the middle and pulled back tight into coils at either side of the head, revealing tracks of pale scalp. In front of a large framed portrait of the spirit photographer William Hope there is a row of smaller pictures labelled 'Hope's Spirits'. There are mediums with ectoplasm flowing around their heads, and seated figures clutched by disembodied hands. Hope had captured a handsome couple side by side in their wedding finery, apparently oblivious to the glowering figure in uniform hovering above the young man's head.

On impulse, she touches the side of the teacup on the table. It's warm. She withdraws her hand, oddly frightened suddenly, as though she is being watched. The Fox sisters stare at her from their glass cabinet, as though the photographic paper was no more than a window, a viewing point from another world to this one.

'Can I help you, miss?'

She starts at the voice and whirls around. A small bald man, waistcoat straining over his stomach, has materialised through the wall. She glances over his shoulder. You fool,

Violet, she thinks, noticing a second door, tricked out to look like wooden panelling.

She takes a deep breath. She is interested in the spiritualist writing of Sir Arthur Conan Doyle, she explains. She was passing and noticed the Reading Room sign.

'Then *sign* is the very word!' He titters, delighted at his own wit. 'Why, clearly you were brought here, miss, to my library,' he replied, 'whether you were aware of your spirit guide or not.' He runs a finger down a tall pile of illustrated papers and, with difficulty, extracts a copy of the *Strand Magazine* from 1915. 'The *Strand* published two articles in response to Sir Oliver Lodge's writings in the *Journal of the Society for Psychical Research*. Conan Doyle writes in fervent support, and Edward Clodd,' the librarian gives the name a sneer, 'who has the gall to claim it is unscientific, firmly against.' He folds open the page at the headline *Is Sir Oliver Lodge Right?* A renowned physicist, Lodge is certain the dead can communicate with the living. 'We have been so fortunate as to have both him and our esteemed supporter Sir Arthur Conan Doyle here on many occasions,' he adds.

'Did I hear my name?' The door to the hallway creaks open. 'Good morning, Levant.' The newcomer nods. The librarian's face goes pink as a piglet. He tugs at his waistcoat, clearly beside himself with joy. 'Sir Arthur! What a delightful surprise!'

Good God, it's him! Conan Doyle turns to Violet, his hand extended. What is she to say? She isn't prepared for such an encounter. She's never met him before so she can't betray that she knows him or anything about his business . . . but he's such a well-known figure that of course she knows who he is, in which case she should show that she is aware of who is addressing her, shouldn't she? It would be wrong not to. But at the same time, she can't let slip that he is the only reason she's here, or, indeed, use her own name, just in case. Oh, get hold of yourself, she thinks.

She takes his hand. 'Miss Chrissie Bullman. It's – it's such an honour to make your acquaintance, sir.'

Levant slips between them. 'This lady is keen to read your writings in the *Strand*. I have just this moment been telling her how fascinating Sir Oliver's articles are – no more so than your own, of course.'

Conan Doyle frowns. 'That article contains a second response to Lodge's piece, one that foolishly negates his research. You would do well to avoid wasting your time on it. Clodd conflates spiritualism with a time of animism, when primitive men believed spirits dwelled in everything.'

'Thank you for the advice, sir. But, if you don't mind me enquiring, how *do* you refute men such as Mr Clodd who use science to decry spiritualism?'

'That is simple. They do so without study, in which case we cannot accept their opinion – *a priori*, it is not evidence. One cannot be a man of science without scientific support, don't you agree? We are back in the realm of conjecture and dogmatic illogicality otherwise.' He sounds as logical as you'd expect Sherlock Holmes himself to be. 'Forgive my impertinence for asking, but are you a Roman Catholic, Miss Bullman?'

'No.' She has read his book *The New Revelation* so the question doesn't surprise her.

'When I was a schoolboy, I was a devout Catholic, and I believed – indeed, I was taught as much – that religion and science were incompatible. Yet by the time I completed my medical studies, I found myself to be a convinced materialist.'

'I'm sorry, but I don't understand.'

'Allow me to explain. Have you ever seen a photograph of the surface of the moon?'

She nods, confused. The picture that comes into her head is the old postcard Chrissie pinned up in the office: *London, 2013 ... Next Stop the Moon!* An aeroplane, with luggage strapped to its roof, and a pair of toffs waiting to climb inside. He's wearing a top hat, she's got a fur wrap over a tightly corseted dress. A huge lamp on the front of the aeroplane illuminates a yellow moon, dotted with greying shadows. 'That's what the world will be like in a hundred years,' Chrissie had told her. 'Imagine going there for your holidays!'

Violet had snorted. 'Aeroplanes taking people to the moon and back, yet we'll still be strapped into corsets? Not much advancement in that, is there?'

'Science has stripped the world back too far. Left it hard, clean and bare. Very much as we now know the landscape of the moon to be, from photographs. But what Clodd and those of a mind with him fail to understand is that science is merely a single light in the darkness. And if you understand that circle to be what is definite knowledge, what is known and proven by science, then what remains *outside* that circle of light?' He pauses, and she is unsure whether or not he is expecting her to answer him. His manner is so practised, he has clearly said these words many times before. Just as she decides she must attempt a reply, he continues, 'Surely by applying the same principles, it is not being unduly suppositious to say that what else could there be but other, larger, more fantastic possibilities? And these possibilities continue to impose themselves across our mortal consciousness in such ways that it has become impossible to ignore them. The spiritual dimension is not a barrel-organ, grinding out the same tunes over and over again in the way of our human, material world. It is wider and broader than any of us can ever know or understand.'

He sounds so calm, so eminently rational. Yet she can't help but think of his son, and wonder to what extent Kingsley Conan Doyle's death has changed the nature of his father's beliefs. Who could blame a man for wanting to see, to hear, his son again? With so many slain, those who loved them must be desperate to believe them capable of rising in appeal against such a brutal end and coming home – even if it is hand-in-hand with a spirit guide.

Levant looks delightedly from one face to the other.

'Levant, have those pamphlets arrived?' Conan Doyle says, his lecture at an end. 'I have an engagement and must not delay any further.'

'This very morning, sir,' he says, rooting out a small parcel on the table.

'Thank you. Goodbye, Miss Bullman, a pleasure to meet you.'

For a large man, he moves quickly and is at the door in seconds. She's missed her chance! 'Sir!' she calls. 'Sir, please, but what of those detractors who say it is all untrue, *all* of it?'

Levant is horrified. 'You must allow Sir Arthur to go about his business, miss!'

But Conan Doyle ignores him. 'I have been slower to form an opinion on this subject than on any other. For several years I regarded it with considerable interest and an equal amount of scepticism. But I *have* formed an opinion, and it is a rigorous, considered one, supported by men of honour and intelligence. In the face of *that*, should one persist in regarding spiritualism as a vulgar pursuit of the uneducated, then of course one must look unfavourably on it.'

With a bow and a wave, Levant signals to him to keep going, then turns to her, hissing, '*Detractors?* What of them? They are the fools.'

II

The volume lifts and falls all night long. Will hears the sounds as waves lashing a lonely, night-black shore. Liberated by the butchered version of sleep their wounded bodies permit them, the men of Ward Five shout and snore and whimper. Some who are the most silent during the day – those whose injuries make talking difficult or even impossible, or who wish to avoid the sheer hell of attracting attention to themselves – are loudest at night. There are men who cry out as others cry softly. In the bed to Will's right, Jem is fast asleep, lying on his back and snoring loudly. On the other side, Neville whistles and moans like a banshee because of the flattened cartilage in his nose. Neville had caught a cold the previous week, and between the snotty gulps and wet sucking sounds, the noise coming from his bed meant Will hardly slept at all. The shell that took Neville's ear and gouged chunks out of his cheek means that he has to lie on his side, facing Will. The ward is always kept partly lit, even at night. ('What? Like a nursery full of babies?' was Davey's typically snide remark, but Will doesn't mind: he's grateful for anything that isn't blackness.) Will is used to waking and seeing Neville's eyes staring into his own. Neville calls out sometimes, too: nonsense about spies as far as Will can make out. He'd become paranoid in France. Plenty did. Will remembers soldiers behind the lines who'd got suspicious of the smallest thing, who could read German plots or codes in the turn of a windmill, in the movement of cows in a field. Men whose worlds were so inverted that watching for Death's stealth attack was all that kept them going.

'All right, Nev?' Will whispered, the first night it happened, but Neville said nothing, just stared, unblinking.

'No!' Neville shouted, a minute later.

'Hush, lad, rest easy,' Will said. 'Hush now.' He's got used to this open-eyed yet sleeping version of Neville. He has no idea whether talking helps calm him or not. Does he even hear it? But it feels somehow cruel not to try, when those big eyes – the eyes of a kid, really: Neville is only twenty and young for it – are trained on his own even as they're trapped in their own private, sleeping hell. Poor Neville. The unlucky bastard had got through the war unscathed, as far as what they'd discovered afterwards was the last day of fire, when he'd tripped just yards from his own trench and landed on a gun buried in the mud. It discharged straight into his face. Every few minutes Neville's forehead contorts, but whether it's some sort of muscle spasm or a continuous nightmare, Will has no idea. He shudders at the thought of the sleeping world of each one of the other nineteen men in Ward Five. What despair do they each live through at night? What rage and pain seep out of their sleeping limbs?

No one talks about it during the day.

Will takes his mask off at night, when the ward falls quiet.

At first, the air is soft against his raw, clammy skin, though his face turns stinging cold as the night goes on. He lays the mask on the locker he shares with Neville. It's odd to see it there in the night, his own metal face staring at the ceiling. Neville can only eat pap, food mashed up like you would for a baby, and he drinks through a brass straw. He leaves the straw on the locker at night. A few nights ago he put the straw standing up in the mouth-hole of Will's mask, which made Will laugh. He'd looked at Neville, who stared at him and smiled, or as good as, his eyes brighter. Neville puts the straw in the mask every night now and Will wishes he wouldn't keep doing it, but doesn't want to say so. Because he laughed the first time, Neville needs him to laugh every time now: Will knows he does.

The skin around his eyes feels taut and thin. Sometimes it's more comfortable to lie there with his eyes open than to close them in the hope of sleep. He knows it's stupid – the nurses told him so, as did the first doctor, the day he arrived. Then one of them must have said something to Major Gillies because he appeared and said the same – but he's afraid that his eyes will rip when he closes them. The skin will just tear away, and his eyeballs fall out. *No!* He clenches his hands. *Don't think about your eyes, don't think about your face.* He thinks about the narrow iron bed, makes himself focus on it, inch by inch. From the sheet folded over on itself and tucked under his armpits to the far corners that his toes can just about reach when he flexes them. He touches the weave of the blanket, his fingers inching along the nearest hem until a tiny dip and flatness tells him he's almost at the corner. He concentrates on the weight of his own head against the pillow. He moves it gently from side to side to feel the pillow

against his ears and sniffs the air for any faint *pfft* of starch.
It's lumpy, the feathers all pushed to one side from the angle
of his head, and even realising what a tiny discomfort this is –
hardly worth naming, it's so meaningless – is good. It's clean –
oh, God, so beautifully bloody clean! – that he feels joy simply
lying under the starched sheet and enjoying the swish as he
opens and closes his legs. The soles of his feet are irritated
from shell-shock. It gives him that funny walk, toes splayed.
Lots of the men, not just the foot-sloggers, have it. God knows
his toes have been shat on by rats, broken, blistered. They
were not far off gangrenous at one stage. Walking like a
pigeon seems the least of his problems. There's plenty who'll
never walk again. Finally, he closes his eyes.

He wakes lying flat on his back in the operating theatre.
The lights over his head are bright, so intently white that
his eyes hurt. That must be what woke him, because he feels
groggy. Drops of salty water sting his temples, where the skin
is cracked, arid as a sand dune. Major Gillies is leaning over
him, his cigarette ash dropping onto Will's chest. He's younger
than some of his patients – he can't be forty yet. His face has
the tired lines of an older man, yet the expressiveness of a
much younger one. There is something gleefully unrestrained
about his manner that is different from that of every other
doctor Will encountered in the field hospital, but when he
asks a question, his gaze while listening to the reply is the
most watchful Will has ever known.

'Oh, honey, I see you're crying again.' Will has met plenty
of Kiwis, most of whom had much stronger accents than
Major Gillies but none who had his habit of addressing men
and women alike as 'honey'. His hair gives the appearance of
having slipped back from his head, like a cloak being shrugged

off to reveal smooth bare shoulders. His large forehead blocks out the light as he leans forward over Will's lips, as low as if he's going to kiss him. His face hovers for a moment – close enough for Will to smell the meat of the man's breakfast, see a tiny crumb clinging to his thick moustache, inhale his sour, smoky breath – then slowly, slowly, Gillies straightens. He is a tall man, yet this movement seems to take an age, his entire upper body moving in a series of small jerks, as though on a pulley. 'And what are we doing for you today?'

Will tries to speak but can't. His mouth is heavy, his lips doughy and cold. He tries to lift his hand to point to his face, but it won't raise so much as an inch from the table.

'Look!' Gillies says, holding up a wicker basket so that Will can see inside it. Ears! Piled high, slopping right up to the handles. A thin, brackish liquid seeps through the sides of the basket. 'How about one of these, fresh in? No one's going to need them now. They're all dead! Won't be hearing much, my boy, will they?'

Next, he upends a tub on top of Will's chest, saying, 'Or what about these?' Nose after nose tumbles down on him, landing as far up as Will's neck, *thwick thwack*. He tries to move, to push himself back and away, but can't. Blood splashes onto his face.

Gillies picks up a green metal fire bucket. His gaze locked on Will's face, he holds it high over his shoulder then carefully turns it upside down. *Eyes*! Red, blue, black, pink, green . . . Like tiny coloured balls, each bounces off him and falls to the floor. But the sound of them landing is sharp and thin, not the soft *thwock* of a ball, and Will realises that they aren't eyes, they're buttons, the sort you'd see on a toy bear.

'Well? How about one of these beauties? You won't know

yourself with these, my boy.' Gillies lifts two buttons from the tumble on Will's chest and holds them up against his own eyes. Amber, each with a black dot right in the centre. They are tea-brown and misty, tiny patches of gold flashing from a peaty soil. Will doesn't understand how he knows it, but these are lions' eyes and, suddenly, he is afraid of Gillies, terribly frightened by this giant standing over him. With a *ping*, Gillies drops the buttons into a metal tray next to him and takes up a needle. He holds it up to the light to thread it. In the harsh theatre light the silver flashes like a blade. Gillies winks at Will. 'You weren't brave. You shouldn't be here.'

Will's eyes are wet. His face smarts. He shudders fully awake, feeling the damp chill of sweat drying on his chest. Dread is a leaden weight, pushing him against the mattress. Neville is staring at him.

'Sush,' Neville says, his lower jaw moving unevenly, failing to make contact with the top. Every word Neville says is hard won. 'Sush, Will, s'be all right.'

The irony of living in Queen's Hospital is that a strange peace is to be found there, among the nightmares and waking terrors. Among the debris of war. The main building, Frognal House, is an old red-brick manor bought by the government a couple of years earlier and converted. Will had overheard Neville's mother talking about it the first time she'd come to see him. They'd visited the house before, when Neville was a little lad. 'Darling, you must remember the Marsham-Townshends?' In common with so many visitors, her voice had the slightly desperate quality that comes from being scared, yet equally afraid that someone might notice it. 'Bobbie Marsham had that gorgeous Irish wolfhound. You were simply wild about that dog!' She was talking too loudly, too slowly, as though Neville's silence meant he couldn't hear, or understand. Neville had shrugged and looked at the floor: a grown man, one who had saved lives – including his own, which matters just as much, as far as Will is concerned – reverting to a truculent child. Later on, Jem had whispered to Will, sarcastic, 'He thinks he's too posh for the likes of us.' And that had made it worse, as though the three of them fighting on the same side, in the same army, living the same life for all that time was worth nothing, now that they were back. The normal order had reasserted itself. It wasn't even the power remaining with the officer class that annoyed him so much: it was the willingness of men like Jem to hand it back, to seek out a commanding officer in every situation.

The main hospital building, the wards and operating theatre are new, a series of low, prefabricated huts, white with black timbering. They look more like a clutch of village cricket pavilions scattered around the grounds than a hospital. When he walks in the gardens he hears the gentle crunch of gravel as a victory march. He avoids walking too close to the trees. Forever in shadow because of the high walls, the earth there is damp and the muddy squelch underfoot is unbearable. Also, it's too quiet: no birds sing in the trees shaded by the walls, and the silence isn't a good one. It's not the sort of silence at the end of a song, where the final notes seem still to be fluttering around. No, it's the pure stillness of the moment before they went over the top. It is the sound of a thousand men filling their lungs with oxygen all at once.

Will leans against his pillow and tilts his head as far back as he can, until he can make out the top of the window frame behind him. He forces himself to follow its line with his eyes.

Around and around until he can feel his breath returning to normal. Quietly to himself, he lists everything he can see. He is in bed. The bed is clean. The bed has a window above it. The bed is dry and above ground. Every window, every sheet, every meal and clean toilet, every pair of laundered underpants and socks is like a prize in a penny lottery he hadn't known he'd bought a ticket for. Each and every single bloody one. The men of Ward Five are already the lucky ones, Will believes: they have outlived their own lives. So why does luck feel so unfair?

'Bad dream, Will?' Nurse Goodfellow is by his bed.

He nods, grateful that his head moves so easily. Did he shout out? He must have. Neville's eyes stare at the back of her head.

'Get some rest before tomorrow,' she says. 'Try not to worry. It's a small operation this time, very straightforward. And there are no safer hands you could be in than the major's. Shall I get you a drink of water? Another pillow?'

He shakes his head, wishing he had his mask on. Her skin! Her smile! Even in the brightest daylight she is perfection.

She leans down and pulls the sheet and blanket tight. He feels the slight rise and drop as she folds them taut under the mattress.

'Tighter, please, Nurse.'

She tugs and folds until he feels the covers pushing down on his chest, firm as the walls of a coffin around him. There's no escaping now. Nurse Goodfellow walks away, the swish and squeak of her getting fainter and fainter. He watches her until the door to the nursing station opens and shuts. He closes his eyes and tries to rest. The skin around his mouth pulls and cracks.

III

He is both of this world and distinct, separated from it, as though it exists on the other side of a length of muslin. Walking through the streets of Sidcup is like moving through a series of giant postcards. It looks like life, but it's not real: it doesn't feel the way life should. It's a tableau, one constructed merely to make a fool of him. Because what part does he, Will Dockery, have to play in the morning-to-evening business of this town? Its sun and moon don't rise for him. He has no money for shopping, or need of anything. He has no business with any professional person or tradesman. No one at all, for that matter. His presence is of no interest or meaning to either the economy or the society of the town.

Being a hospital patient used to mean being in a bed, didn't it? Lying sick in a ward until you left, either cured or taken away in a box. When Harry got pneumonia that time he'd run into the sea at Margate – years before, Will couldn't even remember which winter it was – he'd ended up in the Royal Free. Ma didn't know her own name, she was that scared he wouldn't pull through. 'She says she was beside herself with worry, but she was always bloody beside *me!*' was Harry's comment, when he was home again and Ma had him tucked up in bed, a fire raging and them all fetching and carrying fresh tea, lavender water, and hot jars for his feet. He was in hospital for a fortnight and didn't leave the bed once for the first week, not even to shit, as he said himself. Harry's experience was what 'getting better' had once meant to Will. Illness, convalescence even, wasn't a complicated idea, even though the outcome could be cruel, and people ill-used because of it. It made *sense*. It was a circuit that returned you – assuming you weren't one of the unlucky ones – to roughly where you'd been beforehand.

But this!

Will lives in a hospital where, within reason, he can come and go. He gets dressed in the morning and potters about in the workshop or the art room. There's even a cinema. He can go up to London once a week if he fancies it, which he doesn't much, these days. He prefers the walks through the trees that skirt the grounds, or the road to the town. He's glad January is over. It's only a few days into February, but nature has just begun to send out tiny green promises. Down payments on the future.

A couple of mornings a week he sets up the lectern in the library and talks about books. At first, he'd made the mistake of billing it as a class, *English Literature through the Ages*. Only four turned up for the first session, and none the second. On Nurse Goodfellow's advice, he'd renamed it *What Shall I Read?* and got a full house. They'd all had enough of being told what to do, was her take on the matter. Let them ask questions for a change. The men love Dickens, Sir

Walter Scott and Sir Arthur Conan Doyle. It had gone so well for the first few weeks that perhaps he'd got carried away, because suggesting *The Winged Victory* by Sarah Grand had just confused them ('Too soon, perhaps,' Nurse Goodfellow murmured). Last week he suggested they try putting on a play by Shaw, just reading the parts aloud, not having to learn them or anything, but all he got were shrugs and sarcastic comments about a skit instead.

'"Beauty and a Thousand Beasts",' a voice had shouted. 'That's more like it, eh, Nurse?'

'Best to leave it with novels for the time being,' said Nurse Goodfellow, later. 'Keep it simple. There are plenty of intelligent men here, Will, but that doesn't mean they're interested in the same things you are.'

Apart from the headaches, his stinging, smarting face, and his sore, irritated feet, his body is working all right; he doesn't even have to take any tablets. He had hated the Tabloid they were given in the field hospitals. It was supposed to help with shell-shock, but had left Will feeling sleepy: an unpleasant, half-drunk sort of tired as if he wasn't made of the same stuff as the world. His body is doing all right. But his face? A single look in the mirror is enough to make a man feel sick enough for hospital.

'Finished stuffing teddies for the day, have you?' Davey is waiting for him at the top of Station Road. Davey can't stand hanging around Queen's when he comes to visit, says it gives him the creeps, so they're meeting in the town instead. Will wishes he'd never mentioned the toy workshop. He enjoys it, though he was more of a mind with Davey when he first arrived at the hospital: a group of grown men sitting in a circle, sewing toy horses and bears and the like? Daft nonsense. Passing each other baubles and buttons as if they were little kiddies in a nursery! But, as with his talks about books, it's turned out well enough. Both Jem and Digson – if he's got a Christian name, Will's never heard it – were joiners before the war, so they make little wooden trains. Horses too. Andy, a harness-maker and tooler from Sheffield, makes miniature leather shoes for the patchwork dolls. It's as though the riverbed of each man's former life – he'd have said 'real life' once, but he doesn't make that mistake now – hasn't fully shrivelled and dried: a tiny trickle still flows through their hands and into what they're holding. And what they're holding just happens to be toys, that's all. Because Will was – is, he reminds himself, nervous at how little faith he has in the present tense – a teacher, he stitches a tiny alphabet like a scarf onto each teddy to help the children learn their letters even as they're playing. His first few attempts looked like twine wrapped around the tiny bodies, as if he was trying to strangle them, but he's got the hang of it now.

'Like a bleeding circus, this town. Every sinner in the place must come to gawp at you.' Davey sounds irritated. 'Charabancs on a Sunday, I bet, full of fools come to throw stones at the animals.'

'It's not that bad.' He shrugs. 'People know. Most of them understand. And the ones who don't? They don't matter.'

Why is he lying? There's no need to spare Davey's feelings. People don't understand. Just that morning Digson had told his wife she wasn't to visit him again. 'Repulsive' was the word he'd used: he knew she found him repulsive, and couldn't bear her attempts to deny it any longer. She had to look at the beast, then lie to its face about what she saw. 'It killed me as much to look at her face, as I'd say it did her to look at mine,' he said. 'And the bloody bairns screaming the whole time, like they'd been dragged into a Hall of Horrors.' The broken, bumpy craters of his jaw strained as his face tensed with anger and tears.

But Will tells his brother none of this. Instead he says, 'All around the town there are blue benches for us. People leave you alone if you're on a blue bench.'

'What? Your arses special, are they?'

'It means you're from the hospital.'

'I bet a sodding bench doesn't stop anyone looking.'

He's right, of course. It doesn't. Most likely it diluted the worst of the name-calling, the obvious horrors. The women exaggeratedly clutching their children to their sides, the not-hushed-enough exhortations *Don't look at him!* The Sunday just gone Will had walked into Sidcup and passed the Catholic church just as Mass was coming out. Nurse Goodfellow attends that church. He'd hoped, even as he didn't allow himself think it, that he'd bump into her leaving – maybe she'd let him walk back with her to the hospital. Instead, two elderly ladies in mantillas and black coats crossed themselves when they saw him approach. It made his blood boil. Calling on their God to help protect them! Protect them from what? No, from *whom*? Wasn't he one of *their* bloody protectors? He and the hundreds of others in the Queen's had fought a war so that old crones like that pair could keep going to Mass every day without living in fear for their lives! He'd told Nurse Goodfellow about it that evening, leaving out the bit about it being right outside her church, cornerboying in the hopes of sighting her. But even as he began to talk, he could feel the heat draining from him, until he felt like nothing so much as a child running home to Ma after a silly spat in school.

'Don't mind them, Will,' she said, and looked him straight in the eyes. 'Faith is no proof of kindness, to my mind. And it's certainly no proof of intelligence.' Two years before she'd been nursing in Brighton, she'd told him, and when the Royal Pavilion was converted to a military hospital for the wounded Indian soldiers she couldn't believe the number of people who went just for a look at the place. Ten thousand in a single month – it had been in all the newspapers! Just trooped up to stare and comment, like they were on a Sunday-school outing. People can't help themselves, she told him. The war had crept in everywhere, had leaked into every bit of life. 'It's fear. And you can't be angry with a couple of old ladies for feeling frightened, can you?' She'd been staring straight at him, and smiling, and his whole body wanted just to lean forward and touch her. To take her shining face in his two hands and feel the slope of her cheekbones, the curve of her jaw under his fingertips. To cup the soft roll of skin under her chin in his hand.

Then he'd imagined her flesh and blood lips touching the hard metal of his own and hated himself.

He and Davey are almost at the end of the high street. Along its length, bicycles have been left with one pedal leaning against the edge of the pavement to keep them upright while their owners are shopping. As they pass each set of handlebars, Davey leans over and rings the bell. The constant ting-a-ling is horrible, and Will wishes he wouldn't draw attention to him like that. Passers-by hear the sound, they look, yet all they see is him, not Davey. *Him*.

A few doors ahead, a young couple stare in at the window of the Pianoforte Warehouse. Her hands are pressed against the glass, black-gloved fingers splayed wide. Will, in common with every other demobbed soldier, can assess a man in a second. Age, rank, wounds: one blink and he can hazard a fair guess. They all do it, Davey too, only the difference is that Davey does it aloud. Davey is quick to judge, yet doesn't care a fig for whoever he's commenting on. Will cares but doesn't judge.

'What do you reckon?' It's as though Davey read his mind. 'Stayed at home? Hiding in the barn, I'd say, and sucking buttermilk straight from the cow's tit.'

'Shut up, Davey,' he says, though there's a farmyard air about the lad right enough.

Hearing their voices, the lad watches their approach. He has one hand on his girl's upper arm, the other on her waist. A tiny frown crosses his forehead. Will reads it as the expression of a man who wonders if he has been found wanting, and chivvies himself to make it up in some other way, good or bad.

'That one, there.' She points. 'With the ebony trim. Isn't it a beauty?'

'Too expensive, pet,' he replies.

'But we've not been in and asked yet! Anyway, couldn't we get it on the deferred payment system?'

He tugs her hand away from the window. 'It's not like you'll be giving concerts, now, is it?' His voice is sharp. 'We don't need anything fancy.'

Will silently curses the stranger. Buy her the bloody thing! Be glad there's a girl on your arm, in your heart, who wants to sit at home and play the piano for you, and hang the expense. Don't make her life pulse with whatever hurts in your own. Buy it. Steal it. Whatever. Give your girl her heart's desire.

A child shuts the door to Siskin's drapery behind her, silencing the shop bell in mid-peal. She has a ball of wool in one hand and a brown paper bag in the other. A horse in harness on the street nearby shakes its mane and whinnies at the sight of her. Its reins hang limply to the side, an old candlewick blanket over the side of the small cart behind. Will watches as she takes a sketch around, all furtive. She shoves the ball of wool far down into the pocket of her apron, then fumbles inside the paper bag for a few seconds. White sugar crystals crust her hand – the tiny glint is like slivers of diamond. She licks her fingers one by one, starting with the smallest, as if her hand was made from lollipops. The horse whinnies and lowers its head to nudge her shoulder. Laughing, she dips her fingers back into the bag, then holds them to the horse's mouth. It looks as if it could swallow her hand whole. She is a person made only of that moment, Will thinks. Alone, happy. A child, with nothing more important to worry about than the sly slipping of a treat and not getting caught at it. He envies her: the balance of life is still in her favour. She's not lugging her grimy history on her back. She's not, he thinks, watching her pat the horse's nose and giggle as it nuzzles her hand, sweating behind a sheet of moulded tin. She woke today and knew who she was, just as she will wake tomorrow. What is he? A half-man. Abandoned. He despises his fixed metal face yet is terrified of the one that Major Gillies will eventually return to him. Who is *that* man to be?

Will blinks. It's uncomfortable behind the tin, he is suddenly warm, despite the grey, dull day.

Davey stops outside the Black Sheep. 'Time to wet our whistles.' He nudges his brother. 'Aptly named, isn't it?'

'We're not allowed. The hospital doesn't like us drinking.

Last time a man from Queen's got drunk he went berserk in the ward.'

'You can just watch me, then. I don't mind.'

'No. I'll keep walking and come back for you in a while.'

'All right, suits me.' And the door flashes open – stale beer and fried chops, the cheap promise of company, not companionship – then shuts with a click.

Will goes on down Main Road and onto Downdale Avenue as the rain that was threatening begins to fall. He's forgotten his umbrella, and while he carries a hat, he's stopped wearing it. It wedges the mask so tight that the tin feels glued to his skin.

Drops pelt down, suddenly hard and sharp. He hears rather than feels them at first; he hates the cold, echoing sound the tiny bullets make when they hit his metal face. On his right is the wooden lych gate of a church, so he ducks under it, beside a board. *All Saints' Church, All Welcome.* A smell of ivy and damp earth rises around him. Must be a draughty spot. His feet turn cold and he looks down and realises that he's standing in a puddle. He swishes his foot around gently, stirring the silty water. It barely covers his sole, and the mound of his toecap rises from the water, like the hump of a dead man's back. He lifts his foot slowly, slowly, as if carefully tugging a body from a swollen trench.

The church door is ajar, though the lights are off and no sound comes from inside. The clouds are forcing mid-afternoon to fall sharply towards evening. Yews line the path on both sides, stretching out in rows through a graveyard that wraps around the church. The dead a moat, protecting the living. Rain hammers, heavy and leaden, on the roof of the lych gate. Suddenly he can't bear the smell of earth, the incessant rat-a-tat noise.

He was right: the place is empty. Good. Last thing he needed was to land on the locals at their prayers, appearing in front of them as a living, breathing example of what the vicar was sure to have been telling his congregation to be kind to. An animal in a cage, trained to perform for gawpers.

It's a long time since Will has been inside a church. There was a chaplain with them in the battalion, a kind chap called Emory, but you saw more of him if you were as good as dead than if you were still alive. Some of the lads thought Emory brought bad luck for that very reason. Soldiers are a superstitious bunch, and the saying was that the first man Chaplain Emory spoke to in the morning would be gone the same day. Emory held his church services in the middle of fields usually, and Will had gone along, same as everyone else, but the man could have been reciting penny-paper doggerel or the *Help Wanted* columns for all he was listening. If a shell had your name on it, you'd get it: that was what Will believed. Whether you'd taken your commission for faith or money, no amount of seeking or dodging God would get you out of it.

It's not a big church, though so dim and gloomy in the half-light from outside that it's hard to tell where the shadows end and the walls begin. He walks up and down the side nave first. Then he moves into the central aisle and walks the length of the church to the altar, a groom with no bride. He hears a faint tick-tock, but whether it's a clock in the vestry or beetles, he can't tell. There is calm in the weight of the silence surrounding him, as though the church bells had just this minute stopped ringing. The pew handrails are inset with a series of brass squares, each one a whine from a grave.

The most recent one he can see is from 1910, which might as well be a thousand years before as less than a decade. These deaths come over as quaint by comparison with all the ones he's known. Men and women, died at a ripe old age and celebrated for it. A few kiddies, yes, but that's the way of things: his mother lost two as babies. These polished brass dead belong to another order, a sentential world.

Slam!

Will jumps, turns. The sound has ricocheted around the stone walls. Fear surges through his body even as he feels himself tensing, readying himself. A memory, firing him up to turn, to act. *Move, man, move.*

'Sorry, sorry.' Through the gloom of the far aisle he sees a fat man is walking slowly towards him, his hands held up, as if in surrender. 'I didn't mean to startle you. Desperate draughts in here. Doors slam willy-nilly!' Now that he's closer, Will can see that the vicar is not as old as he had assumed. His hair is grey and sparse but his face is unlined. He extends his left hand. 'Stuart Miall, I'm the vicar here.' His hand is fleshy, damp and soft as dough. It swallows Will's. Will wants to grab it back, rub himself dry against his jacket. He swallows, hard.

'William Dockery. From Queen's.'

'I gathered as much.' The vicar gestures at the mask. 'How is your treatment coming along?'

'Fine.' He knows Miall is waiting for more, the way you'd go through the story for someone if it was a broken bone or whatever (*and then it didn't set right, so the sawbones broke and reset it and, well, you can imagine what happened next...*) but he has nothing he wants to give him.

'I meet one of your fellow patients regularly. Neville Ruther, do you know him?'

Will nods. Neville has never mentioned Miall, but it's no surprise, really. Will hears him whispering his prayers in his bed at night. The desperate lost sound, the suck and gasp as he mutters to himself.

'Poor chap,' Miall says, and gestures to the side of his face, a circling movement, as though a simple turn of the wrist can describe the broken man Neville has become. 'I take some services at the Queen's, but I don't recognise your face—' He stops sharply. 'I don't recognise you from there.'

Before Will can reply they are distracted by a noise from a small balcony set to one side over the altar. A bird. They stare as it beats its wings against the yellow of a stained-glass sun.

'Oh dear,' Miall says. He tut-tuts but doesn't move. The bird flies away from the glass and into the buttresses, blundering and panicked. Will can hear it flapping about, trapped. Shit lands on the altar with a loud *splat*! Miall tut-tuts again. 'That'll give the verger something to complain about.'

Will walks down the aisle towards the door, trying to track the bird's progress as it bumps around the roof, following the noise of wings beating in fright. It's the same colour as the beams. A thrush, maybe? He doesn't know much about birds. There it is! At the wall. He moves forward and pushes the big front door open, hard as he can. Cold air rushes in. The bird slows above Will's head, hovers. Whether it's the gust of air or the sight of an open door that does it Will has no idea, but the bird is gone in seconds.

The church bell peals out the hour. He's been gone ages. Davey will either be drunk or disappeared, there's no predicting which.

'That's my cue!' the vicar says brightly, the bird already forgotten. 'I must go. Next week's sermon won't write itself, will it?' He holds out his hand again. 'Good to meet you, Mr Dockery.'

Will leaves the church, ready to retrace his steps to the Black Sheep. He pauses in the lych gate once more, takes a few deep breaths. It's almost night now, the air sulphurous and sooty. It's still raining, which means the streets will be quieter. People are inside by their fires, the sure roll of evening into night under way. He takes off his mask, briefly glad of the cold against his skin, but puts it back on when the rain begins to sting.

Will had had another consultation with Major Gillies that morning just before he left to meet Davey. Gillies made sure to have several meetings with each patient before 'getting to work', as he put it. Mrs Scott had been there too, silently sketching. She had been a sculptor before the war. ('Everyone says you'll be fine if you get one of Mrs Scott's noses,' Digson said. 'I'm hoping for one of hers.') Will hadn't met her before today, but he'd read about her in the newspaper some years before – six, was it? Seven? – when her husband had died.

'That poor woman.' He recalls his mother commenting on the headlines announcing Captain Scott's death. 'So what if he's a hero? A hero lost in the ice is no good to his family, is he?' At the time it had seemed tragic and strange, and oddly mythical. And now here she is too: a widow without a body to bury, no different from thousands of others.

She had smiled at him when he walked into the consulting room, but didn't speak. Her head moved up and down from the pad in her hand to Will's face. Up and down, over and over, like a little bird after a worm.

'How do you imagine your face looking?' Gillies asked. Funny to think about it now, but he'd never asked him such a straight-out question before. They had only ever discussed details: the angle of a jaw; the relationship between his eyebrows and the bridge of his nose; the fullness or otherwise of lips. Gillies had put his cigarette down and held a hand mirror up to Will's face. Will could see his own dire reflection and then, just above it, the surgeon's kind smile. *Who am I?* Will thought. And then a different thought that belched around his head like a shaken bottle of lemonade: *Who was I?*

'I want . . .' Will had paused. *Mirror, mirror on the wall.* He'd never really considered this. All he knew was that he couldn't bear the face now looking back at him. Or the tin mask over it. He knows it'll never be what it was. The glory of ordinary! When he'd looked like any other lad. He was never handsome, like Davey. Davey always had looks enough for the whole family. Harry was handsome too, and had the personality to go with it, unlike Davey, who was always the in-on-himself type, even when they were lads. Harry was the joker – he'd have charmed anyone into anything. But Harry is gone and Davey is in London, drinking his pension and up to God knows what, and Will is here. A man in a bed in a ward in a hospital. A man waiting to be repaired, like one of so many toys in a doll's hospital.

Mrs Scott, Major Gillies, Will. Three people, who would never have met under any other circumstance, quiet together, uniquely concentrated on this silence. Mrs Scott had even put down her pencil. Her hands were clasped together loosely, resting on her pad so as to obscure her drawing of the side of Will's head.

'I want . . .' he said again, as the quiet suddenly jangled loud and discordant inside his head. He pictured one of the blue benches as clearly as if it was in the room with them, and realised how much he hated them, that he'd never put his backside on one again.

'Yes?' Mrs Scott's voice was clear and soft. 'Yes, Will?'

'I want a face you'd never pick out in a crowd.'

There is no noise coming from the Black Sheep. That's good. Will takes a deep breath, feels the sooty cold of the world fill his lungs, checks his mask is on straight. As he'd left All Saints', he'd spotted a small shape beside the lych gate, partly covered with mud. He'd reached down, touched the tiny, soup-brown body, felt the last of its fading warmth.

Will wants to believe in God, he honestly does. He wants something to hold on to. But how can he? God is nothing more than himself. There is nothing greater and nothing smaller. Praying is as useful as trying to shake hands with a ghost. He pushes the pub door open. His eyelashes bat against the tin as he steps inside in search of his brother.

A toy workshop! For the life of him – and it's worth bugger-all, he'd be the first to swear it away – Davey can't understand his younger brother. It's some sort of joke, that's what it is. What is wrong with Will that he can't see he's been made a fool of? Grown men, who've been to war and lost limbs to it, more than one in some cases, sitting around with pin cushions on their laps, sewing stuffed arms and legs onto teddy bears! Tapping out little wooden toys with their little wooden hammers!

The counter of the Black Sheep is sticky with spilled beer. The cold comfort of other nights spent at bars just like this one rises inside him. He's never been here before yet he knows exactly where he is. There is an order to this world, even when it gets to the mess of kicking-out time. A scratched memory surfaces: in the Golden Hind on Christmas Eve, him shouting and some fat fucking conchie shouting back, telling him to shut up . . . the sharpness of the pain in his arm and shoulder when he was chucked out onto the street. He tries to remember exactly what happened, but he can't. It's like looking at the world through pinpricks in a sheet. Fuck it, it's done now. The hiss of the gas lamp on the wall nearby is making him sleepy. That and the ale. The Black Sheep is quiet: a grand total of three customers, and one a dog. He wonders if it was always like this, and the place is on its uppers, or if the weather or the Spanish is keeping the punters away. The lone barmaid leans against the wall by a window, staring out at the street. She holds a grubby rag for polishing glasses in one hand, but he's not noticed her wipe a single one all the time he's been sitting at the bar. She's standing at an odd angle: one entire side from feet to head rests against the window frame, so she can look out while still facing her supposed customers. Her round face reminds him of Violet Hill's secretary, Chrissie. The yellow hair too. But this girl's the brassy sort, no more blonde at birth than himself. Her expression is unreadable. Is she waiting in hope of someone in particular passing by, or just for time to tick away until she can again bolt the door on the world?

The dog yelps in her sleep, thumps its tail.

Davey is restless again, feeling an irritable current running from his hair to his toes. It goes right into his fingertips, the dirt of it trapped under his nails. Some days he's so full of energy he could do anything, go anywhere, walk to any public house in London and drink it dry when he got there. Other mornings, he can barely drag himself out of bed and into the world. He never knows which it's going to be. He raises his glass again. Beer helps level it out.

What happens if Will's not allowed back to the teaching? His brother's not thought of that, has he? Would any school take on a man who's no better than a scarecrow to the pupils? It's not being mean to think it, it's realistic. And, Davey assures himself, *someone* in the family has got to think straight. Will's got too much hope pinned on that surgeon, that's his trouble. All of 'em going around that hospital as if Major Gillies is God, and all they have to do is believe and they'll be saved, pulled back from the Hell fires. If the last four years have taught Davey anything – and they have taught him a lot, even if he has to keep most of it locked away somewhere so sunless and hidden inside him that he can't reach it – it's that you never fucking know what's going to happen. Will always did take on so about things. He's too quick to take offence or suspect someone of slighting or misunderstanding him. Needs to toughen up a bit, that's what. He's in limbo, as though he's in a boat and fine to drift along, reconciled to going whichever way the stream takes him, not caring whether the churn of a waterfall is waiting just around the bend or a harbour. He'll be left behind. He'll eventually appear out of that hospital and he'll be good for nothing. Just cos the world turns one day at a time doesn't mean it's not turning damn quick, spinning them all dizzy.

Teddies!

For fuck's sake! It's cruel, that's what it is.

'What's that?' The barmaid turns her head towards him. Her body remains perfectly still as if glued to the wall, angled towards the world outside.

He spoke aloud again, did he? That happens a lot these days. He's not really aware of the thought passing through his head until it turns out he's gone and said it.

'Nothing.'

She continues to look at him and her body turns to match the direction of her head. It's so slow a movement as to seem like a shop mannequin being moved into position, some unnatural angle designed to flatter a single object, irrespective of what it does to the entire figure.

'That glass of yours empty again?' She moves to stand across from him, leaning one elbow against the wood of the counter. Her arms have a swollen meatiness to them. Her sleeves are pushed high above her elbows and held in place by two bands. Not that she needs the bands – the cuffs are so tight that red weals have sprung up on her arms. She keeps the rag tight in her hands, like a baby afraid to drop its comforter.

'You know Queen Mary's?'

'Them doctors are bloody miracle workers if you're a Queen's man.'

'I'm not. Do you get lads, patients, from there come in?'

'A few used to a while back, but they got told not to. Suits me. My regulars said it put them off their drink.'

So Will had been telling the truth. He nods, sips. The dog by the fire twitches again, dreaming of rabbits too fat to run. Her tail briefly beats in unison with the clock over the mantelpiece, but time moves faster and wins again, as it always does.

'My brother's a . . .' he pauses '. . . a Queen's man.'

He wants to see her wrong-footed, embarrassed out of

her dull-witted solidity. To apologise for seeming careless, disrespectful. Maybe even persuade him to a drink on the house, for politeness' sake.

She shrugs one shoulder, the gesture so careless as to mock him by the very lack of effort it took to make it. She refills his glass and takes his money without comment, then moves to the middle of the counter and opens a door leading into a back room. The dull throb of a man's voice slips through. Without looking around, she stretches her hand out and throws the rag onto the countertop behind her. But her hand doesn't return to her side immediately. He watches as she flexes her fingers wide, tiny creatures coming back to life. The door shuts behind her, the man's voice silenced.

What's keeping Will? Davey checks the clock above the sleeping dog. He's to be at work for half past seven – there'll be trouble if he misses his train. Assuming there is a train, of course: London is down to the end of its coal because of the miners' strike. The papers say that the Underground drivers will be heading out on strike, and the Metropolitan lads are set to join them. Could happen any time now. He's all right for today at least, but he'd better not take too many more chances in coming to Sidcup. There'll be a right contango if he's late for work, tonight of all nights. He only came to tell Will he'd be going abroad soon. Another couple of weeks or so – less maybe, the boss is getting twitchy to leave – then they'll be away. It can't come soon enough.

He shouldn't have bothered coming to Sidcup. Waste of time. Now that he's here, he doesn't want to tell Will about going abroad, after all. Last thing he wants is a lecture from his younger brother. Yes, he decides. It's best to leave it. No point saying anything without a date, is there? After Will's next operation would be better, anyway. Easier done, while Will is more distracted. Davey lifts the glass again. Yes, should've thought of that before. In fact, the best thing would be to drop him a line when the tickets are booked.

New York! He smiles at the thought, feels again that current in his legs, his arms, a jolt in his dick. He's only been in the job six weeks and hadn't had it a fortnight when the boss said he couldn't do without him, he'd be wanting Davey to go to New York with him – and everywhere else in the meantime! That's the big advantage to Davey's being so *amenable* to all sorts of work, as the boss refers to it. His right-hand man, that's what he called him. Just as well, eh, seeing as how banged up his left is. Stiff as a poker half the time. He might just drop in on that Chrissie again one of these fine days, when her boss is out of the way. She's been useful right enough, and most likely a soft touch for a good send-off if he plays his cards right.

Since demob it's felt like a wind has got up. It comes from everywhere at once and never lets go. Will allows himself be buffeted by it, turned around and around, spinning every which way and no way at all. Davey knows better. He's going to use the wind. It'll power his back all the way to America!

Why won't Will get angry? Davey wants him to stand full-force and shout back, to scream into the gale. The way people look at his brother, for God's sake. It's not like he's the only one with a face like that. And he's still got his teeth. That Neville in the bed beside him, his mouth puckered up like a cat's arsehole . . .

Heroes: that's what they were told they would be, just for making it home when so many didn't. Harry didn't. He imagines hundreds of thousands of Harrys in uniform, growing grey as shadows, then vanishing one by one into thin air. Hundreds of thousands of studio photographs on hundreds and thousands of sideboards, mantelpieces, dressers. Each with one face gouged out. Or two, or three . . . And the people who loved those faces, the mas and dads and sweethearts, all lamenting and wishing their own Harry was home, weeping and promising that they'd have made a hero of him, had he been there to look at, to touch, instead of gone. Snuffed out.

But Davey is back, and Will is back, and where are their rewards? It's only been a few months, and he's full sure the well of gratitude and relief is as good as drunk dry. The stones he throws into it don't disappear into deep, cool water. No, he can hear a sullen thud as they pierce a puddle and land on the hard floor just below. The measly pensions, the assumption you'd be able to take up your life from before the war, as though you'd done nothing more than go on a Sunday-school outing for four years! There has been one pleasant surprise, though: he'd assumed the days of taking liberties with girls had died with the threat of death itself. That they'd give nothing away any more in case you'd take it and just shove off, instead of trooping away to die, your dick still throbbing from the parting gift. Turns out he was wrong: the shortage of men has created a panic in the market. There's no end of women if you want them, all desperate to grab some lad like it's a game of sardines, but unless you're clever and find yourself a well-off widow, there's no living to be had from a woman. Or not the sort that would interest him, anyhow.

Whenever he was home on leave it used to make him furious to hear people going on about their suffering, what a burden it was to keep the home fires burning. The hard labour of constant making do. As though the horrible, huge deeds being done across the Channel weren't for their reckoning! Men who'd never left their own hearth for a night, yet by their own lights were no different from him. Fools. The war had rendered men like him a different species.

One of the double-doors to the street creaks open. It's in the middle of the room, on a line with the one the barmaid disappeared through. There is a pause, as though whoever is outside is trying to look the room over without being spotted. That'll be Will. He enters, his back to the bar. Davey can tell his brother is tired, his shoulders rounded and low. From behind, Will looks soaked. Davey pushes the stool away and stands up. He puts his right hand to the counter, to stop himself swaying to and fro, a forgotten flag caught in a breeze.

Will should be full of rage that he's not being treated better. Angry that he's put sitting on a special bench so as not to upset the locals. Sewing teddy bears for oafs and their oafish children! He's going to grind down to nothing if he doesn't find fire within himself. He'll be discarded like a piece of rusting machinery, and without the strength left to do anything about it.

Harry was the souvenir they left behind in France, one of the thousands who'd got to dig his own grave. A casualty of war, though 'casualty' makes it sound almost accidental, unintentional. But Will? Will has been abandoned by the peace. He just can't see it yet.

January 2018

1

Although I knew roughly where Dunease Court was, I had never noticed its entrance before. The wrought-iron security gates and high, hedged perimeter were tastefully discreet. As soon as I pressed the visitors' bell the gate slid back to reveal a large red-brick Victorian building, a Gothic fantasy of turrets, stonework and ornate chimney stacks. Despite the NW1 address, I had expected something a bit more rough-and-ready from Phyllida's description, yet the entrance and foyer had more in common with a country house hotel than a typical retirement home. Little groups of sofas and walnut coffee tables, Axminster carpets, the works. Every fabric was a riot of flower prints, every couch bolstered and buttoned and padded. It was the *Sunday Telegraph* come to life. The receptionist introduced himself as 'Ron McBride, junior administrator' as he slid a visitors' book across the desk. Beside my elbow a framed photograph was captioned *Welcome to Dunease Court, Director Robert Grain BA (Hons), SBS PGDip Global Business.* In my experience, when people advertise their credentials quite so energetically they're usually hiding something.

'Name and signature, please. Who do you want to see?'

'Phyllida Hartigan.'

'Excuse me?' He frowned.

Christ, maybe she wasn't a resident at all! Had she spoofed me? And, like a fool, I was standing there with a gift for her!

'Is she expecting you?' he added.

'No.' It came out as a whisper. 'I mean, NO.' Police-volume the second time, loud enough to startle him. 'Sorry.'

'It's definitely Mrs Hartigan you want?'

'Yes. Why?'

He ignored my question. 'Take a seat, please, Miss Tenant.'

He moved to one side and called over a young woman. He spoke, she looked at me, he looked at me, she shrugged, she headed off, he looked at me again, he shrugged too. Judging by the pantomime, asking to see Phyllida Hartigan was an unusual request.

Three sets of doors led off the reception area. I could hear tinkling music, a faint pop of clapping. Instead of the pongs of institutional cooking and cleaning fluid that I'd been expecting, the place smelt of flowers, but when I touched the roses in the vase beside my seat, the petals were fake. The magazines on the table beside me were fanned out with military precision. I looked around. Wherever the CCTV cameras were, they were well hidden.

'Stagey, isn't it?' was Phyllida Hartigan's greeting. 'No cliché left untroubled. Perhaps we're to be murdered one by one and a nice chap in a trilby will be sent for to sort it out.'

'It seems, um, very pleasant,' I said, though I secretly agreed.

'Do you have one of those black police notebooks on you? The woman skulking by those fake plants is Maria something.

Write it down. If that tedious Grain man can come up with an alibi, go looking for her – she's a likely culprit.'

'Nobody is going to be murdered, Mrs Hartigan.'

She lowered herself carefully onto the sofa – it was very padded: I had bounced up when I sat down – and gestured for me to sit to her right. She looked tired, paler than she had at the café. She hadn't immediately asked why I had come to see her, which unsettled me. Guilty or innocent, it was the first question most people had when a police officer – even an off-duty injured one – showed up unexpectedly at their door. In my experience, it went one of two ways: an expectation of disaster ('*Oh, Jesus, God, is it . . .?*') or a denial lit as easily as a cigarette ('*It wasn't me, whatever the fuck you're here for*'). To be met by passivity was disconcerting.

'I have something for you,' I said, feeling foolish.

'How lovely.' She turned her face slightly towards mine. Her expression hadn't changed. Sitting on her unscarred side, I could see how remarkably beautiful she must have been. And, though I badly wanted to know what had happened, I was sure asking her outright would land me back on the pavement in seconds. I looked intently at her profile, willing my memory to fire up: almost-violet eyes, thick lashes, small ears and nose. Brows perfectly arched, but I knew to disregard anything that could be achieved by make-up or tweezers. I closed my eyes. The drag of recognition tugged an image to the surface, a picture in black-and-white. Lips fuller at the top and differently made-up. But, unlike my usual way of remembering, which was the fleeting pressure of an invisible hand pushing an unseen door, it felt forced. 'Margaret Warner!' The name was out of my mouth before I realised I'd spoken.

'What?' she said sharply, turning to me. The right side of her face looked annoyed.

There was a famous photo of Margaret Warner, taken on one of her many honeymoons, in which, wrapped in a vast mink coat, she stared straight at the lens, her eyebrows raised as if challenging the viewer to think whatever the hell they liked. Shit, that was probably what I had recalled: a bloody coat. What I had hoped was a tiny charge of memory sputtered and died. How the hell could this woman be Margaret Warner? She'd been dead for the best part of twenty years. Christ, I thought, what was happening to me? Was my brain now conjuring up *false* idents? None would be preferable to the wrong ones. What would happen when I was back at work? Far from being good at my job, I'd be a liability.

'Nothing!' I said, embarrassed and desperate to leave. I pointed at the table. 'That magazine, I thought the woman on the cover was her. My mistake.'

She snapped the clasp of her handbag open, peered inside, then shut it again. It was the closest to discomfort I'd yet seen from her. I imagined the scene from her point of view: a woman claiming to be a police officer follows her to a café, impounds her swag, then appears at her home, talking nonsense. I was lucky she wasn't shouting for help.

'Here!' I said. I handed her a Pavement Books bag. 'I paid for it,' I said hastily, glad I had thought to keep the receipt. 'I returned everything else, but I paid for this.' It had been easy to return the other things. Flashed my ID, murmured something about apprehending a known petty criminal and a confidential ongoing investigation (the more official – even pompous – the language, the fewer questions people tend to ask). The assistant in Claire Voyante's was relieved: the boss would have given her no end of grief, she said. The staff in Camille's and the Primrose Pharmacy hadn't seemed that interested, and in the bookshop I'd done nothing more than browse in the back for a while then slip the book out from my bag, bring it up to the counter and pay. As I suspected, no one had even noticed a battered old book of poetry was missing. A smell of mildew squared up to the artificial scent coming from the vase beside me as she leafed slowly through the pages.

'Listen to this,' she said, holding the book close. '"Our battle is waged as one man for God, our deaths those of men alone in Hell".'

2

The new English Heritage plaque hadn't attracted much interest within the building. On the day it had gone up, Alec didn't notice the difference to the façade. 'Dunno,' he said, when I asked if he had noticed anything new downstairs, looking at me curiously as though it was a game of *Mr & Mrs* he'd forgotten to swot up for. When I pushed him on it, the best he could come up with was a rather unconvincing 'Did someone clean the railings?'

We were only on helloing terms with the other occupants of the house, but on the couple of occasions since that I'd seen any of them, I'd been sure to ask for an opinion. It didn't take long to discover that William, the investment banker who lived in what would once have been stucco-ceilinged Gardiner bedrooms, had applied for the plaque.

'Really?' I said, curious. 'Why did you nominate him? Are you related?'

'Lord, no, nothing like that,' William said. 'I thought he'd be the most likely to get approved. They took their time putting it up, I must say. I was expecting it well before Christmas.'

'What do you mean "most likely"?'

'Of previous owners and tenants – well, the ones I could get any decent intel on anyway.' He leaned closer to me and put a hand on my arm. He smelt of musk and peat. Part cologne, part whisky, I decided. We were on the front step – me going in, him out – so I slipped past him and into the hallway. 'Jack the Ripper could have lived here for all I care,' he added. 'But owning a plaqued property, well, it's bound to have an impact come resale, isn't it?'

How disappointing for poor old Henry Gardiner! His value only monetary, and an English Heritage imprimatur simply because William had decided he was the best of a dull lot!

'Jack the Ripper might have got you a better return on your investment,' I said, and headed upstairs, grumpy.

'At least we have a peer,' was Mrs Gore-Kirwin's opinion, when I bumped into her on my way back from Dunease Court. 'Honestly, have you seen some of the plaques in Highgate? Complete nobodies.' This last word was so pristinely served up, perfectly garnished with a cut-glass stare, that I wasn't sure if it was aimed at the English Heritage selection process or me.

Since the installer's visit I had googled Henry Gardiner a few more times, following odd links here and there, burrowing into military archives and old newspapers, bumbling around, happy to waste my time falling down various rabbit holes and over stopped-up burrows. As with my first search, the results were mainly about his scientific work, which I struggled to understand. There had been a brief falling out with a fellow scientist because Gardiner had queried the inclusion of noble gases in the ordering of the Periodic Table, an irony I enjoyed. During one online rummage, I came across a December 1913 account of an inquest. At first I couldn't understand why it had featured in the search results because the headline referred to a man called Gareth Slatten. He was a footman who stole a 'substantial sum of money and family heirlooms of considerable value' from his employer – who turned out to be none other than Henry Gardiner. With the exception of a rare crystal and gold-leaf bird, the heirlooms had been found, with his fingerprints 'quite all over the items', the article noted. But presumably, as a servant, his fingerprints would naturally have been 'quite all over' the house and its contents. As far as I could recall from training, fingerprinting had first been used in the early 1900s, so perhaps the detail merited a mention because it was still considered a relatively new technique. The missing money had never been recovered. Rather than face the ignominy of a trial and subsequent prison sentence – the piece was smugly confident he would have been convicted – he committed suicide while on remand in Brixton Prison. The verdict of the inquest was that he took his own life while the balance of his mind was disturbed, and the coroner extended his sympathies to the Marquess of Denismore and his family for the suffering the proceedings must have caused them. Like his employer, Gareth Slatten had had a wife and three children, yet the article didn't mention their names. The rich were apologised to, the poor ignored. How little had changed.

The light-fingered footman's sad end made me curious as to who else had lived in the house at the same time as him, so my next port of call that evening was the 1911 census. From castle to slum and all points in between, each entry was a surgeon's knife, a blade that sliced the skin of a household to reveal the skeleton beneath. Census entries appeared mainly to be structured from most important (men) to least (women and children), via those whose labour was of most use to men (servants). With beautiful handwriting, Henry Gardiner listed his occupation as peer, his age as thirty-nine. He lived with his wife, Virginia Penelope (thirty-six); children Hettie (fifteen), Beatrice (thirteen) and Henry Alfred (four). And, to support two adults and three children, to grease the machine of their lives smooth and soft, there were five live-in servants. They bookended the building, their lives and labour a bolster on either side of the family: David (fifty-three) and Noreen Keily (forty-one), a married butler and cook; footman Gareth Slatten, who at thirty-six was the same age as Gardiner's wife; and two domestics, parlourmaid Gwen Parks (nineteen) and her scullerymaid sister, Doreen (seventeen).

An asterisk beside Noreen Keily's name directed me to a small note in the same handwriting that made me laugh: *Age given as 41, and she will not move on the subject, but I find it unlikely, given her appearance.* Who would we have been, I wondered, had we been part of his household on census night? Family or just one of the bodies – the nobodies – there to serve them? I pictured my life a hundred years earlier. I didn't have some bizarre new genetic deviance: presumably there had always been people with super-recognition. All that had changed was how the world viewed it. But spin back a century and who would have believed I was anything other than a charlatan?

By the time the next census was taken in 1921, Gardiner was long dead: 2 November 1916 was listed as his date of death but his grave was unknown, so alongside seventy-two thousand-odd others, his name had been recorded on the Thiepval Memorial, near Amiens. I wasn't sure where Amiens was until I looked it up. I had been to France only once, to see Haynes play at the Paris Jazz Festival – he was very popular in Europe, particularly France and Belgium. He had another European tour coming up, and at Christmas had asked us if we wanted tickets for a gig, but we'd said no, we were too broke.

I bounced around online for a while, reading about the Battle of the Somme and calling out bits of information to an increasingly uninterested Alec. The school history syllabus had included it, of course, and there had been plenty of coverage of the centenary of the First World War over the previous few years, but I was surprised at how much I had forgotten (or never known to begin with). As a military action, it was startlingly ill-prepared; more than one battalion was told by their commander that the attack would be a stroll in the park, that they'd need walking sticks not rifles because the Germans were already dead. Phyllida Hartigan and her book of poetry flashed into my head.

The total of dead and injured was more than a million. Human flesh-and-bone parcels posted from all over the world to war, their deaths reduced to an exercise in numbers. Sixty thousand Allied troops died on the first day alone. I pictured an entire town, every single inhabitant gathering together and simply walking silently into the sea.

'Two of Joey's great-grandfathers fought at the Somme,' Alec said. 'We buried the widow of a veteran last year – I overheard him telling the family about it. Irish in France fighting the Germans for the British, he described it.'

'Did they survive?'

'Only the one on his mum's side. Joey said he was treated like a traitor back home. He ended up moving town, denying he'd ever been in the army.'

Gardiner cropped up again, with a photo this time, in an

obscure magazine piece about peers who had died in the war, written for the hundredth anniversary of the Somme. 'Standard-issue Edwardian nob with a moustache,' Alec commented. The article dripped with *noblesse oblige*, adamant that to offer up one's son to the slaughter remained a worthy sacrifice. Alec sighed. 'If you're so curious about random dead soldiers, why not read about one who went so his family would get separation money, like Joey's great-granddad? Some poor sod who hadn't any power over his life and was abused by propaganda or strong-armed by his employer. Some fight for freedom that was – you can be sure thousands of the men who died never knew what freedom was when they were alive.'

There wasn't anything else of interest about Henry Gardiner. I didn't spot anything about Gareth Slatten, and without his wife or children's names I didn't know how to go about finding them. I closed the archive and census tabs and began to flick through the *Guardian*, but the more news I read, the less I cared. I didn't like feeling that way, because it was hard not to let the sense of dull dislike seep into my life. And if I stopped understanding, stopped caring, I would no longer be a good police officer. I'd watched colleagues get disillusioned – we all did at times, it was inevitable – so much so that I was suspicious of those who never got ground down by the job. The trick was in knowing how to gear yourself back up. Disillusioned by the world, I could live with. Disengaged from it, I couldn't.

What was Henry Gardiner thinking about, the day he left this house to go to war? Perhaps he believed war was like science, necessary for the progress of humankind. Life must have been miserable for his family, waiting at home and reliant on newspaper reports. Desire for and fear of information in a permanent relay race, and all the time waiting for a telegram.

Alec looked up from his tablet. 'Why does this man suddenly matter so much? It's not like you, this . . . nostalgia.'

I shrugged. 'I'm interested in the people who used to live in our building, that's all. Now I know who they are, I'm curious to find out more about them.'

I wondered if he thought my interest was rooted in something more prosaic than history: that because the intense pitch at which I was used to operating had dropped to nothing, I was bored and filling the gap with a long-dead man and his household simply because they had, in a manner of speaking, fallen into my lap. I wished, later, that I had whispered the truth: that since the accident I was uncomfortable in the present and felt safer ducking around in the shadows of the past. That I felt haunted. Hunted. But I didn't have the energy for another conversation about head injuries, concussion. About giving myself time.

FEBRUARY 1919

As with other events she has been to, the crowd is predominantly female, yet within seconds of arriving at the London Spiritualist Association, Violet can tell that this evening, which has been organised by private invitation rather than ticket purchase, will be of a different order entirely. Unlike her visit to the Reading Room earlier in the week, the place is thronged. She has attended many meetings recently – ones not led or attended by Selbarre – to try to understand what showman tricks are being played, and how. She has seen the same desperate faces over and over, has heard personal revelations from the stage that would never be uttered in other circumstances, yet even as the audience were surprised, dumbfounded by the detail, no one ever appeared to be *shocked* by the nature of what they heard. Something about the atmosphere of spiritualist and mediumship events appears to shrink the space lying between reality and secrecy. Confidences she can't imagine even the closest friends sharing have been aired in front of hundreds of strangers, yet she has seen no embarrassment displayed. Mrs Johnson's unpaid account came to mind when she watched a woman being told that her late husband had had another family this last twenty years – three children, a grandchild on the way too – but in death the man was racked by guilt at his infidelity. Yet instead of being angry or shamed, the woman had marvelled at the medium's skill in ferreting out from her husband's newly loquacious spirit what he had never revealed in life, despite her often-expressed suspicions.

She watches the well-to-do crowd assembling around her and wonders what this evening's performance will be like. At every spiritualist event, she has walked around, made it her business to talk to people, to mention Selbarre's name. All for nothing. Most of those she's spoken to have heard of him, frustratingly few have seen him – though those who have are united in their adoration. It irks her that he has appeared at so few public events. None, in fact, since Wigmore Hall a month earlier. He seems to spend his time at private gatherings, with wealthy clients. To her, this alone marks him out as different: he quickly achieved notoriety and fame, yet seems to have shunned it almost immediately. Does this suggest he is worried about being found out at a big public event where the audience is always more skittish, or merely that he has identified a lucrative territory and is determined to exploit it?

Unlike the variety hall giddiness of the event at Wigmore Hall, the atmosphere here is that of a cathedral: an expectation of uniting with hundreds of years of devout worship, a grateful anticipation of adding to the thousands of prayers that pepper the rafters. The audience is a far more exclusive group, most of whom appear to know or at least recognise each other. A frisson runs through the room at the arrival of Sir Arthur Conan Doyle and his wife. She recognises him immediately, of course, but has never seen Lady Conan Doyle clearly before. There is no sign of the librarian, Levant, for which she is grateful.

From single armbands to obviously new georgette crêpe outfits, the Gathering Room is united by the colour black. Clearly, some of society's most enthused spiritualists are equally devoted to maintaining a stylish appearance. Just recently, the *Sketch* magazine had referred to the thorny topic of finding suitably becoming mourning wear as the 'most pressing problem of the day'. Violet is relieved she wore her best outfit after all. Her coat is bottle-green boiled wool, which she doesn't particularly like but is not nearly old enough to consider replacing. She had wondered if her best would be too much, but if anything she might stand out as not well-dressed enough. She recalled a conversation she'd had with Chrissie about mourning when Chrissie's father died. Chrissie's bossy aunt Aggie told her she was to wear full mourning ('With pleasure, in his case!' Chrissie snorted) for a full year: ten months of all black, then the last two of half-mourning: black with white, grey or mauve. Chrissie's mam, who didn't give a sop for mourning her late husband, but was vexed by Aggie throwing her weight around in the etiquette of death, claimed half-mourning was three months, not two. To solve the dispute, Chrissie asked Violet to check what *A Bachelor Girl's Life* said on the subject. Mrs Miller's index ran *Mop O'Cedar, Mourning, Moving*, which seemed about right for most women's lives, Violet decided. You cleaned, you lamented, you died. In the end Chrissie hadn't bothered with making more than an armband, and forgot to wear it half the time.

As Sir Arthur Conan Doyle's business manager, it had been a simple matter for Mr Forrester to give her a letter for the secretary requesting admission for the niece of a late friend, a devout adherent of spiritualism, visiting from the country. Forrester has become increasingly irritated by her slow progress: with Selbarre travelling between private houses all around England, her investigation had come to a standstill. But tonight! What there is to be found out will be found out. She is determined. It was only when she arrived at the door she realised she had foolishly forgotten to ask what name, if any, Forrester had given this supposed niece or the good friend. So as not to take any chances, she had simply handed over the envelope to the secretary in the front hall taking guests' invitations as they arrived. Thankfully, he had demonstrated no interest in who she was, or from where. He glanced at the letter, nodded and pointed her towards the Gathering Room. It makes her doubly glad not to bump into Levant, who, assuming he recognised her at all, would remember that she had introduced herself to Conan Doyle as Chrissie Bullman.

Most of the people are in groups, which makes it easy enough to find a single unoccupied chair just two rows back from the stage beside a couple of women dressed similarly to herself. To a casual onlooker they might pass for three friends out together. Just as the Reading Room above it, the Gathering Room is long and narrow, running the length of the building. One end has a makeshift stage, with a plain wooden chair its only furniture. A curtain hangs from a rail at either side of the chair. There are two fireplaces but only the far one has been lit, so the coving above the stage is thick with shadows. The wallpaper is a strange choice for such a public room:

an old-fashioned horizontal pattern of closely interlocking peacock feathers. Iridescent blue and orange circles stare out at her. She looks carefully around the room. There must be hundreds of them! Harsh, unseeing eyes, surrounded by fronds the colour of an autumn pond. Staring from just under the surface of the water and imprisoned by weeds. She feels overheated all of a sudden, and discreetly tugs at the collar of her dress.

Selbarre appears from the back, not from behind the stage. He walks up the central aisle and onto the stage, then slowly turns to face the assembly. He bows, his face neutral. If he is disconcerted by the full room and the society audience, he doesn't display it. He turns and walks behind a screen on the platform, and when he reappears, the same girl as before is standing by his side. The same as last time, it is as though she appears from nowhere, that she has materialised from the very walls of the room. She looks thinner, if anything, the whites of her eyes shining clear against the dullness around her. She blinks several times and the effect is almost of disappearance. She's wearing the same brown dress, her feet again bare. She moves ahead of him to the chair at the centre front of the stage. Surely she must feel his breath on her head – he's that close behind her. If she were to pause even for a second he would topple her, a giant felling a dwarf.

There are no requests for volunteers this time, no searching of the girl's clothes. No one touches her feet. All that would be considered too common a business for this stage. In a dressing room upstairs, several female representatives of the London Spiritualist Association would already have inspected the girl's naked body, then checked her stage clothes and watched her as she put them on. Violet feels shamed on the girl's behalf: to have strangers' hands and eyes run over her like an animal! That slight body, on display, so entirely vulnerable and naked, while gawping women stare at her most intimate flesh.

'Is she that colour all over, do you think?' the woman beside Violet whispers to her friend.

There is no *Roses of Picardy* this time. Selbarre doesn't speak of truth and understanding. He doesn't tell the audience that they have been brought here not of their own volition but by the desires of those who have passed over and are desperate to contact them. Instead, to Violet's mind, everything he says sounds as though he's saying it the other way around. His manner is slightly different too, less of a performance. He is more a professor lecturing to a classroom full of knowledgeable pupils, than a . . . What? She realises the word she wants is 'magician'.

'All of us here in this room, we are trustees of a great body of knowledge,' he says. 'And with that comes a very great responsibility for its safekeeping. We must guard it even as we share it freely. We must house it well, and keep it warm and nourished. We are missionaries of the truth. And that is no facile calling, but the truest one – for body and spirit alike.'

He speaks of the charge of credulity, how to dismiss the fallacies of the unreceptive. How the London Spiritualist Association – at this point he holds his arms up and wide before slowly closing them, as if wrapping his audience in a tight embrace – is enlightened, and has a duty to humanity in these testing times. 'As the world struggles to find a new peace,' he concludes, 'it is *this* world – the world of mediumship, of you, dear ladies and gentlemen, of *us* – that has the power to remove both new and old barriers to understanding. We are between those barriers. We hold the key to both worlds.'

The approval of the crowd swells around her. Hats, heads, fans, all nod. *Yes,* they seem to be saying, *we understand. We have a power that those outside these walls do not.*

'We must,' he implores, 'pity those living a life cast black by mortal shadows!'

She glances across the aisle to where Sir Arthur Conan Doyle and his wife are seated. He is leaning forward, nodding approvingly. He holds his hands in front of him and raised slightly from his lap, as one might tilt a child's head to kiss its forehead. His wife holds an expensive fringed silk evening bag ornamented with tiny pieces of jet. She has removed her gloves and is running her fingertips over and back across the silk. He notices Violet and nods. His wife's head turns too, better to see the object of his greeting.

The girl sits impassive as before as Selbarre puts her into a trance. In the long, slow silence, Violet is aware of her own pulse. Of the heat of the room, the feather pattern on the wallpaper. She feels jammed into place, trapped on all sides by strangers. It is a sensation she hasn't experienced at any other séance or gathering she's been to. She stares at Lady Conan Doyle's fingers as they shift rhythmically to and fro, as though casting a spell.

'It's you!' The woman next to her is nudging Violet's ribs. 'She's pointing at you!'

'What?' She's startled. The gentle trance of the fringe bending and swaying is broken. But her neighbour is right: the girl is pointing directly at her! A single brown finger, slightly raised and revealing a pinkish pad underneath. Dark eyes look straight and unblinking into Violet's own, even as the stare itself appears unfocused and blurred.

'Please, speak further to us. Will you tell us your mortal name?' Selbarre says, his tone smooth as butter.

'Slatten,' the girl replies, in a voice that is hard, rough, strangely male, though there's no doubt that it's coming from her mouth. She continues to stare into Violet's face. 'Gareth Slatten.'

Violet starts in her seat.

'You remember me, don't you?' the girl says. 'You remember me and I will never forget you. I will never leave you alone, I promise. How can I, while you're breathing and I'm not?' She begins to sing a variety hall tune from a few years before that Violet recognises. '*Sweet violets, sweeter than the roses . . . covered all over from head to toe . . . covered all over with sweet violets.*' The girl's words trail off though she continues to hum, her eyes never dropping from Violet's. It feels as if she's humming for ever, though it can't be more than ten seconds. The woman beside her sways in time to the tune and Violet has a violent urge to slap her, hard.

Suddenly the chair the girl is sitting on begins to tap against the ground, jerking her up and down. Her head slumps to her chest, her speech fast and suddenly unintelligible as the seat bucks beneath her. Violet's dress is tight as a noose around her neck, her back suddenly hot and damp. She is aware that she's panting, rather than taking air in.

The chair abruptly stops. The girl's pointing hand drops to her lap. She closes her eyes. Violet gulps, swallows, gulps again. Sir Arthur Conan Doyle and his wife are staring from across the aisle. He smiles enthusiastically – surely she's imagining it, but is there something congratulatory, almost conspiratorial, in his expression? – and nods, his eyebrows raised. There is a long pause before the girl speaks again. A different voice this time, a dead captain searching the room urgently for his mother. He needs her, this captain says: he has something of great significance, great value, to explain. Won't she just listen? Violet breathes properly at last, tearfully grateful that the attention has been diverted from her. Her throat aches from the effort of not crying. She looks cautiously around, unsure what to do next, but the focus of the room has shifted entirely. A woman – the captain's mother, she presumes – can be heard weeping loudly from the back of the room. Lady Conan Doyle looks back, frowning at the noise.

Violet's stomach churns. She feels imprisoned. Over the Conan Doyles' shoulders, hundreds of blue and orange eyes blink down in horror from the walls. The peacock feathers are lost souls, each one of them, and now they have captured hers. She is being slowly tugged away to a gasping, ugly death, her lungs shredded from lack of air.

Gareth Slatten: her secret history, thrown for scraps to a room of strangers. The roar in Violet's ears is that of a blacked-out train hurtling through a closed station.

II

Half an hour later, she has been trying to lift her cup to her lips for some moments but can't keep it steady. Her hands are shaking. She's sure she's going to drop the tea and draw even more attention to herself. As soon as the girl came out of the trance – she didn't fall to the floor this time – Selbarre announced what a remarkable success the evening had been. So much so, in fact, that he promised to hold a spirit-writing séance for the devout membership of the London Spiritualist Association as soon as his other commitments allowed it.

Violet had wanted to run out of the room and never come back. But she held her ground, aware that she'd have got as far as the pavement before regretting her cowardice. It is only now, her breath somewhat returned, that she groans to herself. What will Mr Forrester say? He commissioned her in the surety she would prove his suspicions correct. How can she? He won't pay her a single farthing when he hears what just happened. But what *has* just happened? She stands alone by the side of the tea table, eavesdropping, hoping to get close to Selbarre without drawing too much attention to herself as a woman alone with no acquaintances in the room. That the gathering went well appears to be the verdict of the crowd as well as that of its main attraction. Heads lift and drop *peck, peck, peck* into their cups. It reminds her of the way birds appear when Chrissie scatters crumbs on the office windowsill. Unlike a variety hall, it would appear that in spiritualist circles smaller gatherings had a greater expectation of results, and this crowd was pleased with what they had been given.

'You clearly have a most particular distinction within the world of the spirit.' He appears from behind her as if through the wall, reminding her once more of the librarian upstairs.

'I beg your pardon?' There is a loud clink as her cup bangs against the saucer. Flushing, she slips it back to the tea table, surreptitiously running a finger over the rim to check whether or not she has cracked it.

He takes her hand. 'Jean Claude Selbarre.'

She tries to keep the panic from her voice. 'Miss Chrissie Bullman. A pleasure to meet you.'

His eyes widen. 'At your service, Miss . . .' he pauses, bows his head '. . . *Bullman*, you say?' She nods. A woman passes close by them, her shoulder nudging against Violet's. She stares rudely, almost angrily, then swishes on, her gown shining sleek as crow's feathers. His eyes follow her for a moment, then turn back to Violet. 'There will always be those disappointed when the doors do not open for them in accordance with their expectations. That is human nature, after all.'

He is standing close to her, too close, and she is aware of warmth coming from him. He doesn't look warm – his face is quite pale, if anything, his lips fleshy, pink. He has wide cheekbones, a broad nose and a narrow forehead, hair slicked back. He's not heavy-set yet the overall effect is large, almost overbearing. There is too much of him, too near. His frock coat isn't, as it looked on stage, black, but an inky blue with grey stitching on the lapels.

'You looked quite . . .' again he pauses, as though weighing up every syllable, '. . . taken by surprise.' He raises his hands and clasps them together. It's an odd pose and it takes her a second to realise that he reminds her of a clergyman in a pulpit. 'So much so that I would not have taken you for a believer. But how can that be the case, Miss Bullman,' his hands separate for a moment as he gestures around the room, 'when here you are, in a room for believers? It made me wonder what else you could possibly be, if *not* one of us.'

'Ah, there you are, Selbarre!' booms a familiar voice behind her. Loud and resonant, the name reverberates. She feels it as an echo inside her head, a shout into an empty cave. Selbarre and Sir Arthur Conan Doyle greet each other enthusiastically before he turns to her. 'We meet again, Miss . . .?'

'Bullman, sir. A pleasure to see you.'

Selbarre lays one hand on Conan Doyle's arm as though he wants to move him out of her company, but it's too late: Conan Doyle is talking to her. 'Mr Selbarre here is such a master of the higher spiritualist arts, don't you think, Miss Bullman? It was a privilege to be present here this evening. Lady Conan Doyle and I are both most impressed by his work. I have been trying to persuade him to extend his visit to England by another month so that I can incorporate a study of his methods in a book.' Conan Doyle smiles at Selbarre and touches his shoulder. Selbarre beams in return, yet when his gaze flickers over Violet's face it turns cold and hard.

Conan Doyle adds, 'And please forgive me saying so, Miss Bullman, but you looked somewhat distressed during the channelling. A loved one lost, I presume. And a favourite song for you both? I know how painful the powers of mediumship can be.' He blinks hard, several times, and tugs his moustache as though it is a careless gatekeeper of his words. 'But please trust me when I tell you that you will shortly go on to discover relief – sustenance, even – in the occurrence, though that sensation is not always immediate.'

She swallows and says, 'Forgive me, but what did you mean just now by *higher* spiritualist arts?'

He gestures at Selbarre. 'This here, what you witnessed – what, indeed, you were part of! – is an example of the higher spiritualist arts. A considered insight into the phenomena of the world outside our own. The business of flying chairs and tables and suchlike, they are of a cheaper spiritual order entirely, a lower plane that holds no interest for me, or indeed – if you will permit my speaking for you, Selbarre – for either of us.'

She remembers their conversation in the Reading Room, and Levant's furious hisses. She is about to risk his ire, she knows, but what choice has she? 'And, sir, do these higher arts require much defence from talk of fakery and tricks?'

He doesn't appear offended this time. 'As I believe I told you previously, the charge of credulity is one I can dismiss with ease. A gullible man does not spend many years reading and experimenting before coming to his conclusions, as I have done. And consider this: when intelligent men of science and superior knowledge than I come to endorse it, then *I* would be the uneducated fool to disregard their opinion, would I not? Life, as I have said several times to Selbarre here, is far more baffling and curious than anything fiction can invent.'

She smiles, nodding her agreement, though it was not Conan Doyle's reaction to her question she was interested in: it was Selbarre's. But his face is impassive, blank as a mask. He stands facing her, his hands clasped tight, his eyes fixed on her. She wants to wriggle away from his gaze. She feels captured by it, speared. It's as if she were an insect pinned to a display.

The nine o'clock bell chimes; the crowd begin to shift away from the tea table and towards the door.

'And now, Miss Bullman, please excuse me, I see Lady Conan Doyle is ready to leave, so we must bid you farewell. Selbarre, I have received a fascinating letter from the Society for the Study of Supernormal Pictures, which I'd like to discuss with you.' He bows his head to Violet and the two men turn away. With one hand raised in a wave to his wife, Sir Arthur Conan Doyle looks back at Violet and adds, 'Dear Selbarre leaves us again tomorrow for a series of private engagements, but perhaps you will attend the spirit-writing séance, which he has kindly promised for his return. Spirit-writing is remarkable, and may indeed result in greater success for you in hearing from your departed. Allow me to give you my card. If you have success with it at any stage I should be glad to hear of it, for I am compiling accounts.'

She takes the card and slips it into her bag, noticing Lady Conan Doyle's glance isn't addressed to her approaching husband but, rather, just beyond him, to Violet herself.

'Miss Bullman?' Selbarre is back at her side, his voice low. He is far too close, looming over her, leaning into her face, as though his pink lips would swallow her. 'Despite Sir Arthur's generous invitation, I feel obliged to inform you that the world of the spirit is no simple matter. I think you should reconsider your interest. For the ignorant, it can prove quite dangerous.' He bows, his pale face impassive once more.

She wants nothing more than to run from the building, but instead forces herself to cross the room to the stage. Her hands are shaking still; perspiration continues to roll down her back. Holding a single glove high in one hand, she forces herself to make a show of studying the floor under the front row of seats as though hunting for its lost mate. No one pays any attention as she moves about in front of the stage. There is nothing unnatural to be seen. No strings, no unusual divergences in the floorboards or suspicious bumps in the walls that might suggest hidden spaces. It is a flat platform in an ordinary room. The single chair on it is plain wood, same as all the others in the room, as if plucked at random from one of the rows. Nothing more.

She is so clearly alone, and the crowd has dispersed to such an extent that she will look suspicious if she stays any longer. There is nothing for it but to leave. She pretends to find the glove, suddenly desperate to put the London Spiritualist Association behind her. She pauses in the front hall by the secretary's desk. It's just possible Forrester put her real name in the letter, isn't it? Gareth Slatten was in service all his working life, so perhaps at some stage he was employed by someone in the room who could now be in league with Selbarre. Maybe, she admits, begrudging her wobbling logic and paucity of facts, just maybe. Mr Forrester's note is lying open and abandoned on the table. There is no one else around, though voices are approaching from the far end of the corridor. It is the work of a moment to swipe the letter and its envelope.

'Gareth Slatten.' The name falls, stuttering, past her lips when she is alone outside. It feels sharp as bile against her tongue.

She waits until she is several streets away to stop and read the letter. A misty drizzle has started up, so she holds the page up to the gas light above her. It's only three lines long. Forrester doesn't name either her or his supposed friend. Rain spatters onto the paper and ink the colour of Selbarre's coat bleeds down the page and onto her hand.

III

She walks home, not caring that her good clothes are getting soaked. Her mind is full of Gareth Slatten and his horrible end. She has a sudden image of a woman begging, a clutch of kiddies around her skirts, the lot of them pauper-pale and mottled with cold. The spirit, the presence . . . How is she to explain the voice that channelled itself through the girl? What is she to call it? There is no doubt the message was for her and her alone. But *how*? It's been years . . . and Hannah would never willingly have revealed either her own or Violet's part in her husband's death. Violet's name was not mentioned at Slatten's inquest. The despicable Henry Gardiner was dead too – Violet remembers his death notice in the newspaper – not that he would ever have breathed a word of his part in Slatten's death, that was for sure.

In the legions of lost lives between that day and this . . . that *he* should be the one to come back? And to her, in a place where nobody knew who she was, by either name or face? It seems impossible to believe and yet she had witnessed it herself, so it is true. But that makes no sense: how can something be both? If it is true, and the girl did channel Gareth Slatten, then Violet has proved Forrester wrong and has lost the twenty guineas. If it is untrue, and Violet is the victim of some sort of fakery, she has no means to prove Forrester *right*, in which case the money is equally lost to her.

Sodden and shivering, Violet puts the key in the latch of her room. Inside, it is grey and cold. She hangs up her sodden hat, coat and dress. She makes tea on the gas ring, but there's nothing to eat. (*Tut-tut*, murmurs Mrs Miller, from between her warm paper covers.) She feels suddenly feverish, though her feet are like ice. She hasn't the energy to do anything other than climb under the blankets in her underthings and lie there, trying desperately to make sense of it all.

Has she discounted every possible theory, logical or not, as Sherlock Holmes would have done? *All right, then,* she reasons with herself. Consider Sir Arthur Conan Doyle's part in all this for a minute. Didn't he create one of the cleverest men in the English language? Sherlock Holmes would believe in spiritualism if every single other explanation was discounted or discountable, wouldn't he? Well, then, why wouldn't his creator? That stands to reason. Could a man that intelligent really be taken in by fools and fakers? Violet has never subscribed to the belief that a man knows more than she does simply by virtue of his sex. Sir Arthur Conan Doyle has no reason to lie and every reason to be cautious when he stakes his money and his reputation – not to mention his time and intelligence – against anything. Putting Gareth Slatten to one side for a moment, isn't it possible that there is falsity *and* truth to the whole business? That it is a spectrum, with a baseless, common version – a land of sharps and liars – at one end and a new, honest truth at the other? After all, it would be only the same difference as that between a respected surgeon in a hospital and a travelling medicine man dispensing liniment from the back of a cart.

If only she'd been able to talk to Conan Doyle without Selbarre! She wishes she had been more ready, less guarded, with her questions when she met him in the Reading Room. She should have enquired about Selbarre then and there. It's not as though she thinks Gareth Slatten is a ghost come to haunt her, a vengeful apparition unleashed from beyond the grave – she knows it doesn't work like that. Whatever was going on, she knows that nothing else can happen without Selbarre and the girl channelling, pushing a door open. Without that brown, pointing finger.

But what to do about Forrester? As it stands, he has been proved wrong and his employer right. And she herself is the evidence! She shivers under the blanket, horrified that she is, once again, proof of her own failure.

The next morning, just before daybreak, she climbs out of bed and tugs the armchair across the room. Her only window is fitted into a recess just wide enough to accommodate the chair. It's so tight she has to climb over the arm and haul her bedspread up after her. She wraps herself up entirely, tight as she can, toes grasping the tufted nap of the seat. It's like being parcelled up in a box. During the night she heard herself wondering aloud how Mrs Miller would have indexed such failure, her *folly, foolishness, frailty*. She watches and waits, needing the sun's spin, needing the light to bring goodness with it. Night-time London disappears with the dawn. It is comforting to follow each second of the change, as the leering topsy-turvy world of night transforms yet again into neat, sober day. She is relieved that what happened is now a day behind her, that – like Gareth Slatten – it has been shunted backwards, to the past where he belongs.

She sends a neighbour's lad to the office with a note for Chrissie, pleading illness. Chrissie sends him back immediately. *You bad, Vi? Should I visit?* Violet knows this is Chrissie's way of asking if there is a chance she might be contagious. It makes her feel more isolated, no matter that Chrissie's only being sensible. *Bad tooth,* she writes back. *An abscess. I can't talk properly. It'll need draining.* She runs her tongue around her mouth, choosing a tooth, deciding what in her mouth is rotten. No investigator worth her salt would invent a fiction, even such a minor and hard-to-disprove one as this, without having first considered it as real. She touches the top of a back tooth with her tongue, feels the rough edges, the pit in the centre. Yes, that's it. She imagines it sitting in a pool of pus, diseased.

Evening comes and she is still there, watching those same lights reappear as the moon and sun change guard. But, like a prayer mumbled with no real hope of its being heard, there is no comfort in it. In fact, today the constancy makes her feel worse. All those tiny bright circles that can't be seen in daytime are rendered visible at night, that here are definitive as a map but in daylight are useless . . . she can't see them in daylight but they are still there; she knows they still exist. Her head is hot and sore, and she leans into the crook of her arm.

She finds herself trying to work out the actual route of the Underground trains. She knows the lines aren't aligned with streets: the network makes the city appear angular and stubby, constructed in lengths that come together and break apart like pipes to a gutter. Purposeful. Neat. But that's not really the case. Imagine the trains bursting to the surface to show the city the true paths they follow, the shops and firms and houses – the lives! – they cut through as they hurtle people from one destination to another. She imagines hundreds, thousands of people, dirty and dishevelled and pushing through cracks in the pavements, furious as winter. She shivers. What else could that be but the buried come back to life?

Are the Slatten family represented by even a single light in the city? For Hannah, making herself lost would have been easily done. A tweak of a name, a late-night flit to a different part of the city – even putting the grubby flow of the Thames between the old life and the new would be enough. She stares in the direction of Cranford Crescent, but whether she can see the house where he worked or not is irrelevant: the building exists, she knows it. He existed. She doesn't continue to need proof for that to remain true. Every paraffin lamp, every electric switch, every bloody candle in the place must have been extinguished and relit thousands of times since 1913.

Before the war, a year felt like no time at all, but now! Four years of incessant chaos has left the city reeling, as if the entire population fell as one from the side of a merry-go-round. The world has been lost and found, made and remade. She looks out the window and tries to picture a different city, one in the hands of foreigners. Invaders, translating the city into a new tongue, making it no longer understandable, legible. It's impossible that such a thing could ever happen. Imagining a London run by children, or rats, would be as easy. Everything scrabbles around her head, all at once, and none of it makes sense.

She considers both conversations with Sir Arthur Conan Doyle, goes over each again and again. She returns to *The New Revelation*, flicking through the pages as though expecting a clue to drop from between them. Just as he had told her that morning in the Reading Room, he wrote that he was a Catholic first and then a materialist. If he can move from one set of beliefs to new and entirely different ones, then has he done the same thing now? Merely swung the pendulum of his creed to the far side? He didn't come across as a man who could be indifferent to anything. For good or for bad, he would take the time to form an opinion. To forsake the rituals of religion she can understand, when religion allows horror into people's lives, then insists God Himself is the only respite from the pain caused. Yet it still feels like a leap instead to glorify a force that is demonstrated through material things.

She's a detective. She prides herself on being logical, reasonable. So why can't she make sense of this? Why does she keep oscillating between the truth as Sir Arthur Conan Doyle would have her believe it and what she has always understood to be the truth – which is its opposite, isn't it? Belief is at the heart of the whole business. Sir Arthur Conan Doyle believes in something and Selbarre animates that belief. But for her to trust in that same truth – and to do so in the way her eyes and ears tell her she must – she has to forsake so much else. The very act of believing breathes truth into what happened in that room: Gareth Slatten spoke to her and nobody else. She heard his name, heard his words issue from the girl's mouth. She can't prove it was him any more than she can disprove it. And in that case what's left? Belief is a vessel equally full and empty.

An errand boy appears early the following morning. *Dear*

Vi – Mr Forrester sent a telegram you're to call on him at eleven o'clock today or else!!! (The !!! are from me, but he didn't half make it sound like that.) What should I do? Hope tooth better. Love, Chrissie.

Or else. Or else *what*? she thinks. Or else no money. Fine. She can come to terms with that. It's not as if she'll have any choice but to do so. She won't be moving out of this room. Not ever, it feels like. In her imagination, that long voile curtain the colour of ripening pears gives a final flutter. The pale wooden window slams shut, the entire mansion block quivers, then folds in on itself. Her future collapses to the ground in a cloud of dust.

IV

Spring has come to Cheyne Place. The pavement is as grey as it was on Boxing Day, but the gardens are green and budding, desperate to shake off the dead of winter. Little crocuses have winkled their way above ground and bow their purple and yellow heads to each other politely. The colour reminds her of the Spanish flu, the way it takes over a person's body, turning it a rich amethyst. A flare of beauty presaging death. She preferred the chalky stucco flatness of the Christmas snow.

The maid shows her into the study – 'You're to wait here' – and leaves the room without offering Violet so much as a cup of tea. Has he told her not to bother? Or could the maid simply tell, the way women always can, that Violet, too, is an employee of Mr Forrester, which makes her an equal and therefore not worth bothering with?

She waits by the window, and watches daily life being performed silently on the stage of the street below. Laden delivery boys disappear down basement steps only to reappear a minute later, empty-handed, mouths pursed in a permanent whistle. A nurse pushing a perambulator bends over to talk to the sailor-suited little boy beside her. The poor tot trips, scrapes his knee on the pavement. Violet watches his face crumple. The nurse pulls him up by the hand and tugs him until they move slowly away in the direction of the Physic Garden. A motor car pulls up and a chauffeur jumps out. An elderly couple emerge slowly from the back, neither of them looking at him as he holds their doors open in turn. They walk up the path of the house opposite without speaking. She is dressed in the old way, a bustle at the back and matronly bosom trussed up, her posture rigid as a ship's figurehead. Where have they come from? What day is that woman, that man embarking on? She watches all these people and more pass each other without acknowledging each other's existence. Maybe we, too, are nothing more than underground trains, she thinks. All of us on our separate tracks, clacking along through our lives, not seeing the passage of those around us, or caring how we might ever join with them. Her gaze follows the nurse and her charges as they turn out of sight around a corner. The nurse's shoulders are low and slumped; she leans on the handle of the perambulator as though the baby is a dead weight she is compelled to push for the rest of her life.

Violet has shown herself to be good for nothing and nobody. She envies Selbarre and the girl. To have such dominion over the hopes and dreams of others. To be able to bring life back to those who feel it stolen from them . . .

'Miss Hill.' His words are lost as the grandfather clock in the corner begins to strike the hour. He shuts the door behind him and takes a seat at his desk, waving at her to sit in the straight-backed chair facing it. The chair is narrow and low, forcing her to look up at him from an angle. She feels like a naughty schoolchild facing the headmaster – which presumably was his intention. As soon as the clock has finished chiming she begins, 'Mr Forrester, please forgive my silence, I—'

He speaks over her, as though her voice is of no more interest to him than the chimes of the clock. Indeed, possibly of less. 'I have been most anxiously waiting for news from you. Selbarre has once more gone out of town?'

'Yes. He had a number of private engagements and commissions to fulfil.'

'This is the most tedious time-wasting, Miss Hill, and a cause of exceptional concern. The most pressing issue is what proof you have accumulated. We must do the best with what you've got, so explain yourself and be quick about it.'

'I cannot.'

'You clearly have no perception of what is at stake here. Only yesterday Sir Arthur spoke to me in the highest possible terms of Selbarre's performance earlier this week and how he plans to commit himself to the promotion of the man's work. Once more, as to proof. Tell me what you have discovered.'

'I think you must misunderstand me, sir. I have no proof that Mr Selbarre is anything other than who and what he purports to be.'

'*Nothing?* That's ridiculous. He was to—' He stops himself short, angry. 'It has been well over a month since you undertook this commission, Miss Hill. And yet you have nothing?'

There is something else under his exasperation, something unexpected. Confused, even. She clenches her hands inside her gloves.

He continues, furious: 'He is back in London at the end of next week. Go to whatever ridiculous charade he holds then and do not leave that room until you have what I require.'

'I apologise, but I have not made myself clear, Mr Forrester. I have not discovered anything. Neither can I continue to investigate the matter. I am resigning your commission.' She is nervous yet hating herself for it. 'Now.'

He frowns. '*What?* But it's a simple matter. An idiot could do it!'

'I am not in a position to discuss the matter further, Mr Forrester.'

'I should have known a woman wouldn't be up to the job.' He lifts a sheaf of papers from his desk and slams them down again. 'And don't consider for a moment that you can present me with an account! As if there wasn't enough money wasted already. In fact, I should be serving a writ on you for wasting my time so wilfully. Sir Arthur's literary output is drying to a trickle as he lets himself be exploited. He is committing ridiculous sums of money to Selbarre, the Lord knows who else. Charlatans, all of them. I considered you an unlikely victim for this type of stupidity, but clearly I was misled.'

'Your principal concern is what you perceive to be a cruel exploitation of your employer's time and financial resources?'

'I have told you so.' He is impatient now.

'Yet at our first meeting your concern was for an old friend's health.'

'Our contract is at an end, Miss Hill. You have failed me completely, and I have no hesitation in saying so. You have yet to learn that the world turns on the beliefs of the gullible:

those who are determined to favour belief over disbelief, regardless of the expensive nonsense such belief leads them into.' He leans over to ring the bell but she is already standing. As if she would wait for the snooty servant to appear! She will find her own way out.

January 2018

January 2015

1

Alec worked at least one weekend a month so I was home by myself on Saturday afternoon. He had two funerals, and expected the first to be a big one: former politicians always drew the crowds, he said, and not necessarily grief-stricken ones.

Just before he left for work that morning I asked him if he had noticed that the weird noise the dishwasher made just before the cycle started sounded like Kim Deal blowing a whistle under water in *Cannonball*. 'You're beginning to sound stir-crazy,' he replied. He had a point. It didn't seem possible that in a few weeks I'd be sitting in the small and crazy-busy Super-Recogniser Unit, staring at CCTV footage for hours on end, looking at grainy shot after grainy shot as my brain processed images firing past my eyes as quick as bullets. I felt so distant from myself that the idea of being back at my desk was ridiculous, as foolish as if I'd been told to report for duty as a plumber or a brain surgeon. 'Or an undertaker?' he added. 'Look, if you really feel that way about it, why not drop into work next week, just for half an hour, to see what's happening?'

I shrugged, sullen as a teenager denied extra phone credit. I was nervous about meeting the other super-recognisers. It wasn't as though they could tell something was wrong just by looking at me – I would have to 'fess up for them to realise – but, still, while I wasn't myself, I wasn't one of them. Until I'd joined the unit I'd felt my entire identity was bound into the fact that I was somehow different from everyone else, that I was a gang of one. But when I found others like me, I found empathy. A tribe. Without that tether of connection, humans are just magnets dancing around each other, in thrall to whatever mood, whatever meme, exerts the strongest attraction. What would happen if my brain didn't fully return to normal, *my* normal? How long could I hide that at work? Because my ability to do my job well – or even at all – was controlled by the way my mind worked, my occupation defined me.

I'd gone for a walk after Alec left for work but it was cold and spitting sleet, so I headed home after half an hour. I made a coffee and stood at the window, looking out at the low grey sky that leaned over the city, chewing it up. Halfway down the street a young woman sat alone on a doorstep. A small figure in a trench coat, she stared straight ahead, rubbing her face over and over with a cotton pad, hard, in the constant swooping motion of an ad for cleanser. The long belt of her coat trailed down the step like a dog's lost lead.

Since I'd begun in the police force I had regularly encountered people whose worlds were ripped apart in a second, changed in engulfing, dramatic ways. Families broken into tiny pieces by horrific accidents, by murder. Lives serrated by assault, vicious indignities, betrayals. But most of our lives change in small, gradual ways, micron by micron. The descent from the summit to unhappiness below can be gradual, and when the journey is taken in small steps, you can be halfway there before you realise where you're headed. She looked like a woman on that path, trapped yet unable to change course. Her fragile solitude made me wonder how JD was getting on with the sexual assault case. I'd have heard of any arrests or more recent attacks. I texted JD. His *All fine get better* response was immediately followed by a text from Leon telling me to relax and stick to *Murder, She Wrote* on daytime TV. *Does 'all fine' mean no leads?* I texted back, to which he replied, *No + no snaps since yours.* The perpetrator's silence worried me. It felt like an uneasy pause that only he had the power to break.

My mobile rang. It was the station on Kentish Town Road.

'Susanna Tenant?'

'Yes.'

'Detective Constable Susanna Tenant?'

'Who's this?'

'It's Gary. Gary Cook? I thought it was you all right – we met on that profiling course last year?'

I could picture him perfectly. Burly, blond guy. Blue eyes, mole under the left. A few of us had gone for a drink together at the end of the course, spurred on by that giddy holiday sense you get when you're technically working but don't have much to do other than sit there and be talked at. Gary had featured recently on the cover of the staff newsletter *The Job* because he'd saved the life of a woman who'd overdosed in a secluded part of Hampstead Heath. He was off-duty and walking his dog when he came across her, and carried her the best part of a mile to his own car because there was a forty-five-minute delay on the ambulance.

'Hey there, PC Famous,' I said. 'What can I do for you?'

'It's Sergeant Famous now.' He laughed. 'But,' he lowered his voice, 'it's the other way round, I'm afraid. We've got a woman here asking for you. She didn't have your number, just your name, but I remembered you. You super-recognisers aren't the only ones with long memories, you know.'

We heard this sort of thing a lot about our unit from other Met officers, how un-elite, how essentially un-super we were. How they'd all be doing it, if they weren't too busy on the beat, or keeping pushers off the streets or whatever. People also occasionally assumed super-recogniser ability was the same as hyperthymesia: Highly Superior Autobiographical Memory. Hyperthymesics can remember every detail of their life, going right back to childhood. The recall is often involuntary, which sounded horrendous to me; a Groundhog Day of horrible, inhuman proportions. Life lived in split screen: one side in thrall to the waspish buzz of the past while the other tracked the present.

'Yeah, yeah,' I said. 'Like an elephant, I know. So, who is she?'

'Phyllida Hartigan.'

I was so surprised I forgot to reply.

'You still there?'

'Sorry, Gary. Yes.'

'Well? Do you know her? She's pretty distinctive-looking.'

'Her face.'

'Yeah.' I could hear the sympathetic wince in his voice. 'That's her.'

She'd got herself nicked! And only days after I'd visited her and given her the book. Either she hadn't believed me when I told her she'd get caught, or simply didn't care either way. Why on earth had she asked for me rather than someone in Dunease Court? Then I remembered the wary expressions on the faces of the staff when they'd looked at her, and it made a bit more sense that she wouldn't have wanted to involve them. 'Have you nicked her before?'

'No. Should we have?' Gary sounded suspicious. 'What's her deal, then? Bipolar? Klepto?'

'I honestly don't know. Eccentric certainly, but . . .' I had no idea where that *but* should go, so instead I asked, 'What did you get her with?'

'Hang on,' he said, and there was a rustle of papers. In the background I could hear a door bang, a shout. 'Here we go. Bluetooth speaker from Hill Sounds.'

'A *what*?' Fuck's sake, I thought, what was she doing with that? 'Anything else?'

'When they brought her in, she'd a serious-money diamond bracelet with the maker's sticker still attached, but no tag to say what shop it's from. Nothing matching the description has been reported stolen, and she says it's hers. The owner of Hill Sounds is really pissed off. "Make her a warning to the rest of them," he goes. What do people think we're going to do? Cut her hands off and pin 'em to the door?' He sounded exasperated, which I understood. I remembered that feeling well. 'Look, Susanna, you know what it gets like at weekends. You coming in to take her off my desk, or what?'

Much as I wanted to exercise 'or what', I knew he wasn't suggesting it as an option – and, anyway, I couldn't leave her sitting in the station. God knows how long she'd have been there before they got around to sorting out a crime as low-priority as pinching small electronics, particularly if she wasn't doing anything to help her cause.

'Okay.' I sighed. 'I'm on the way.'

She greeted me: 'You're looking thin. Are you tired?'

'Mrs Hartigan, I came to take you home, so let's just leave me out of this, okay?'

'Phyllida, please. And how can I? You're here.'

'That's down to you!' I was getting exasperated. 'You asked him to phone me!'

'I can't leave you out, that's all I was saying. You put yourself into my story when you started following me around Primrose Hill. Surely you don't want me to exclude you now?'

'Why did you take that speaker? The owner wants to prosecute you.'

'I can't prevent him doing that, of course, though I'd rather he didn't. I had never visited that shop before. It's rather marvellous.'

'I wouldn't know. It's too pricey for me.'

'It was on the expensive side, yes.'

'For you it will be, if you end up in court.' She didn't seem the slightest bit interested in the trouble she was in, and trying to explain it was merely dragging the two of us up a blind alley.

'Well?' Gary appeared and took me aside. 'Look, Susanna, let's make this easy. I'll call Bob in Hill Sounds and talk him down so we can let it go with a caution. But will you please tell her to knock off the knocking-off? You know as well as I do that she'll get more than a caution next time.'

'I have absolutely no influence on her, Gary, but, yeah, I'll try.'

He shrugged. Luckily, he was too busy to ask me any more questions. I didn't want to admit that I already knew she was a lifter, but didn't want to lie to him either. Now that I had accepted responsibility for taking her off his hands, Gary had moved on to sorting out the next of a dozen human-shaped problems waiting for his attention. 'Are you ladies ready to leave or will we have the pleasure of your company for an overnight visit, Mrs Hartigan?'

'We're going,' I said quickly, gesturing at her to grab the fur. 'Thanks, Gary.'

'Mind that arm now, Susanna,' he said. 'And goodbye, Mrs Hartigan. It's been a pleasure making your acquaintance but, please, let's not do this again, okay?'

She rose, wrapped the mink around her shoulders, shook his hand.

When we were safely outside the station, I glanced back up the steps. Gary's head was framed in a small window to the left of the door. He looked out, grinning, his hands a whooshing motion. Across the road a dark-haired man was hurriedly getting into a black taxi. He had his back to us, yet there was something about him, about the way he moved, that made me uncomfortable. I forced myself to concentrate, to see if I could tug any information to the surface, but got only a jumble of features that refused to settle into a single photofit. My brain felt full of static, a radio tuned halfway between two stations. I was about to signal to Gary, to ask if he recognised him but, anticipating the slagging I'd get for not knowing a face, changed my mind. The man slammed the door and the cab drove off. I was just about to note the registration when Phyllida tottered to one side and stopped, slumped against the wall.

'Are you okay?' She was very pale, her breathing quick, shallow. I shoved my phone back into my pocket. I had missed the reg. 'Wait here. I'll hail a taxi and get you home.'

She held up a hand to stop me. 'No, no, I'll be fine. It was too stuffy in there.'

What was it she had said when I arrived? *You put yourself*

into my story. The more time I spent in her company the less suited she seemed to the neutered charms of Dunease Court. I flagged down a cab. 'Here's what we're going to do,' I said, opening the door and helping her in. 'It's nearly six, so you're going to phone Ron and tell him you'll be late. Tell them you'll be home before lights out, or whatever it's called.'

'It's not a prison, you know,' she said. 'Yet it does feel rather like one.'

'Believe me,' I said, thinking of the stuffed sofas, the hushed tones, the jugs of chilled water with fresh mint and cucumber, 'it's nothing like prison. I'll make sure you get back in good time.'

'That sounds delightful.'

I hoped she was smiling, but because the scarred side of her face was nearest to me, I couldn't be sure. We drove down the road in silence. There was something rather magnificent about her. A wonderful exuberance, tamped down.

'Golden' was the word she used. Margaret Warner and Philip Harrison were golden. The most famous screen couple of the age, their actions defined a particular narrative of the sixties: a glamorous, hard-drinking existence that played out just as intensely off screen as on. Their relationship began in 1965 when they were cast in the romantic thriller *The Illusionist's Dream*. The affair was initially denied by the studio until, with perfect choreography, she was 'caught' by the press leaving his town flat early one morning that summer, her long silver ballgown a mist about her ankles, beautiful face pale and drawn, hair artfully undone.

'And not to care whether reporters knew was not to care whether your spouse – and your lover's spouse – knew too,' Phyllida added. Within weeks, Warner's husband was cast out, Harrison's wife cast aside. They married swiftly, almost as though they were both seeking to annul the memories of their first weddings, of her witnesses-only registry office event the previous year, his drab ceremony in Hove a decade earlier.

Phyllida sipped her wine and looked around the room

without comment, which was, I suspected, perfectly in character. Her mink lay draped across the sofa, like something out of a B movie. It was the first time I'd seen her without it – she'd even been wearing it when I'd called into Dunease Court a few days earlier. She was still very pale, and far slighter than I had realised. Her skirt was the dense blue-green of a cold sea viewed from a beach, her high polo-neck jumper a fine-knit metallic red. She took a lighter from her bag and flicked it on and off several times. With each click, loose threads in her jumper flared to life, the last sparks of a dying fire.

She took a photograph from her bag. I recognised Margaret Warner and Philip Harrison immediately. They were at a table littered with cigarette packets, glasses, ashtrays. There were no other tables visible, yet it looked like a restaurant. A nightclub, maybe. A woman sat on Harrison's left, a man on Warner's right, one on either extreme of the frame, as though they had been told to budge out of the way while the picture was taken. Philip Harrison wore a white shirt with a slim tie, and a dark jacket. He was handsome certainly, yet not outrageously so. He might have been a middle-management heartthrob from an advertising agency out on the town with a client: a man who has been drinking all day, whose tie is coming loose, hair dishevelling. A man who will not recognise this version of himself the following morning when he wakes up in his suburban house, resenting the tawdry ordinariness of his hangover.

Margaret Warner, on the other hand, could never have been mistaken for anyone but her incandescent self. A pale fur stole was wrapped loosely around her shoulders, her dark dress just visible beneath it. Her hair was a sleek twist, folded and pinned into a thick coil at her neck. She was sitting close to Harrison on one side of a table. Their bodies were angled towards each other. Her elbows were on the table, a small evening bag sitting between them. A long white glove stretched up her left arm. Her right hand was bare, except for a cigarette and a huge ring on her middle finger. In profile, she stared across and slightly up at her husband, focused on his face, as if her kohl-rimmed eyes could hypnotise him. Her stare was so intent, it was as though she was trying to capture him with a lens of her own. But he was looking elsewhere, at a point over her head outside the frame of the picture. His expression was not that of a man out on the town with his new wife, the woman who, the newspapers and magazines kept telling him, was the most desirable and desired woman in the world. Rather, it was the fretful face of a man who senses trouble impatiently tapping its foot just around the corner.

I felt as though I was spying on them, a lonely voyeur staring into a neighbour's bedroom. Their expressively disconnected faces gave the photograph the intensity of a private moment. Which would have made sense – they were together, they were drinking, they were intensely, obsessively, in love – except that it wasn't private. In the background there were a dozen gawping strangers. What was Margaret Warner thinking? That what she believed was love was in fact a ravening jealousy, fuelled by sex and alcohol (this would turn out to be true)? That they were already at the high point of their careers, and that she would, a mere decade or so later, dulled by an aggressive addiction to prescription medication, be pimped out by her managers to third-rate movies, like a bear in a travelling circus?

'No and no.' Phyllida whipped the photograph out of my hand. 'She never thought about anything other than herself, and certainly never about the future. Philip thought she adored him, but she wasn't capable of it. What she adored was the light he cast on her, and that's not the same thing. Anyway, you're looking at the wrong people,' she said, and pointed to the man sitting to the side, on Warner's right. His face wasn't visible – he was nothing more than a black suit, white cuffs and hankie in the breast pocket, a signet ring, a clinking highball tumbler. It was impossible to identify him; he could have been anyone.

'He's not *anyone*. He's Jack Hartigan, my husband.'

'What?'

She nodded, glancing at the picture again, her eyebrows raised as if to say, *Go on then, copper, surely you can figure the rest out yourself.* I stared at the woman on Philip Harrison's left. Feature by feature, as if I was at work and under pressure to make an ident from a single, tricky shot. She was in profile, and slightly tilted away from the camera. She was pouting, her lips ready to receive the cigarette in her raised left hand. From what I could see of her – one thickly lashed eye, one perfectly arched brow – she, too, was beautiful. From the angle she was sitting at, Jack Hartigan across the table was the subject of her disinterested stare, though without seeing his face I couldn't assess exactly who or what either of them was looking at. The even-handed perfection of her face was almost made bland by the neatness of its symmetry.

'That's *you* with Warner and Harrison,' I said, immediately disliking my magazine-style adoption of their surnames. 'Were you friends with them? They're legends!' She dismissed my use of the word. I considered the photograph again: it was more than a paparazzo snap of a famously tempestuous couple on a night out, it was a tale of two marriages, one framing the other.

'We depended on them for our livelihoods,' she said. 'We loved them, we couldn't stand them. No, that's not it. *I* couldn't stand them. Is that friendship?'

'I'm confused,' I said. 'Can we start at the beginning?'

She threw her eyes upwards at the word 'beginning' but shook open a packet of cigarettes, which I read as acquiescence. I scurried off to find the ashtray we kept for when Joey came over. Joey always smoked outside on our tiny terrace, but I couldn't imagine Phyllida sitting there, her mink bunched out on either side of a cheap folding chair.

Jack Hartigan was a bit-part actor who had known Philip Harrison since the late fifties, their friendship forged in heavy-drinking rep tours up and down the country: 'Jack used to say that "rep" was an abbreviation of "repetition" rather than "repertory": pub, stage, pub, and repeat in town after town.' The two men looked alike and were the same build, so when Philip began to get movie work, he made sure his former understudy was hired as his stand-in on set. 'The studio saw the value in Jack. Philip could drink him under the table, yet Jack was somehow always able to keep him on track. I think it was a sort of security blanket for Philip to have him around. He used to ask his advice all the time.'

'And what about you?' I asked.

'I met Jack in 1965. I was a switchboard operator in his agent's office. It was horribly boring, spending all day listening to voices whose lives were more thrilling than mine would ever be . . . but isn't that what every young woman believes, before she discovers that the future is equally unattainable for everyone, that there are no real victories to be had?' She paused to smoke, her elbow resting in her free hand. 'Jack and I had been out a few times. He kept a stable of girls on the go, which I knew, but he was such good fun that I was happy with any crumb of attention. He was filming *The Illusionist's Dream* – well, Philip was, but obviously Jack was there too – when he dropped all the other girls, suddenly, for me. Afterwards, I wondered if Jack figured it all out in advance when Philip and Margaret's affair began. Did he play out a sequence further than anyone else would have imagined? The similarities between him and Philip were obvious, but perhaps he would never have gone after me had I not looked like her. Nobody had noticed the resemblance before he did. Neither my mother nor I had spotted it, and we used to devour the movie magazines, much to my father's disapproval. I was naturally fair so Philip had my hair dyed Margaret's colour and asked a friend in the make-up department to do my face the same as hers. My eyes were smaller, but the same colour, and copying her eyebrows and lashes made a big difference. Another friend dressed me from her rails. Jack had pals everywhere – he collected useful people as easily as some actors picked up venereal diseases.'

I laughed. 'So you became her body double? What movies were you in?'

She frowned. 'Because I was getting paid to be there anyway, I occasionally appeared as an extra, but generally the studio only used me for very basic work on set, blocking out her positions for the camera, that sort of thing. Anyone with her build could have done that. No, our real value to Margaret and Philip was off set.' She pointed to the photograph again. 'Two married couples who were the best of friends and went everywhere together was the story the studio would trot out if anyone asked. The reality was very different. We weren't their equals. We were servants.'

Margaret was surrounded by fans wherever she went,

Phyllida explained. And much as she thrived on the waves of adoration flowing towards her, she hated that they wanted her time and attention in return. To her, fans were no more than vampires. 'That night we all got up from the table together, and went to the private cloakrooms. As usual, she and I were wearing the same dress under different jackets, so she took my wrap and I put on her fur and hat, and turned the collar up. Margaret and Philip slipped out the back door and went back to the hotel to carry on drinking. It was Jack and I who posed outside, as them.'

I found it hard to believe that a switch-trick could work with such easily recognised celebrities. 'But,' she said, 'faces familiar from grainy black-and-white newsprint, or made-up and in character on screen, will appear different in real life. We weren't *identical* to them, of course not, but we resembled them as closely as we could without being mirror images. I was taller than her, so I wore the same style and colour shoes, but with lower heels. Who's going to look at your heel height? And you have to remember that we were not only dressed as them, we *said* we were them, and the restaurant staff and studio people all said the same. If it was just one of us being seen alone, it probably wouldn't have worked. That's what Jack realised, when he met me: neither he nor I by ourselves was enough, but *together*? It would have been too implausible a coincidence to be anything but true. Life is a confidence trick, Susanna. Surely as one of London's finest' – she was being sarcastic I assumed – 'you know that.'

'I've certainly met enough people who live as though it is, yes.'

She was right, of course: add convincing visual evidence to the fact that people were prepared – no, willing – to believe they were in Warner and Harrison's stellar presence, and hey presto! Two screen icons, living, breathing, signing autographs, fuelling anecdotes for months to come.

'Margaret used to say, *No matter how hard you try to be me, Phyllie, you'll never have what I have.* And she was right. When I was styled as her, when I was being her, I could turn heads. But the way I looked had nothing to do with *me*, merely what had been sculpted using me as clay. She was different. What she had was far more than beauty, than sex appeal. When she walked through the door it was as though the air supply to the room became suddenly charged.' She frowned. 'Do you have any idea what it's like to be dependent on another person's appearance for your livelihood? If she gained or lost five pounds, so did I, and quick too, because I'd have to catch up. She chose what we wore, but I always had to keep my outfit covered. The purpose of my life was to be there when she was tired of hers.' She sounded bitter. 'Margaret was a completely consuming person. She swallowed you whole, which was enormously flattering. I adored her at first, until I realised that we weren't friends. To her I was just another one of the staff.'

'And what about Philip Harrison? Did he like having you two around all the time?'

'Philip loved the idea of having a double, and even more so, being in a *couple* of doubles. And it meant he had a constant drinking partner. He was besotted with Margaret, yet rather nervous in her company. His first wife – according to Jack, I never met her – was very sweet but a complete milksop. She never argued with him, no matter how unreasonable he became. Margaret was the opposite. She argued simply for the attention. I think for him I diluted what he found most overwhelming about her. Occasionally I would catch him looking at me oddly, as if trying to figure out where she stopped and I – the real me, a person he never really knew – began.'

Out of nowhere, I recalled a couple I'd met on a trekking holiday in South America. I had just finished university and went travelling for six months with my then boyfriend. We met Juliette and Mick in Brazil, about a month into our trip. As two couples rather than four individuals, we bonded over a common dislike of a tedious trek we had signed up for. We spent three weeks with these people, the only other English speakers in the group, yet all the time I knew that once we were back home, our mosquito bites fading, free to like the trek now that it was over, we would secretly despise Juliette and Mick for our similarity, our timidity, and never want to meet them again.

Their lives as the Warner-Harrison doppelgängers lasted two years. Phyllida and her husband were conjoined shadows. Paid to preen, while their employers hid. Paid to skulk around corners, waiting, always waiting, to appear, to glow and glimmer. 'We were permanently available, ready to be switched on so that they always had an audience to perform their relationship for, or an escape route, whichever she wanted. Even now,' she added, 'I can hear Margaret's voice shouting, "Someone, go and get me the bloody Jack Hartigans." Jack once likened our lives to a state of constant dry arousal.'

I laughed.

'The Jack Hartigans . . .' she repeated slowly, as though the idea of two lives packaged in one man's name was newly alien to her '. . . three words and I'm not to be found in any of them. There was no space for *me*, for the person I was, in that name.' She leaned forward to tap ash from her cigarette.

I was aware it was beginning to feel like an interrogation but decided to keep asking questions until she told me to stop. 'And what did your family make of your job?'

'I was her assistant, as far as they knew, employed by the studio. My father never came near the place. My mother was different. She adored the glamour of it all. She visited us on set a few times, and of course Margaret charmed her. Jack had finished with school by the time he was twelve, so my father saw only an ill-educated man in a precarious and rather distasteful profession.' She clicked her lighter on and off again. 'My father had a scarred face too – isn't that a curious coincidence? – and I always suspected that for him, the idea of being on a film set, where everyone is obsessed with appearances, defined by them, was torture.'

'What happened to his face?'

'War wounds. From the first war, I mean. He had eleven operations and occasionally wore one of those awful metal masks when the scar tissue was sore. I hated that mask because it made it impossible to know what was going on in his head. "He's not thinking any different," my mother used to say. "Leave him be. He's exactly the same man as when he's not wearing it." But I never believed her, I don't know why. As I child I was scared it wasn't him under the mask at all.' She gestured towards her face. 'He didn't live to see this, and though he would have been the only person who could really have understood, I'm glad he didn't, because he would have foretold my future from his past. For him, education was the route to a better life, the film business no more than vulgar nonsense. He never believed me when I told him that movie stars were treated better than royalty.'

'They still are.'

She smiled. 'He never accepted that, despite weekly proof

in the movie magazines. I was an only child. My parents were both in their forties when I was born, and by the time I met Jack they not only seemed like a different generation but a different species. I changed my Christian name – well, Jack did, he thought my real name horribly brown-brick – and my father was upset, insulted really, about that too.' She moved her hands gently, her fingers waving towards the dark corner of the room, as if conducting a small and invisible orchestra.

'What was it?'

'Violet,' she said. 'Violet Dockery.'

FEBRUARY 1919

Of course a man must die. What other tale is there to tell in a story such as this? But to choose *this* man? One who has suffered so much already. No heroic deeds, no dramatic rescues will be recalled by those who cluster around his bed. No one will speak of the complete bravery in every hard-won exhalation, because it is too ordinary, too commonplace to praise: such is the cruelty of life as it throws up its hands in surrender to death. But that his final, rotten breath should be into a tear-soaked pillow in an iron bed in a room shared between twenty men in a hospital hut built to repair – some say hide – the ugly detritus of a war that, even now, is still lumbering towards what will be a lumpen peace? Life is cruel. Even in death, life is cruel.

Greedy and bloated, the Grim Reaper swoops in above their heads. 'This one?' he says. There is no reply, so he shrugs, helps himself.

'A blessed release,' says the ward orderly, his fingers running over the rosary in his pocket.

'And to say so suggests a speaker entirely unaffected by

the man's life.' Mrs Scott has one hand on the rail at the end of the bed. The sketchbook slotted under her arm is open at a page of faces without noses.

'It will never be possible to save them all,' Major Gillies says, his usually bright tone flat and despondent, 'but every failure feels so huge.'

'The Lord takes to Himself His own,' Stuart Miall – sent for 'in the nick of time', he claimed – says to anyone who will listen.

Nurse Goodfellow gently shrugs the vicar's hand from her arm. She dabs under her eyes with a handkerchief. 'Don't keep tears to yourself, I told him once. Tears have their own language, and should be heard.'

'The Lord Himself would agree,' Miall opines.

'Holy Mary Mother of God, pray for him,' the orderly chips in, feeling the need to find his God a front-row seat for the proceedings. He makes the sign of the cross on his forehead, lips and breastbone, then drops his head in a not-silent-enough decade of the rosary.

'Is there really a need to practise one's religion quite so enthusiastically?' Mrs Scott murmurs. She looks down at the body in the bed. 'What a beautiful boy,' she says, and passes through the ward and on, into the corridor.

'If you could all leave please?' The ward sister appears from behind Major Gillies and gestures towards the door. 'My nurses need to prepare the body for removal to the morgue. Not you, sir, of course,' she says, but Major Gillies merely shakes his head and walks away in Mrs Scott's slipstream.

Of course a man has to die.

'But why this one?' says a voice from under the bed. He

is lying on the floor, searching for a metal straw that should have been on the locker. Where is it? He's flat out, one hand swishing around in front of his face. The linoleum is spotless. He wriggles out, feet first, grateful he's there at all. That he's not rising from a shell hole, climbing in the dark, escaping water so sticky he doesn't know if it is muddy blood or bloody mud. That his hands are not touching submerged faces, fingers. Not feeling the horrors of ordinary things: buttons and belts, the kiss of unseen hair.

'What?' Nurse Goodfellow says. 'Are you all right under there? Here, let me help you up. You have to leave now, just for half an hour or so.'

The Reverend Stuart Miall trots behind the man as he walks towards the door. 'Perhaps I can be of some assistance to you in the loss of your friend,' he begins.

Only if you can sodding well find him again. Will shakes his head and slips the brass straw into his pocket, feeling as stupidly guilty as a schoolboy caught filching apples. His fingertips play along its smooth surface, registering the change from warm, where it had been clutched in his fist, to cold, where it had once been in Neville's broken mouth.

'Perhaps a prayer together?'

'No.' There's no need to be rude, he thinks. If Neville liked the vicar well enough, can't he, in his memory? He sighs. 'I appreciate your concern but, no, thank you. Prayers are no good to me any more, so please don't waste your time.'

'Time spent with one of the Lord's children is never wasted.'

'I don't want to be one of the Lord's children.' His voice is louder than he'd realised. 'Sorry, I don't mean to shout. But I've had enough. Enough of believing in things. I might as well be reciting nonsense as a prayer for all it means to me now. Shouldn't a man know what he's saying and understand why he's saying it?'

'Know, yes. But *understand*? No. Imagine our Creator with the world in His hand. The flattening of the poles shows us simply where He has held us gently, before setting us down to spin for all eternity.' His hand is close to Will's face, thumb and index finger a few inches apart. 'We are His handiwork, but He alone understands everything. The purpose God gives us is to interpret His role in our lives, not the essence of His actions.'

'Well, I don't want to. I don't know why I should pray or even how to, and lack of knowledge doesn't make me want to go and learn, or change, or get help to overcome it. It makes me feel exhausted, as though I could put my head down and go to sleep and never wake up, just like Neville. And I'd be glad of it.'

He feels so tired suddenly. Of course the vicar is going to bring God into Neville's death; it's his job to do so. But why is it so hard to make him believe that this life – the one he is living, that Neville has just left – feels so different from any plan God could have had? Or any of the thousand others who have been treated at the Queen's? And they're the lucky ones – if being alive is still considered lucky.

Will strides down the path towards the big house, the vicar beside him. Christ, the man is still talking! '. . . but God is more important now than ever before. Mankind needs His light and His love more than ever. God had been forgotten, and war is His way of reminding us to think of Him and His plan for us. Why else was there this urge for self-mutilation?'

Will bristles at the harsh choice of word. Does religion

restrain man from fighting or push him towards it? He remembers soldiers who fought as though God was pushing them towards the Front, as though it was some sort of warped honour to be in battle, defending Him. He remembers others, too, who fought despite it.

'So,' he says slowly, 'God seeks to remind us to revere Him by killing us?'

'It is men who kill, not Our Lord.'

'You've an answer for everything.'

Miall's smile is a cold twitch of his lips. 'You must allow me this, Mr Dockery: the word "theological" does hold the word *logic* at its heart.' He folds his hands across the black terrain of his stomach and taps the tips of his thumbs together.

'I allow it only as an expression of language, not of creed. Tell me, Vicar, have you seen the end of the world?' He imagines stretching out an arm and pushing this fat man over, then watching him roll, like Humpty Dumpty, down the gentle slope of the lawn and out the gate. Like a child with a hoop and stick, he would bowl him all the way to Sidcup and return him to the dead arms of his graveyard and their futile desires.

'Scripture is very clear as to what we can expect.'

'I didn't ask if you had *read* about it. Have you *seen* it? The end of the world.'

'No, of course not. I—'

Will holds up a hand. 'Well, I have.' He walks away across the grass, certain that Miall won't follow him. He keeps going until he realises he's skirting the perimeter wall. He's never been this close to it before.

Should life mean more now? Now that there is an *after*, is there a *before*? The gauge of the world has shifted. Will's mistake has been trying to go back to what was once there, to an old way of being he'd never considered, just gone along with, instead of seeing that this is the new world. Davey understands that. There's something rum going on with Davey. All that talk a while back about going to America with the man he's working for – a right charlatan by the sound of it – then silence for the last week. He can't have left yet: he'd have let Will know. Wouldn't he? Will's brother is a lost cause in many ways, but he's sure Davey wouldn't leave the country without telling him, if for no other reason than to warn him of what debts might find their way to Will's door in search of a Dockery – any Dockery other than Davey himself – to discharge them.

Poor Neville. They are all equally subject to the randomness of Fate. He really was an unlucky bastard, after all.

Will's own most recent operation went well. He is 'on the slate', as Major Gillies calls it, for his next surgery in six weeks. Two, maybe three more procedures to go and then he will be finished with hospital. He should be back out in the world by the end of the year. What a thought. In the garden, by the wall, he stands totally still, aware of every breath as it enters and leaves his body. Some day, one will be his last, but how is he to know when that will be? Being so close to death so many times already has given him no insight into that moment, no sixth sense as to when the oily claw will land on his shoulder, when he will fall against the door only for it to creak open. No, if anything, his proximity to Death has dulled his senses, worn him down with its incessant taunts. *Not yet, not yet.* Davey thinks he's cheated Death, but he hasn't: he's just not that important to the Grim Reaper. *Not yet.*

He heard Neville at night, pleading in prayer not to

die. Doesn't everyone do that, he thinks, in a thousand unconsidered, unacknowledged ways? Every action begging continuance, to be allowed to stitch itself quietly into the next.

The grey stone is damp. It looks greenish-black in the dim light created by the trees overhead. He touches the surface, expecting it to be hard, but it's soft, yielding. Moss, not shadows. It's so quiet here. He knows the noises of the town continue, the rattle and clink of commerce unabated, but he can't hear them. The hospital, too, with its low babble of voices, the metronome of shoes on endless corridors. He hears none of them. The only sound now is the clear, true note of a brass straw tapping against a metal mouth.

January 2018

1

Phyllida leaned back into the sofa and exhaled. Her smoke ring travelled up, thinning to nothing in the corner of the room. I could see now why she had described herself as a mongrel when we'd first met. At the time I assumed she was referring to a mixed ethnicity, but actually she'd meant she was a blend of different people's versions of her.

'But my father's scars aren't what you're interested in, are they?'

'No, well, I mean, yes, but . . .' I was hesitant. 'Your face – did that happen after you stopped working for Margaret and Philip?'

Silence. I was desperate to know yet didn't want to say anything else. Just as I lost my nerve and was about to change the subject, she replied.

'I'd never had a drink in my life till I met Jack, but after the best part of two years I'd learned how to hold it just as well as the others.'

I nodded, afraid to break the spell.

'Margaret and Philip broke up in 1968. It had been very

unpleasant between them for about six months before that, though they were good at covering it up in public. She persuaded herself Philip was seeing someone else. Jack said he wasn't. She was even suspicious of me at one stage because Philip and I got on well, though there was never more to it than that. Even had I wanted to have an affair with Philip I wouldn't have.'

'Because of Jack, you mean?'

'*Jack?* No, I doubt he'd have cared. I liked Philip a lot, but an affair? What horrific narcissism that would have been. Perhaps she didn't truly believe it, I don't know – I had long since stopped looking for the truth in what I was being told. I just waited for instructions. Neither Jack nor I ever said as much, but we both knew that when Margaret and Philip broke up it would be the end of our marriage too. If Jack had to pick one of us, he'd have chosen Philip.'

Once more her fingers moved gently, like fronds in water. 'One evening they'd been drinking heavily, and arguing, which always made Jack and me scrappy as well. He found it hard not to take Philip's side, then I'd tell him to stay out of their marriage, which meant he'd get angry with me. It was exhausting, the simulacra of their fights that he and I would end up having. I'd get confused sometimes, and wonder whether we were fighting simply because we were so used to copying them, or arguing as ourselves. That evening we had gone to their suite for a nightcap and Margaret started screaming at Philip, accusing him of eyeing up a waitress earlier. It was very late, and I was tired and drunk and fed up. She was lighting a cigarette just as I stood up to leave. She threw the table lighter at him, but it hit me. The catch was faulty, the flame hadn't gone out. I had half a can of lacquer on my hair, and the side of my head went up in seconds.' She pushed her hair back and held it with one hand, exposing the entire left side of her face, more so than she had that day in Gordon's Kitchen. From forehead to chin was scarred. The worst areas were her hairline as far as her ear, and across her cheekbone. Pools of puckered skin were connected by fine white lines, as though someone had put a razor to her.

'What . . . happened then?'

'I panicked. I was shaking my head, screaming – I had no idea what I was doing. Philip shoved me to the ground and hit me with a cushion. He put the flames out quickly, but I was wearing a hairpiece. The nylon fused with the skin around my ear and cheekbone.'

'That was quick thinking on his part, considering he was drunk.'

'He'd have got to me quicker if I hadn't been running around so hysterically.'

'You're very hard on yourself. To run is a perfectly understandable reaction.' Panic affects everyone differently and, as I knew well, no one was ever able to predict their natural response to trauma.

'His pushing me to the ground saved the other side of my face from going up too.'

'That's appalling. What a terrible accident.'

'Accident?' She gave another of her slight shrugs, her left shoulder lifting higher than the right. 'I had a lot of time in hospital to think about it. When she threw the lighter I was standing up and he was sitting at the other end of the sofa. She was drunk, and never a good aim, yet to be that far off the mark . . . Margaret always got what she wanted. I can't help but think that had she really wanted to hit him she would have.'

'So you were her real target, not him?'

'I'll never know.'

'How did Margaret react?'

'She screamed louder than I did and ran to Jack, as though she was the one who needed protection. It was instinct in her, I think – immediately to seek out a man who would make saving *her* his responsibility, regardless of the situation.'

'But why . . . I mean, how come she wasn't—'

She cut me off. 'I presume you mean why have you never heard that Margaret Warner was charged with assaulting an employee?'

'Assault at the very least, yes.'

'Because it was a terrible accident. I caused it by smoking while taking down my hair when I was drunk.'

'*You* took responsibility for what she did?'

'The studio offered to pay for a private hospital and convalescent home, pay for everything, in fact. They gave me money to go away, to become someone else – my original self, I suppose, the management didn't care. I had no other source of income, or any prospect of one, so I agreed. What was I meant to do? Go crawling back to the switchboard? When I got out of hospital, not only did I not recognise my face, but I didn't even know who I was meant to be. My appearance had changed, but so had my entire identity. Changed twice in fact – first by Jack and then by Margaret. I think I went a bit mad from it all. Perhaps,' she looked at me, her restless eyes focusing briefly on mine, 'you have come to the conclusion that I still am.'

I knew by now that she was teasing me. I had never met anyone less interested in the opinions of other people, so I ignored the remark and instead asked, 'And no one ever found out what happened?'

'No, why should they? It wasn't as though the press were bothered with Jack and I. We weren't actors, just two friends hanging around, often with others, studio people, agents . . . There were plenty in their retinue apart from us. Margaret and Philip divorced and she was on to husband number three within a year. There was that Henry the Eighth quality about her marriages even then: *divorced, beheaded, died, divorced, beheaded, survived.* Awful, to be reduced to a sixth like that, as though one's final fate at another's hands is the most significant part of one's life, not the living of it.'

I topped up her wine. The heavy-drinking years must have stood her in good stead, because she was on her third large glass and the alcohol didn't seem to be having any effect.

'We'd have lost our jobs anyway – I would, at least – as soon as they split officially. So, no, no one ever found out. The studio imposed the condition that I could never tell the truth, even after Margaret died. She insisted on *that* clause, apparently.'

'But you're telling me?'

'As you said earlier, I owed you one. I saved her from prosecution, you saved me.'

'There's a world of difference between the two crimes.'

'That depends on your point of view. And it was years ago, and I'm tired of holding other people's secrets. By keeping faith with what she asked me, I've been protecting her all these years, as though I was still in thrall to her. No . . .' she frowned '. . . not *in thrall*, that's not it. In servitude. And that's no way to live.'

That must have been a bitter pill, the realisation that by agreeing to what Margaret Warner had asked at the time of the assault (I couldn't bring myself to use the word 'accident', even if she could), Phyllida had signed away part of her future, swapping power over her own life for financial security.

'And did you ever see her again, after that night?'

'She came to the hospital a couple of times, Philip too.'

I pictured her lying in a hospital bed, unable to escape the unwelcome attentions of her assailant. During my childhood hospital stay in Sidcup, when I began to recover and the constant low-level fear began to abate, I got very bored, scratchily desperate for company. The stifling irritation of lying in bed waiting for crumbs of attention! Yet by visiting time, I'd be irritable and resentful, worn out by anticipation. As soon as my visitors left, I'd turn clingy and tearful with the nurses.

'She must have felt terribly guilty about what happened.'

'It was hard to tell. She was sorry I'd been hurt, of course, she repeated that over and over, but never once did she say she was sorry *she*'d hurt me.'

'Did you see her after you were discharged?'

'No. When they divorced he moved to France, she went to Hollywood, and that was that.'

'And Jack?'

'I was in hospital for four months. Two weeks after the accident Philip and Jack went to France to shoot a movie. I didn't want Jack beside me all the time I was in hospital. What good would that have done? Until then, my salary had always gone into Jack's account. Apart from a post office book I'd never had an account of my own. I insisted the studio set up a new bank account in my name and pay the compensation directly into it. It was a lot of money too. Before I signed the waiver the bosses must have been terrified I'd insist on prosecuting. I gave Jack a quarter. It seemed fair to me, that he was worth a quarter. That's all we each were, a fraction of a person. My former employer was still Jack's agent and he advised me how to invest the money so that I'd have enough to live on without needing to work. Jack visited me regularly until I was discharged, then began to split his time between here and Nice, where Philip was living. His visits became less and less frequent, until he was never here at all. I had never even had a boyfriend before Jack, so of course I'd believed I was in love. He never felt that way for me, of course, just with the idea of us being Philip and Margaret – or maybe of him being Philip. But he was very fond of me. It was another fifteen years before we divorced, and that was only so he could marry again. We couldn't have stayed married, even had we been in love. We had seen too much servility in each other for that.'

'Is Jack still alive?' I asked.

'I don't know.' She leaned forward, put out her cigarette and picked up the photograph, her thumb obscuring her face. Her fur slid obediently from the sofa at her touch and wrapped itself around her. 'Margaret gave me this, you know. One of her cast-offs, just like myself. Will you call me a taxi?'

'Are you sure? There's no need to go yet.'

'I'm tired. So are you.'

She was right, of course. I was exhausted. Plus, it was half past seven and Alec was due home around eight. Just as before, I wanted to hold on to Phyllida's tale for myself. I didn't know how I could have talked about her without sounding melodramatic, making her appear ridiculously eccentric – or worse. I imagined the story as Alec would hear it from my lips: implausible-sounding impersonations, drunken rages, disfigurement, isolation. Phyllida's tale with whatever accidental shifts and shadows my retelling would give it. A slant of emphasis here, an implied judgement there, by the end it wouldn't have been her story at all: it would have become my Hall of Mirrors version, distorted and unrecognisable.

I walked her down to the street door to wait for the taxi. The sky was low over our heads, full of rain. I pointed at the blue plaque, though it was too dark to read it properly, and began to tell her some of what I'd discovered about the Gardiner household, but she cut me off mid-sentence. 'Not all elderly people are interested in those who went before us, you know. You may not realise this for years, or perhaps you never will, but the only person one can ever be entirely tethered to is oneself. I only discovered that when I no longer knew who I was. Trying to understand the motivations of the past is just guesswork, and it doesn't interest me.'

'I've met plenty of twenty-somethings who'd agree with you.' And, clearly, unless the shoplifting was some unusual manifestation of alienation – which I doubted: in common with other skilled thieves I'd come across, she was good at it because she understood the consequences yet wasn't afraid – her considered self-interest wasn't doing her any harm.

Her taxi turned the corner, and in the glare of its headlights I noticed a figure pause in the shadows on the pavement opposite. I waved as the car slicked away down the wet road, but she didn't look back. As I closed the street door behind me I glanced at the pavement opposite. It was empty. My head was aching, but I felt jumpy, stringy. Simultaneously tired and full of false energy, like a sugared-up child. I didn't want to go upstairs alone and wait for Alec. I opened the door again. I'd go for a quick walk, I decided, just a quarter of an hour around the block. It had begun to drizzle once more but I was grateful for the chill of it against my forehead. I had taken the sling off earlier and couldn't be bothered trudging back upstairs for it. Instead I tugged the sleeve of my hoodie onto my hand to protect the edge of the cast from the rain and turned in the direction of Primrose Hill. I'd cut down the side-streets to the park, then loop home. Ten, fifteen minutes would be enough to dissipate the fizzed-up feeling in my head.

I headed down Cranford Crescent, thinking about Phyllida and her father in his tin mask. It was such an odd parallel, that they both ended up scarred in terrible circumstances. How scary it must have been for a child to watch a familiar face disappear and an emotionless, fleshless stranger take its place. And yet she had grown up to experience something similar, given that her becoming an identikit Margaret Warner was in its own way a disconnection from her real self, even before the scarring.

I imagined coming across her face on CCTV. I could see her a hundred times yet never once have the slightest insight into what made her *her*. All the faces I had recognised over the years, thousands of them, each a unique mix of DNA and coincidence, of luck and forebears all stirred up together. And every single one of us no more than happenstance in the lives of the others.

As a small child, of three, maybe four, I believed that the world had once been monochrome. It made sense to me because the photos of my parents and grandparents on display in the house were black-and-white, as was our first television, to which my parents stayed stubbornly loyal long after all their friends had moved on to colour, to remote controls. My mother told me how disappointed I was when I realised I'd got it wrong. I'd liked the simplicity of it, she said. It made sense to me, that colour meant *now*, and black-and-white *then*.

I kept going, head down, hood up. A burglar alarm yowled

from a few streets away. About five doors ahead on Regent's Park Road a woman walking her dog was struggling to keep hold of a phone and lead while also lighting a cigarette. Her collie entangled itself on a lamppost, then managed to wrap its lead around her legs. 'Absolutely,' she said, as she extricated herself, her loud voice bouncing around the silent street. 'Yes, no, absolutely— Oh fuck off! No, not you, the damned dog!' Across the road, a tall man carrying an umbrella walked quickly in the opposite direction, under the shelter of the trees that hugged the park railings. I turned onto Fitzroy Road. The streetlight on the corner was broken – I could hear it pop and fizz.

Was it because I was so absorbed in thinking about Phyllida's story that I didn't notice the man pause, didn't notice him turn and walk behind me until he was close enough to grab me, the shaft of the umbrella suddenly tugging across my neck. Its metal tips were broken and I felt the sudden sting of skin ripping under my chin. I opened my mouth to scream but only a harsh *pfft* of air came out.

'No flowers today,' he said.

But they were my words, weren't they? I breathed in as hard and quickly as I could. I smelt rain and a familiar woody, mossy cologne. I blinked. In that second of darkness I saw—

The snaking queue for another ride shuffles forward and brief gaps open up between groups of people. His hands are clenched. His eyes roam, scanning the crowd. My peripheral vision drops away, I am concentrating only on his face. I grab his upper arm. He turns, startled, his face only inches from mine.

Snap.

Phyllida and I are outside the station. I glance back up the steps. Gary's head is framed in a small window to the left of the door. He's smiling, glad to be rid of us. Across the road a dark-haired man gets into a black taxi.

Snap.

A confused pixelated blur becomes a lean, pale face, dark hair and high cheekbones, on a screen. The static around the face disappears, my mind is perfectly clear.

Snap.

'Got you,' he said, his voice calm. Soft. 'Got you, Detective Constable Tenant.'

I had been taught what to do when blindsided. Knew that I had to force a reactionary gap between us or I'd be in serious trouble. Elbow, elbow, turn, jab: I'd done it a hundred times in training, and several times on the beat. But with my left arm heavy and useless at my side my reactions simply short-circuited. He began to shove me towards a narrow car park, open on one side to the street but surrounded by bushes and head-height brick walls on the other three. All I could think was that I knew what had happened to the previous three women, and that knowledge drained the fight out of me rather than the opposite. His hand slipped under the back of my hoodie, grabbing the top of my leggings. He shoved me forward so quickly that my feet, already heavy as lead, tripped over each other. Fear is a tornado. In a single second it grabs hands, toes, every strand of hair, every eyelash, and turns them all against you, rendering you powerless. It turns a scream for help into a hoarse, crunched-up whisper. It turns a woman into a child, a freak alone on a dark street. His hand moved inside my waistband. Years of self-defence sluiced away at the touch of his fingers on my skin.

No, I thought. Not again.

The shock to my wrist as I slammed my cast against the side of his head was excruciating, but judging by his cry of pain, I wasn't the only one it hurt. I pushed back from him, my legs buckling under me as I ran out of the car park and onto the pavement. The woman with the collie had doubled back and was coming towards me, scanning the ground, loudly cursing the dog for distracting her into dropping her lighter. I had the strangest sensation when I looked at her, at once completely familiar and entirely strange. As though the air pressure had dropped suddenly, there was a painfully sharp crackle in my head. I immediately knew I'd seen her a number of times in the area, months before. And just as I stumbled and tripped over the dog I felt the click of recognition as clearly inside my brain as if a control switch had flicked back to 'on'.

My lips were moving, soundless. The collie lurched forward, tugging the woman behind him, and jumped towards me. I tried to sidestep him, tripped over the lead and fell hard onto the pavement. Leon paused the CCTV footage at that point, me on the ground, half in shot, half not. The dog stared upwards, as if gurning for the camera. My mouth moved again. I watched my lips silently stutter, *Help, help me*.

'Seen enough yet?' Leon kept looking at the door. It was ten p.m. and we were alone in the office, but he was worried that someone would appear. 'You do know the trouble we'll both be in if Colin finds out?' had been his first reaction when I phoned to ask if he'd meet me three days after the attack.

'Please, Leon, I'm nearly done. Please, just a few more minutes.' I was off the case, of course. Or, as Colin put it, now that I was a victim rather than an investigating officer, 'You can't be the bloody gamekeeper when you've been bloody poached.' He'd have done his nut if he'd known I was there: it could ruin the integrity of our case if it came out in court that I'd reviewed my own attack. Leon clicked on footage recovered from a camera on Regent's Park Road, about twenty feet away from Fitzroy Road. We watched a few seconds of a silent, rain-spattered street before my attacker ran past, his face a brief white flicker under the halo of a streetlamp. It was the same man, no doubt about it. I nodded. Leon clicked again. There I was once more, standing now, groggy, listing from side to side as if I was pissed. The woman stood beside me, one hand on my arm, her dog nowhere to be seen.

Run, run as fast as you can . . . I recalled Phyllida's odd comment. 'Go back to seven thirty,' I said. 'The cameras closest to Cranford Crescent.'

He was reluctant but kept flicking, shot after shot revealing the extent of the man's movements that evening as far as they could be pieced together from the cameras that covered the immediate area. JD had already catalogued nearly all the images retrieved from the council, and Colin had a trawl team working on accessing privately held footage. Leon told me that JD had shared some images with the other super-recognisers, but hadn't got an ident. Jessica recognised him from shots taken at Oxford Circus months earlier, but as she hadn't been searching for him, she hadn't paid any attention. That happened to us all the time: recognising people going about their everyday business, milling around unknowingly among the criminals we were looking for. We knew the daily routines of complete strangers.

I couldn't be certain if he was the person I'd seen on the pavement across the road from the flat, but the CCTV picked him up shortly after that, trailing me. I blushed in shame at my ignorance of his presence. With my head down, as absorbed in my own thoughts as if I had been sleepwalking, I looked frighteningly alone and vulnerable. I had never seen myself on CCTV before, had never been forced to look at myself the way I had viewed thousands of others. I was just another face, caught on camera. Captured in a simple, grainy image. How unjust those pictures seemed to me then; how flat and lacking in dimension, in humanity. My features were blurred – I could have been happy or sad, anything or nothing. It was impossible to know.

No flowers today . . . 'Do you think he'd been after me since the funfair?'

'The previous assaults were planned, not opportunistic, so, yeah, it's likely. In the footage we've seen so far, he's been in your street on at least seven occasions, I guess hoping to catch you going in or out.'

'My accident was in the news. It wouldn't have taken a lot of digging to discover where I live.' I cursed how glibly I'd reacted at the time: much as I wanted to blame the concussion for my stupidity, the reality was that I was embarrassed about such a ridiculous accident, and thinking only of the slagging I'd get for being hit on the head by a watch.

Noticing the awkward way in which I'd landed on the pavement, I saw how easily I could have broken my other wrist. I'd been taken to hospital, but let out after a check-up because, even though I'd banged my head on the pavement, I hadn't lost consciousness. A bad headache, a black eye and soft-tissue damage, but nothing serious. There was a hairline crack in my cast, but as it was due to come off soon the doctor decided just to patch it. The paramedic who'd treated me at the fair passed through the emergency department while I was waiting to be seen. 'Not another head injury?' He whistled under his breath. 'You're one unlucky woman.'

I shook my head. 'No. I'm the opposite.'

'Perhaps it's coincidence and he just spotted you on your street that evening and grabbed his chance because it was dark and you were alone,' Leon said. 'We won't know until we find him. But it's clear that on Saturday he was tracking you shortly after you left your apartment and you didn't realise . . .' He hesitated, put his hands into his pockets then immediately took them out again. I put my hand over my eyes. I couldn't bear to watch myself any more. What sort of police officer was I that I hadn't noticed I was being followed? Leon touched my arm gently. 'It happens, Susanna. Don't give yourself a hard time about it. Come on, I'll drive you home.'

I took one last look at the crumpled figure on Leon's screen. The jerky movements, the flattened-out, grainy features. The way she landed on the ground, the dog jumping, its lead knotted around her legs. I hardly recognised myself.

FEBRUARY 1919

I

Without the prospect of Forrester's twenty guineas, there is nothing. And because there is now, finally, nothing, what else can she do? To her surprise, acknowledging the end of Violet Hill Investigations brought with it a perverse relief. She tugs down a sheaf of papers from the shelf behind her desk and spots the corner of a book wedged behind them. So that's where her first *ABC Guide to London* went! Best threepence she'd ever spent. How on earth did it get trapped there? She'd given up looking and bought a new one just a month earlier. Violet shrugs. Doesn't matter now.

She drops the papers into a crate without looking at them. It's not much more than half full and she's nearly finished packing. Is this all that her years of work have generated? Chrissie's Underwood was on the never-never, so it'll be going back and Violet can get by without a typewriter. She won't need the third container at this rate. Probably better off: the crates will only take up space at home. She'd be better off throwing the whole lot away and starting again. She might have done that too, but Chrissie had looked so shocked when she suggested it. Might as well be written in invisible ink for all the use she has for them now. Her books of case notes tell of successes, failures, or just the dissatisfaction when a case turned out to be neither but just stumbled to a halt; a half-finished story.

'All your notes what you've been writing up for years? Oh, Violet, you couldn't!' It's typically good-natured of Chrissie to take such an interest, but if Violet had ever shown her the files Chrissie would soon realise that every scrap of paper has turned out to be worthless. Chrissie will be all right: she'll find another position easily enough. A job where she can meet more people would be better for her anyway. She's been very cheerful since the new year began, and seems to spend most of her time either looking out the window or into the mirror. Violet suspects she has her eye on someone, though it's unusual for her to keep that sort of thing to herself. Must be someone special, Violet thinks. Too good to share news of, in case talking about him becomes one of those quick, hard frosts that burns off affection.

Chrissie had cried when Violet returned from Forrester's and told her she was closing the office. 'I'd work for free for you if I could, Vi, you know I would, but I've Mam to think of.' Violet told her she doesn't have to work out her notice, but Chrissie only shook her head and turned up the following day anyway. The end of the fortnight will come around soon enough, and Violet knows she should be glad of the company until then. In the week since she said she was closing, Chrissie has brought some little thing in with her every morning – a piece of cake, an article cut from a magazine, 'What Does Your Future Hold? A Guide for Single Women', a couple of cheap ribbons – as though Violet is an invalid of uncertain appetite and needs tempting with dainty morsels and genteel distractions. Yesterday, Chrissie had bent over, reached into her handbag and produced a ball of wool. Violet, exasperated, said, 'If you think I'm going to bounce around the room after that, like a bloody kitten, you're very much mistaken!' Chrissie – straightening up with a pair of knitting needles in her hand – said, 'I thought I'd keep going on a scarf, unless you've something you want me to do?' She sounded hurt, yet her expression was more wary than upset, as though she suspected Violet was going mad. Well, maybe she was.

Erwin Tanner Esq. Bespoke Outfitters, whose name appeared to have expanded in line with his business ('what happened to 'Tanner's Tailors'?' Violet muttered), jumped at the chance to take over the lease on the office. He must be cut from magic cloth. It's not just the alterations to the demob clothes, but new suits for men going back to work. Wedding outfits too. Chrissie had smiled when Tanner had told them this, which was enough to convince Violet that she's got something going with a man. News of weddings usually made Chrissie frown: additional proof of her own failure, rather than an orange-blossom-scented testament to enduring love.

'He'll find out how much it costs to heat this place soon enough, won't he, Vi?' Chrissie had said and nudged her, but even appealing to Violet's sarcasm about Tanner's parsimony didn't cheer her up. Poor Chrissie, Violet thought again, she's trying so hard when plenty of others in her position would be playing up, all miffed and self-pitying.

Violet reaches in and takes the *ABC* back out of the box. She bought it on the day she set up the office in December

1912. A guidebook to the city: surely a good omen. A promise of a new world waiting for her. The adventures she would have! The guilty acts and hidden deviances, the cruelties and mean injustices she would uncover within the criss-cross cuts of these thousands of streets! She believed no building to be closed to her then, no secret heart inaccessible. Everything was there, just waiting to be seen, and when seen, understood. Decoded. All you had to do was look in the right way. Even when the war came, her attitude hadn't changed as much as she had suspected it would have to. She had expected the war to turn everything upside down, as if one morning you'd woken up to find the ground floor of the house where the attic should have been, and everything jumbled in such a way that meant you could recognise your possessions but they weren't of any use. Only it hadn't happened like that, not really. The life of the city was shaken up for sure, everything dislodged and grubby and vulnerable, yet the ordinary betrayals continued. While there are humans to draw breath, she had soon discovered, there will continue to be cheating and lying, petty pilfering and the sharp knife of ambition. If anything, there were people who took the war as licence to behave in any way they saw fit, justifying their own small crimes by comparing them against the larger tilting of the world around them. When it felt as though there was nothing left to lose, some folk didn't care what they risked. It was like watching a child punch his brother: he'll get away with it because their parents are already heaping blows on each other.

Did she see everything the wrong way? *No*, she remonstrates, that's not so. What about all those successful cases too? There had been plenty. The stolen property retrieved, the errant spouses doggedly tracked down. So, why do they feel like cheap victories now? Anyone could have solved those, she thinks. They were puzzles, no more. Everything she thought she was – what she believed made her different – had been undone by that girl's words. Could there possibly be another world floating all around them? Simply there, waiting for her, for Selbarre, to push an invisible door open a crack? Now that she's witnessed it, it's hard to put the idea to one side. Everywhere she goes, she imagines another existence just outside her vision, outside her understanding. Yet still *there*. Crammed full and pulsing. Waiting.

The map sections of the *ABC* are tattered, the pages folded and marked. So many of the places have an association that has nothing to do with geography, with looking down at a map or understanding scale, but instead everything to do with real lives, where scale is transmutable, and truth found in details, not outlines. *Hammersmith* says a landlord scam, where an elderly man had taken on the lease of three buildings by the river and sublet them, cramming people in room by room, under a false name. He'd taken a fortune, yet not paid out a penny in rent himself. Got away with it for seven months too. He turned a knife on her when she confronted him. She managed to get away and he did a bunk, but the police had caught up with him soon enough. At *Putney* she pauses to think of runaway seventeen-year-old Jacob Astley-Rodgers, whom she eventually tracked down to Abernethy Avenue in Lewisham. His former governess answered the door. She wore a loose, low-cut gown, and blue veins ran across her full breasts, like tributaries. The smile she gave Violet was that of the victorious as she folded her hands under her bulging belly. Major Jacob Astley-Rodgers, the young man's father, responded to Violet's information by cutting his son off entirely, which had surprised her: all that trouble and expense to find his son only to renounce him – cursing him and his unborn grandchild to the devil for good measure. Had his father ever wanted his namesake back? Or was it just about control, about the need to assert his agency over his son's life? Jacob and the governess had died in a fire the following year. A nasty business involving an abandoned husband, it had been in the papers. There was a much older child too, to whom the governess had never admitted. The newspaper reports didn't mention the baby, so Violet doesn't know what happened to it. It would be nice to think it had survived and Major Astley-Rodgers had taken it in, but she knows the baby is probably dead too. Any other ending for it would be the stuff of sentimental serials.

Each page whispers its own tale to her, which only she and it know. *Brixton* is the most resonant map of all. It spells failure, humiliation. She tears that page out.

Her suit is hanging on the hook next to the washstand. 'Nice bit of tweed that.' Tanner had rubbed the lapel between his finger and thumb. 'Belongs to your beau, does it?'

She'd scowled. 'Take your grubby paws off it and get back to your own room. This place isn't yours yet.' She hasn't worn the suit in weeks.

The street door slams, followed by a swift thud-thud up the stairs. But when the feet reach the top – where Violet and Chrissie are accustomed to hearing a pause followed by the creak of the door into Tanner's workshop – it's their own door that is thrown open instead.

'Davey!' Chrissie beams. 'Where've you been the last fortnight? I've been getting worried. You said you'd be gone a week at most. No,' she squeals. 'Don't look!' She shoves the knitting into a drawer. 'It's supposed to be a surprise! This is my – this is Miss Violet Hill. Violet, this is my friend, Mr David Dockery.'

'Davey, please. It is a pleasure to make your acquaintance, Miss Hill. I've heard so much about you.'

'I wish I could say the same.' Violet turns to Chrissie, who is grinning like an idiot.

He's familiar. She's seen him before, more than once, too. Violet has a great memory for faces, always has had, even from a tot. His expression is more of a smirk than a smile. He's handsome, no doubt of it, but trickiness comes off him like heat. Violet could put her nose in the air and inhale it, as you'd sniff a flower, and just know that the smell was owned by the entire thing, not just by a single petal. Poor Chrissie. He's sure to break her heart. It's only a matter of time.

'Chrissie dearest,' he begins, 'you'd never be an angel and help me out, would you?'

Violet sighs. That time, it would appear, has just begun.

'You'd never pop down to Queen Mary's at Sidcup and give a package to my brother Will – him I've told you about? Who comes up to see me sometimes?'

'Can't you give it to him yourself?'

'I've got to go away for a week or so again – no, don't look like that! I can't bear it when you look sad! I've got a bit of business, haven't I? Abroad, this time! I'm on the night boat, so it's not likely I'll get to Sidcup and back before I go, is it?'

'Tonight? *Abroad?*' He might as well have said Saturn as Sidcup, she sounds so incredulous.

'The Continent. I'll be back in a few weeks. Bring you a present too. Something really special.'

'A few weeks? You said a week or so a moment ago.'

'Same thing, isn't it? Now don't take on so, Chrissie, or how can I look forward to seeing you again?' He has been walking around the office while he's talking, roving from the window to Chrissie's desk and back to the window. He turns to the dresser where they keep their teacups and opens a drawer. Lifts the lid of Chrissie's cake tin and peers inside.

'Can't you just post it to him?'

'Course I can, but it's valuable. Anyway, I thought you'd like to meet my brother and have a day out.' His voice is sharper, ready to slice through all resistance. 'And seeing as how he's family and what he goes through with his operations and all . . . He'd love to meet you – he's told me as much, lots of times. And, well, you know how I feel about you, Chrissie. But if you're not bothered, I can take it to the post office now and just hope it gets there, no matter that I'm in such a hurry.' He picks up the parcel and nods, suddenly formal. 'I'm sorry to have troubled you.'

Chrissie goes to him, takes the package from his hands. 'No! Course not, Davey, it's no bother. I was just asking, that's all. Course I'll take it. I'd love to meet your brother. And, you're right, I'll enjoy a day out. You're ever so good to think of me.'

Violet has noticed his restless eyes travel over her desk, pausing over a measly cheque lying on the table next to the ledger, bumping one-two-three over the few coppers half hidden under her pen wiper. It's clear he knows the room as well as Violet does. He looks at the man's suit hanging beside the washstand, then smirks at her, as if to say *I've got the measure of you*. She stares straight back. No man has the measure of me, she thinks. Least of all you.

Chrissie stows the parcel so gently in her bag it could be her firstborn going into its cradle. Now he's at the window again, twitching the curtain aside as if checking for something – someone – down below, but when he catches her looking he pretends to be adjusting it instead.

'I've seen you before,' Violet says abruptly. 'Across the road, outside the pawnbroker's.' She stares at him. But there's something else too. She knows him from somewhere else ... This memory is trickier, shaded. Harder to reach. It's not about his face, it's ... She stares at his back, at the jacket silhouetted by the light coming through the net curtain, and forces herself to account for every detail. It's to do with the slight slope of his left side, an unevenness in the way he holds his arm. She has watched him walk somewhere, somewhere crowded, the angle he was at higher than her, which meant she had been sitting ...

'You might have, indeed you might.' He is at the door, Chrissie hot on his heels. Violet wants to push her back into the room, annoyed with her for being so foolish, for padding along beside him like a puppy hoping to be taken for a walk. 'Goodbye, Chrissie,' he says, and Chrissie pads off back to her basket with her tail between her legs. He might as well have kicked her in the backside.

'Miss Hill,' he turns to Violet. 'It's been my pleasure, believe me.' His eyes are fixed on hers, cold and mocking, as he begins to whistle. The tune is immediately familiar. Eyes bright with tears, Chrissie joins in, singing in a low whisper to herself. '"Sweet violets, sweeter than the roses ... covered all over from head to toe ... covered all over with sweet violets."'

The door shuts behind him, his slow whistle already fading.

'Chrissie!' She can barely get the words out. 'Tell me –
when has he been here before? Quick, Chrissie, the truth. I
know he's been here. When?'

Chrissie looks frightened. 'A few weeks ago, before you
were off with your tooth, he was here one time.'

'Just once?'

'Well, a couple of times, really, when you were out. The
poor soul used to get so cold from waiting on the street like
that, and all I ever did was invite him up for a cup of tea. Oh,
Violet, he's ever so good, I—'

'Did he look at what was on the desk? Anything?'

'I'd never let anyone read your private papers! I've told
him a few things about your work and the old cases and that.'
Flustered now, Chrissie waves her hands about. 'You know
how people love to hear what you do.'

'*Old* cases? What do you mean? Chrissie, have *you* read
them?'

'Well, yes, but, Vi, but you never said not to, and all those
times when I've been here by myself all day ... Your notes are
so interesting. You should write them up into books ...' Her
voice cracks as Violet's face changes from confusion to anger.
'You know, stories of real life, just like in the magazines.'

'Oh, Chrissie, what have you done? Call him back, quick!'

Chrissie doesn't need to be told twice. She's out and
leaning over the banisters in a tick. 'Davey? Davey! You, um,
dropped something.'

Feet on the stairs again, impatient this time. 'What?'

Violet moves in front of Chrissie. 'Wigmore Hall! Last
month. I remember you. You were one of the volunteers he
chose to go up on the stage.' She hears her own words and
realises with fury how stupid they are: *one of the volunteers*

he chose. 'You've been here before. Chrissie's told you things about me, things that . . .' She pauses. *Are you sure about this, Violet Hill?* Be very sure: things that *what*, exactly? Just say she's imagined the whole thing and he's nothing other than a feckless charmer set on breaking hearts. Is she going to be as stupid as Chrissie and spill her own bad business to him? Beside her, Chrissie looks from one face to the other, horrified.

'Pick me, sir!' he says in falsetto, and laughs. 'I'm an honest working man, I swear I am.'

She grabs his arm. 'You work for Selbarre, don't you?'

He shakes her hand away. 'I don't know who you mean.'

'Were you at the London Spiritualist Association with Selbarre on Tuesday last week? It was you set up what happened to me, I know it! You twigged I was investigating Selbarre so you got information out of Chrissie, or went through my notebooks, to use against me.' She's as furious with herself as she is with him. You sap, Violet, she thinks. He is Selbarre's stooge, but you've been his!

'Got proof? Course you haven't.' He's mocking her. 'Because there's none to be had. If you've seen me at a séance it's because I'm an honest devotee of spiritualism.'

'You're a fraud.' She feels red-hot suddenly. He's lying, she knows it. What this man has put her through in the last few weeks!

'*Fraud?* I'll tell you what's fraud, Miss Hill. *This!*' he hisses. 'Everything in this city, this bloody country. Everything I went off to fight for.' He gestures around them. 'And what did I come back to? Nothing, that's what. *That*'s fraud. Them in charge taking advantage of men like me because they have money and we haven't. Have you ever picked up a newspaper and seen your friends, your own bloody family, described as cannon fodder?' She opens her mouth to retort but he cuts her off. 'And tell me, how many poor people did you spot at that fancy séance you went to, eh? *None*, that's how many. Séances are where rich people pay spirits to talk to them, like they're ringing a bleeding bell for a dead servant. Visitations and mediums are for people who can afford them. Poor people, like you and me and Chrissie here, have God and grief and no bodies to bury. Poor people don't get spirits, we get ghosts.'

'Ghosts?' squeaks Chrissie, looking from one face to the other, confused.

'There's a cost to everything, and if folk are willing to pay it because they get what they want that's fine by me. Next time you're at a séance, Violet Hill, think on this: the question isn't whether there's a spirit present or not, but why fools like you are so quick to believe it to be true.'

The door slams behind him. Tanner's door was ajar, and the impact shuts it too, the sound no more than a tiny echo of her own.

II

She is about to use Chrissie's name at the door but the secretary, not interested in who she is, merely waves her in. The crowd is bigger than it was on the previous occasion, though once again she notices many familiar faces. There are two newspaper reporters this time, and she overhears their conversation (variously: the extra column inches to be gained by the presence of the Conan Doyles; the filthy weather; their imminent print deadline; Lady Conan Doyle's modish appearance; the journey time to the nearest public house). Violet takes a seat in the front row, facing the dark, empty stage. She's sweating and nervous. Her stomach twists and she desperately needs the WC but doesn't want to leave the room in case she loses her place. There'd be nothing to evacuate anyway: she's been three times in the last hour, her nerves are that bad.

By seven o'clock every seat is taken. There is an expectant hum, a swish and glide of voices, waiting to be led into silence by a conductor's baton. She hears his name spoken over and over around the room, a sibilant whisper that comes at her from the walls, the floors. *Selbarre, Selbarre.* Taunting her.

What a fool she was to think that a spirit could come for her: Violet alone has been the ghost. Gareth Slatten remains as dead and gone as he was the day he hanged himself in his cell. Her part in his death is unchanged, the fate of his family unchanged, yet everything feels different. He is no more haunting her than she could him.

A quarter past seven. The same plain wooden chair as before sits on the stage, and it remains empty. The entire room seems focused on that single thing, everyone silently filling it with their own expectations, their desperate desires. The soft hum of voices drops: their owners know they must fall silent for him to appear.

Twenty past seven. People begin to grumble. The man next to Violet consults his pocket watch and his neighbour. 'Rum sort of business, isn't it?' he says. 'I've a nine for nine thirty supper to get to. This had better start up sharpish.'

Twenty-five to eight. The crowd are beginning to realise that wherever Selbarre is he's not at the London Spiritualist Association. The secretary walks onto the stage, his hands held aloft. He is flustered and sweating. 'Ladies and gentlemen, it would appear that our guest this evening has been detained elsewhere. Please accept my most sincere apologies, but I think we must assume that this evening's gathering will not now proceed.'

The man next to Violet nudges his neighbour. 'And if Selbarre doesn't appear, you can be damn sure nothing else will!'

It's time.

She rises from her seat and dashes forward. 'Wait!' She

jumps onto the stage. 'Please listen to me! Jean Claude Selbarre is a fraud, an exploiter. He's not here and he won't be here again. He makes a living taking advantage of grief and loss for his own financial gain.'

'Young woman!' The secretary lumbers towards her, one arm raised. 'How dare you! Leave these premises at once.'

She moves further down the stage, bumping into the empty chair. It totters, then falls to the floor with a loud clatter. The room falls still: everyone turns to stare at her. She can feel blood pumping around her body. She has a moment, a second, where it's as though she leaves her own body and understands what it's like to be Selbarre's girl, with all eyes on her, the crowd waiting, desperate to hear words that will mean something to their lives, to their loves. She gulps.

It's as though a fog of sickness is clearing, as though she has shaken off some contagion. The city is just the city, the world just the world, and for good or bad it is nothing more than itself, made up of millions of tiny actions and inactions, decisions and indecisions. They sit together like cogs, even as they all believe themselves to be independent, different. Special. There are no ghosts, no spirits. The living merely haunt each other.

'Selbarre has an accomplice called Davey Dockery, who used underhand means to find information about me, which was then communicated through the medium.'

Levant, the librarian, is on the stage now, too, and between him and the secretary they manage to grab her arms and push her from the stage. Her body is rigid as a shop mannequin. Tight still at her elbows, Levant and the secretary haul her down the aisle and out the door. As she passes where Sir Arthur Conan Doyle is sitting, she says, 'Please, sir, it's true.

I know it. I've met Selbarre's accomplice. I found out their methods. Selbarre means to defraud you!'

'Miss Bullman!' Conan Doyle's voice is loud, so loud that all other sound falls away and everyone turns to him. 'Do not insult this gathering or the Association any further.'

'But, please, it's the truth. Don't you want the truth?'

'I will not hear another word from you!' His voice is thunderous. 'Leave and do not return. You will find no welcome here.'

January 2018

1

The Eurostar from London to Lille and a weekend in a hotel. Alec booked it before telling me. All I had to do was pack. Haynes was on a short tour: Switzerland, Luxembourg, Belgium, finishing in France, where he was a regular fixture on the live jazz scene. Chantelle rarely went with him, preferring to stay at home with their dogs. At Christmas, he'd suggested Alec and I go to the first French gig, in Lille, because it was on a Saturday night. We'd originally said no, we couldn't afford it, but in the days after what I was – once again – forcing myself to call 'the event', Alec changed his mind. He wanted to get me out of London, he said, even for a couple of nights. He'd got such a fright when I'd phoned him after the attack. I managed to stay calm until I heard his voice, but when I started crying that night I thought I'd never stop.

On our first morning in the hotel I woke up exhausted. I had dreamed that Gareth Slatten was in the room with me, standing by the wall, his liveried body visible but his torso and head lost in the flickering shadows. His features weren't distinct, and I had never seen a picture of him, yet, in the curious way of dreams, I just knew it was him, and that he was dark-haired and handsome. It was clearly our flat but also his home: I knew I was waking up in his room, just as he was going to bed in mine. The space was filling with early-morning half-light, soft and milky, as he walked towards me. He was holding a table lighter, but high, so his face and neck were partly obscured. He lowered it to expose the single thick red weal that formed a chokehold around his throat. He stood there, staring at me. Then two hands reached around my neck from behind, softly at first. Once again, I automatically knew who the second man was: Henry Gardiner. As he tightened his grip, I began to struggle against the lurid pink bloated fingers, their skin peeling, splayed around my throat.

I woke with a start, sweaty and dehydrated. For a moment I had no idea where I was. Somewhere down the corridor a door slammed, a woman laughed, a lift began its mechanical clunk and whirr. My hand was twisted up somewhere around my ear and the hard edge of the cast was rammed into my shoulder. I had haunted Henry Gardiner and his servant online and now they were taking revenge in my dreams. I couldn't get back to sleep, and by the time Alec woke up an hour later I was worn out and fractious, not wanting to do anything. On the way to breakfast I scooped up a pile of leaflets in the lobby: if we didn't make a plan to leave the hotel soon I'd end up wasting the morning in our room, irritated and uncertain, flicking between some Europop channel and that repetitive version of the BBC you only ever see when you're abroad that makes you suspect you don't know your own country at all.

Haynes had recommended the hotel – perhaps he had a more *frou-frou* side that France brought out. Old-fashioned buttoned barrel chairs in the dining room were upholstered in a giddy cherry-red velvet, and bright green flock wallpaper was decorated with old movie posters. The frightened faces of *Le Village des Damnés* stared just above my head, and from across the room the shadow of Philip Harrison loomed over a pouting Margaret Warner in *Qui sait?*. I stared at her, picturing Phyllida's features in that perfect face.

'Well, mademoiselle,' Alec said, once we'd both had coffee and I was beginning to feel more human. 'What do you want to do? Palais des Beaux-Arts? The zoo?'

'How about this?' I passed one of the leaflets across the table.

'"The Centenary of the Great War: Commemorating the Battle of the Somme at the Thiepval Monument".' He turned the page over. 'Ah, Suze, I get enough dead at work.' In Alec's frown the perfectly ordinary morning he would have chosen – a ramble around the town followed by lunchtime beers at a pavement café and a boozy snooze on the open-top bus – disappeared. 'Isn't a battlefield tour a bit, I don't know, macabre?' We both hated escorted tours, information squirted like cream from a can into our slack-jawed mouths.

'It's only an hour away, and it's not a group thing. Anyway, I'd like to see some of the countryside. Who knows when we'll be in France again?' Since reading that Henry Gardiner was recorded on the Thiepval Monument I'd been curious to see it. Phyllida struck me as someone who believed that the previous generations are our footnotes, but I had come to realise that wasn't accurate. They aren't our footnotes, we are *theirs*. As the living can't inherit the experiences of the dead, what else can we do but preserve the meaning of their existence?

I knew Alec was worried about me, concerned that the attack had affected me more than I'd said – or understood

– and that my apparent okayness was masking a deeper anxiety. But it wasn't. I *was* okay. I had been terrified, yes. But it wasn't the first time, and it most certainly hadn't been worse than the first time. I was happy to be out of London, happy to be away together. I felt safe. I'd escaped my attacker and, for good or bad, I was *me* again. Every stranger I saw was a face to be automatically recalled, ordered, classified. The familiar constant buzz of recognition had replaced the horrible silence. When I had lashed out with my cast and escaped, the bizarre sensation I'd experienced was like a power surge in my brain. But it was an oddly familiar, comforting feeling, though it had taken me days to understand why: when I'd had glandular fever all those years before, there was a moment when I'd grasped I wasn't ill any more. I was no longer aware of the edges of myself. I was back to being *me*.

My assailant remained unidentified, but Colin was confident they'd get him sooner rather than later. I suspected he was smart enough to steer well clear of me now. Colin had uniformed officers making their presence known outside and near the flat, and as Leon said, 'One more makes too much of a crowd.'

I left the dining room to organise a hire car. When I got back Alec was finishing a phone call and, I was glad to see, looking more cheerful.

'Who was that?'

'Dad. Wondering if we liked the hotel.'

'What surprises me is that *he* does. Where was he ringing from?'

'Brussels.' He picked up the leaflet and sighed. 'Okay, if you're sure this is what you'd like to do. Let's go.'

Years of childhood summer holidays spent in a tour bus had left Alec with a confidence bordering on enthusiasm for European motorways, so we were within a few kilometres of Thiepval, at the northern part of what were the Somme battlefields, by late morning. The landscape had been giving hints as to its secrets for a while. The wide, low end-of-winter fields had faded away, replaced by less natural shapes. There was a large hollowed-out crater at the centre of an otherwise characterless plateau, huge ridges and banks of earth forming a distinct undulation across a huge field, as though the grass had been bumped like a carpet runner, and a long, low line of tree stumps that ended in a thick coppice. I couldn't properly visualise the landscape covered with men and machines, that strange canvas simulacrum of a town that springs up at the edge of battle zones. The best I came up with was a saccharine stew of black-and-white photos and jerky newsreel footage of Tommies smoking and larking about. But what had the land been like a year later, ten years later? Before memory became history.

I stared out the car window at the passing fields, imagining soil mulched by flesh and bones and full of fat worms, producing harvests of rusting barbed wire, shells and bullets, belt buckles and identity tags. The Somme Remembrance Trail road signs began to multiply, a mixture of English and French. Most were official, respectful, though others appeared to be more focused on tourism. I noticed a hand-painted *Centre des visiteurs et boutique de cadeaux* and, just metres later, in the same rough script, a larger sign *Battle site here!* with *Fresh farm produce for sale* underneath. Judging by the number of ads for escorted tours in the guide I downloaded, commemoration was a thriving business. On the remembrance circuit the dead continued to provide a pension for the living.

For thousands of people this area wasn't a roll-call of the dead or a place of memory: it was day-to-day existence in all its benign, pointless ordinariness. They lived here, worked here, travelled these roads every day to school, to hang out with friends, to go to piano lessons, parties and football matches. A place of the present and the future, not the past.

'Do you think we could have missed it?' I asked, as we passed a sign saying *Private Property: The Somme Association – Thiepval Wood Keep Out* and *Warning: Live Munitions. Do Not Step Off the Paths.* 'Shouldn't we be there by now?'

'It's nearly a hundred and fifty feet tall, Susanna! So, no, I don't think we'll miss it.' He was right, of course, because we rounded a corner past yet another wooded area and suddenly there it was: a huge structure looming over a lane leading to Thiepval village. A giant stalking the land, halted with both feet on the ground. Made from great red blocks and lighter-coloured stone piers and plinths, it was all arches: one huge arch holding up smaller arches, arches holding up a tower. High at the corners, white plaster wreaths stared out from the sides like so many empty eyes.

'Wow,' Alec said. 'Talk about putting the mental into monumental.'

We parked at the visitors' centre, a long, glass-fronted building tucked under a ridge of trees and sheltered on either side by higher, grassed ground. It was a low, unobtrusive building, more like a modern railway station than a museum. A reflection of trees and a stripe of oatmeal sky waved gently back at us from the windows. By comparison with the memorial it served, the visitors' centre merely whispered its stories, its voice that of the pond-green leaves overhead.

It was a cold day and there weren't many people about, which always made life easier for me. Because super-recognisers tend to be hyper-aware of their surroundings, very crowded environments can be difficult. When I'd been part of the police team at Notting Hill Carnival it was so crazily crowded that I'd had the oddest sensation of every voice, every whistle grinding to a halt around me as my brain scrabbled to process all the faces. At the till in the visitors' centre I overheard the assistant telling two elderly men in identical coats that it had been an unusually quiet week, but they were expecting the following day to be hectic because a big choral event was planned. Both men wore poppies in their lapels, the plastic red petals shiny as lipstick against the pale grey wool.

To one side of the memorial I noticed a huge cemetery of *les inconnus*, the unknown, laid out in neat lines. Hundreds of pale headstones and crosses pushed through the grass, like rows of baby teeth. We walked between the huge arched legs of the monument and up the wide steps to the plain stone altar at the centre inscribed *Their name liveth for evermore.*

More than seventy-two thousand names had been carved into the stone. Letters, ranks, titles . . . Lives swirled around me, as if lifted from the surface of the stone by a huge wind. A notice explained the unexpected gaps between some entries as newly discovered bodies: since the memorial had been built, identifiable remains continued to be found across all the former battlefields. As they were removed for military burial their names were gently expunged from the stone and the letter-spaces filled with cement. Walking past Pier 6, I noticed small but regular shades in one of the limestone steps. I bent down. Fossils! Tiny ancient creatures that, too, were dead, their remains trapped for ever in the giant's feet. The view across the altar top and through the open sides of the memorial was beautiful: a tall cross in direct line of sight and, past it, a jigsaw of fields and hedgerows on the hill opposite.

'This place is overwhelming, isn't it?' I said. 'It forces you to remember what happened.'

He looked at me curiously. 'We're not *remembering*, Suze. All we're doing is sticking a toe into history. Remembering is what I watch people do at work. And it's sad and messy and sometimes horribly angry, but weird as it sounds, it's a living thing. It's real. Without a personal reason to be here, we might as well be at whatever the equivalent is in Germany.'

'You think I'm being sentimental, don't you?' Perhaps this was what he'd meant when he'd queried what he called my 'nostalgia' about the history of our house. Perhaps nostalgia was nothing more than tragedy plus time.

'No.' He paused. 'No, not that. But you could legitimately view this entire place as a monument to folly, at a time when wars are being fought all over the world for similar reasons. If you think about it, you have a more legitimate human connection with the memorial at Ground Zero. No one inside the Twin Towers signed up to fight a war. They were murdered.'

Alec was right. I had no historical link to Thiepval but, unlike him, I did feel a living one. My being there – Alec too, whether he liked it or not – was an echo of strangers' actions, played decades into the future. Memory was not about looking backwards: instead it helps future-proof our actions. Only two weeks earlier, remembering the terrified child I once was had saved the adult me. I didn't have to lay claim to a soldier in order to be curious or to care. The names on the memorial were more a summoning-up than a summing up, permission for the living to maintain contact with the dead. They proved something I understood only too well: terror is never further from you than a warring bullet, a dark street, a strong hand.

We had walked about ten feet away by that point. I was silently scanning the lists of names. 'Look!' I said. 'Up there! Pier and Face 4 A.' In the car earlier I had checked the Graves Registration Report. My dead snap was just another 'G', a ripple in a stream of other Gardiners, Gardners, Garlands, even a Garter. Who had last looked for his name here? Presumably his family would have visited a memorial that included him, but what about his children's children? His grandchildren would have been of the Second World War – maybe for them a bayonet-wielding grandpapa was just another unknown body. But eighty, a hundred years later, curiosity can recharge. The past becomes safe to visit.

The thick red mark around Gareth Slatten's neck in my nightmare was a reminder of his tragic fate. But had he not committed suicide, he could have sat out the war in prison.

Unlike Henry Gardiner, Slatten might have survived and gone home to his family afterwards. Starting a new life must have been a relatively straightforward business in the general upheaval after the war. His best bet, I realised – ironic as it was to the memory of his former employer – would have been to reinvent himself as a returned soldier rather than a shamed servant.

The two elderly men I'd noticed earlier shuffled past. The smaller of the two wasn't wearing his poppy and I wondered if he had lost it or left it on a grave. 'Uncle Al never spoke about it,' his friend said. 'No matter how many times he was asked. I suppose he just wanted to get on with his life.'

'Yes.' His companion nodded. 'I think we should get our cup of tea now.'

I wondered if Phyllida's battle-scarred father wanted only to get on with his life, though from what she'd said, every glance in the mirror must have dragged him back. But the present will always paper over the past, and two, three, four generations back needed Uncle Al, and Phyllida's father, and the hundreds of thousands of men and women like them, to keep going about the business of creating us, the future generations.

Alec pointed at the *Known unto God* inscription on a headstone. 'I wonder how many atheist soldiers there were? Seeing these going up can't have been much good.' He had an uneasy relationship with religion: he had no faith, but he was surrounded by it at Winterson's. It was the pitch of belief he encountered that made him uneasy: in grief people either cleaved to their God or berated Him for the loss they had suffered. Either way, Alec found it suffocating.

'Dad!'

'*Dad?*'

'DAD!' Alec called again. 'Over here!' Haynes rounded the corner of the memorial, waving. The contrast between the handsome man in a black suit striding confidently past the hushed and respectful Home Counties visitors made me want to giggle.

'What are you doing here?' I asked, when he'd hugged us in turn. Alec looked delighted, a prisoner of war-tourism liberated by a single soldier. From his lack of surprise I assumed they had arranged the encounter on the phone that morning.

'Pit stop on the way to Lille.' He smiled.

'From *Brussels*?'

'Why not? I thought you might like a late lunch.' Haynes moved past me and turned to the horizon. He didn't seem particularly interested in the memorial, more the landscape it was set in. 'The Harlem Infantry Regiment band brought jazz to France in the First World War,' he said. 'Impressive, huh? They were such a tough regiment, the Germans called them the Hell Fighters. No man captured, no trench surrendered, and not a single foot of soil lost to the enemy.'

'Do you want to look around?' I asked, hopeful I'd found a more kindred spirit in Haynes than his son. But much as he loved the legacy of the 369th Regiment band, he declared himself a conscientious objector to battlefield museums.

'Playing their music is the only worthwhile tribute I can think of. Come on,' he added. 'I know a restaurant in Albert – it's the best food for fifty miles.'

Haynes and Alec walked ahead towards the car park. The memorial was behind me, the shadow it cast creating an enormous monochrome version of itself on the ground. Haynes turned. 'I was just telling Alec how some of the regiment never went back to the States. They stayed on because the French treated them well, the way they should have been treated back home. That's why the jazz scene here got such a good start. I'll play a few things later, see what you think.'

'Thanks.' I nodded. 'That'd be great.'

He smiled. 'You know what the Harlem Hell Fighters' motto was? "Don't Tread on Me".'

It was an almost oppressively calm and ordered place, both soothing and sad. Back at the visitors' centre I watched a woman choose souvenirs and wondered if Alec was right after all, and when the blood-warmth of chaos drains away, an artificially heated curiosity gets pumped in. He smiled and put his arm around me. 'Yeah. When you think about it, commemoration is nothing more than taxidermy.'

Because of the unexpectedly long stop for lunch – the restaurant Haynes took us to, a small, unassuming room set up for no more than twenty people, was fantastic, as his choices always were – it was after three when we set off for Lille. While the roads were still quiet country ones, I asked Alec to pull in. He drove down an unsigned laneway for a hundred metres or so and stopped by a gate. I got out of the car. The air had that tang of cold that shivers up from the ground as the sun begins to drop. I listened hard, just as I had weeks earlier, lying on the ground on Primrose Hill. Birdsong. Ticks from the car's cooling engine. In the distance, something weighty, throbbing. I leaned on a metal gate and stared across the fields. A horse ambled over, only to lurch away when I extended my hand to pat its nose.

Lille was somewhere north of me, and home was another planet. An uneven hedgerow bisected the field, a stubby green monster rising unevenly through the crops, studded with bits of scrap metal. A kilometre or so to my left was a small wood, the trees dense, secretively close. I had shadowed Henry Gardiner from life into death. Had he found himself nearby and wept, wishing for home? Silently desperate for the touch of his family, the feel of fresh newsprint on his fingers, the heat of his own fire? The battlefields seemed more real to me at that gate than anywhere else. The very soil, fertilised by death, was the memorial. I thought of Phyllida's remark about the men who held their greatest works inside them as they died, that there was no enemy in poetry. What words, what incredible, unknowable ideas had drained away into these fields?

The underground dead sighed and stirred, then settled back to sleep once more.

I got into the car and Alec drove us back to the hotel.

FEBRUARY 1919

I

Sir Arthur Conan Doyle's front door is opened by a butler who could teach even Forrester's maid lessons in rudeness. He looks Violet up and down. 'The master sees callers only by prior appointment.'

'It's urgent,' Violet replies. 'Tell him it's important business concerning Mr James Forrester.'

With ill-grace, he allows her in. She is shown to the study. Her instinct is to have a flick through the papers on his desk, but she resists, because either the master or, worse, his wife would be sure to catch her, and she's about to be in enough trouble without getting herself accused of deception into the bargain. She takes her gloves off and pushes the fingertips of her left hand into the palm of the right. Her ankle still aches from being shoved off the stage the night before. She breathes hard, trying to steady herself, willing herself to be as lucid, as definite, in the conversation as she is sure *he* will be. She remembers a similar room, over five years earlier, which had also smelt of woodsmoke and cigars. How she had appealed to Henry Gardiner, begged him to help Hannah – who had once been, as Violet reminded him, his employee, too – in her distress, but in return had been threatened with ruin and thrown out of his house. Well, that will not happen again, she is sure of it. She had stayed quiet then, accepted his threats as law, because she had felt as though she had too much to lose. But now? It's all gone already, so why stop?

Just as she had at Forrester's, she stands at the window and watches the street below. These are grander houses, set further back from the pavement, but aside from that, the world appears to be going about its morning business in a way that feels uncannily similar to her visit to Cheyne Place the previous week. As if to prove her right, a front door opens and an elderly woman appears. She is dressed in full mourning and leaning heavily on a silver-topped cane. A younger woman, plainly dressed, hovers behind her, fussing with bags and coats. A nursemaid dressed identically to the woman employed by Forrester's neighbour passes by, hand in hand with a little girl. That this tableau is so similar pleases her: she wants London's children to have constancy, because clearly its old no longer do.

The door opens. He looks surprised, confused, but she can't blame him for that. 'Miss Bullman? What on earth are you doing here? Leave at once.'

'Please, Sir Arthur, just a minute of your time. Please. I've come to apologise and to explain.'

'With regard to the former, you most certainly should. As to the latter, I don't want to hear your explanation. I believe I had already told you that the unsubstantiated claims of doubters are of no interest to me.'

His clock strikes the quarter past. She's been silently counting for the last two minutes. *Sharp*, she said on the note. If he's late, she'll already have been sent packing. From below she hears the doorbell. Finally! The study door opens but before the butler can speak, a man is pushing past him, 'Arthur? I got your card. What is—'

'James?'

'Miss Hill?' Forrester's already flushed cheeks turn a brighter, mottled red. 'What are you doing here?'

'Who's Miss Hill?'

'She is. Violet Hill.'

'No, this lady is Miss Chrissie Bullman.'

Forrester glares at the butler, who backs slowly out of the room, clearly reluctant to abandon the farce now playing on the stage of his master's study. Violet takes a deep breath. 'I apologise for lying to you, Sir Arthur. My name isn't Chrissie Bullman, it is Violet Hill. That much of what he says is true.'

He ignores her. 'James, you know this woman?'

'I don't understand . . . I received a note asking me to call at a quarter past eleven sharp. A matter of emergency, it said.' Forrester holds out the calling card to show the few words scribbled 'in haste' on the back.

'That was from me,' she says. 'Sir Arthur gave me his card when we met at the London Spiritualist Association two weeks ago. You wouldn't have come at my request, would you?'

'Arthur, send for the police at once, for your own safety. Whoever this woman is, she's obviously lost her reason.'

'What do you mean, James, "whoever this woman is"? You yourself just told me her name is Violet Hill.'

She is gratified to see the beads of sweat forming on Forrester's forehead, and before he can reply, she says, 'Sir, please, my name really is Violet Hill. I'm a private investigator. Mr Forrester wants to end your association with spiritualism and hired me to find proof that Jean Claude Selbarre was a fraud. But Selbarre was too good. He fooled me. Until yesterday, when I found out how he'd acquired the information on me that he used at the séance. I followed his accomplice, who led me to Selbarre. But not only to him . . .' She pauses for breath and Forrester opens his mouth to protest. Conan Doyle raises a hand, signalling he should stay quiet. 'Please, sir,' she continues, nervous. 'Will you hear me out?'

He nods. The men are silent as Violet Hill tells her story.

The previous day, she had followed Davey Dockery as soon as he left her office on Cleveland Street. 'Window now!' she shouted at Chrissie. 'Keep watching him, and signal me when I get downstairs.' Violet grabbed the suit and cap from the peg by the door and was dressed and at the front door in what felt like seconds. Cleveland Street is long, and it was easy enough to keep him in her sights. She had shadowed him for the best part of ten minutes when he turned onto Ebury Road, a street of narrow white plaster and brown brick, a blend of private residences, small hotels and a loose scattering of shops. He stopped about halfway down. From across the road she saw a sign: Merton House Private Hotel. White-painted façade gone grey, black door, shutters on the windows – the sort of accommodation that looks so perfectly ordinary as to be invisible. She wasn't able to make out who opened the door to him before he vanished inside.

Within minutes, he reappeared with a suitcase. The girl from the séances walked slowly behind him, dragging a carpet bag. Violet lurked in the shadows of the milliner's doorway across the road. (She looked like nothing more than a small man in a cheap suit and hat, leaning against a wall flicking through his newspaper, but does not tell her two listeners this.) The girl's face was impassive as ever. Davey said something to her that caused her to shake her head. He touched her arm and smiled that wolfish grin. She turned away from him. The girl stopped in the middle of the pavement and lifted her head to the sky. She blinked slowly, several times. Her skin was rich as ebony against the cheap decaying greys that surrounded her. A hansom pulled up and Davey ushered her in, shoving rather than helping her. The front door opened again, and Selbarre himself appeared, holding a suitcase. He pulled down his hat to shade his eyes and tugged a scarf over his chin and mouth. He might have been a soldier hiding a wound. He, too, stowed a case in the hansom, but didn't get in immediately because . . .

She pauses. 'But didn't get in immediately because . . .'

'Yes, Miss Bullman – Hill? Whatever your name is.'

She breathes out, feels her body relax ever so slightly. Whether Sir Arthur Conan Doyle believes her or not she has no idea, but he is going to let her finish her story at least. '. . . Selbarre didn't get into the cab because Mr Forrester appeared from around the corner and stopped him.'

'*What?*'

She crossed the road and waited nearby, as if slowly counting pennies from her pocket for two soldiers begging in the doorway beside the hotel. She watched as Forrester ran forward and grabbed Selbarre's arm, his voice loud and angry. 'And where the damnation do you think you're going?'

'That's none of your business,' Selbarre snapped, his accent harder and with less flourish than she had heard it before.

'It's my business when it's on my account, damn you! I paid you to fail, so why do I continue to hear reports of your success?'

'Your account? Why, that's worth less than nothing! You might as well have robbed me, with the amount you offered to pay. Our deal is off. The real money's still out there.'

'You will fulfil your contract, Selbarre. I've spent hundreds on you already!'

'And was it part of our contract to have me followed by that bitch? It wasn't enough just waiting for me to make a fool of myself, was it? You wanted to do the job for me. Your intention was to tell me I hadn't earned my fee and leave me broke and disgraced, I suppose. Well, if you want your money returned, go and tell your boss your plan.'

The cab window opened and Davey looked out at Selbarre.

'What do you think, Dockery?' Selbarre continued. 'What would Sir Arthur prefer to hear? That his employee here was playing a trick on him or that he sought to publicly humiliate him?'

'Well, Mr Selbarre, sir, I'd have to say that either of those awful fates would haunt a man for life.' Davey grinned. 'Lucky, isn't it, that we're so talented in that department?' Selbarre laughed, climbed into the hansom and slammed the door.

She relates the events as carefully as she knows how, watching Conan Doyle the entire time. She does not say that as the cab pulled away a figure appeared at its window. The girl stared straight at Violet, as though she knew who was watching, and why. A pale, pinkish palm appeared and pressed the glass. Was it in farewell or distress? Violet had an urge to run across the road and grab the door handle. Suddenly the palm disappeared, as though her arm had been pulled back sharply.

The girl, Davey and Selbarre were gone.

'And that was the last I saw of them,' Violet says. The grandfather clock chimes the half-hour as if to underline her words. The two men are staring at her. Forrester is standing by the desk. Conan Doyle had sat down while she was speaking. Forrester is furious – even his silence tells her that. He's also thinking fast, she can see that too. He paid Selbarre to ingratiate himself with Conan Doyle, then contracted her to unmask him. It was clever: by hiring a fraud to begin with, he didn't have to take the risk of there *not* being proof. But Selbarre had realised he could make a great deal of money, far more than he would ever earn in two months or so as Forrester's lackey. To honour their arrangement would mean a fee, of course, but also disgrace and a swift return to wherever he had come from. He knew if he left town quickly that Forrester would never take the risk of unmasking them: he had too much to lose.

'He hired me to prove him a fraud and I couldn't. I failed. But Selbarre knew he'd been too greedy and pushed too far, that Mr Forrester wasn't prepared to put up with it any longer. I think that's why he kept leaving London for engagements around the country – to stockpile as much as he could, knowing he'd have to get away in a hurry. I'm terribly sorry, Sir Arthur,' she says, then stops. Year after year she has given clients information that they'd thought they wanted yet couldn't bear to hear, and each time is as bad as the first. She is used to walking into a room a saviour and out of it a leper. 'I don't want to bring you any further grief, but you have to know the truth.' But she knows well that a private temporary embarrassment is nothing compared to the public shame he will suffer should the whole business be revealed in the newspapers. She wishes him no humiliation, and certainly no harm.

She faces Forrester. 'There was no one to connect Selbarre to you except me, and as far as you knew, I was taken in by the whole business and had resigned your commission. It didn't succeed, yet its failure could never find its way to your door.'

'Is this true, James?' Conan Doyle's palms rest heavily on the edge of his desk as he rises. The backs of his hands are pale and dotted with liver spots.

'Of course not! I tell you I've never seen the woman before. I was confused about the name. I don't know who she is.'

'But you do know,' Violet says. 'Sir Arthur, here is the letter he wrote to the London Spiritualist Association, claiming I was his friend's niece visiting town and requesting admittance.' She holds it aloft to show Sir Arthur. Her name isn't on it, but there is no denying Forrester's hand or signature.

'Explain yourself, James,' Conan Doyle says. 'Immediately.'

Forrester blinks, several times. 'Of course,' he says, ignoring her and looking at his employer, his face serious. 'Yes, of course.'

His story is a good one, she has to give him that. He's clever. He was dubious of *some* – he leans on the word, gives it as much weight as he can – of the spiritualists and mediums he encountered with Sir Arthur. He wanted to try to separate the wheat from the chaff, so to speak, so as to avoid any pain for his employer – no, so much more than that! – his dear friend of many years, especially now, at such a time of loss for the family. He lifts his hands in supplication as he says, 'My motives were solid, Arthur, though perhaps my methods lacked finesse. I can appreciate that now.'

'What fee did Forrester offer you?' Conan Doyle turns to her.

'Twenty guineas, sir.' She blushes.

'And Selbarre – is that even his real name?'

Forester shakes his head. 'I don't know. He is a – a magician. I met him during your last speaking tour in America. I saw his performance in a hotel I was staying in, after you had left for an engagement in Ottawa.'

'A conjurer is paid for his time, a man doing a performance of fakery. But *you*? You have purported to be a friend, an ally, to have sympathised with me in the very depths of my grief. You, sir, are the fake. You are a sinner in a way that Selbarre – or whoever he may be – is not. Yours has been the cruellest sort of deception.'

Violet looks from one man to the other. The silence in the room feels oppressive. It excludes her. She has no place there. She puts the letter on Sir Arthur Conan Doyle's desk. She has no further need of it.

She opens the door and trips over the butler, who is kneeling with an eye at the keyhole. 'Show's over,' she says, pushing past. She walks away, down the stairs and out into the bright street below.

'Wait! A moment!' Conan Doyle lumbers down the steps behind her.

She sighs. 'I'm sorry, sir. I don't want to bring you pain, but I felt you ought to know the world you're involved in.'

'Miss Hill, you must not think me so faint-hearted as to conflate the entire world of spiritualism with a single man!'

'But if Selbarre is a fraud, then surely so are many others?'

He shakes his head. 'I'm talking about Forrester. Tell me, do you like Robert Browning's poetry? His line "There may be heaven, there must be hell" is pertinent. Human nature is more aligned with wicked spirits than good – or even benign – ones. That does not mean good spirits don't exist, of course it doesn't. It merely means that sometimes we must work harder for them. With them.'

'But it was Mr Forrester who set out to trick you first! How can it not affect what you believe?'

'What it affects is my faith in my business manager. Do you know how much he paid out to Selbarre?'

'No.'

'Presumably it included the passage from America and all his upkeep here, in which case it must have been considerable. For James, pecuniary disadvantage will be punishment enough, I suspect. I knew he didn't share my convictions. He believes in money and power and material possessions. That is not a world I want for myself, but it is a world I recognise as important for the man I pay to run my affairs.'

His determination to wring logic from his beliefs, no matter how thin events render them, dumbfounds her. When Violet decided to be a detective – and the decision had been that, to *be* one, rather than to work as one – she had believed that the truth was the only answer. But for this man, just as with Hannah Slatten, with Henry Gardiner, what a person does with the truth matters just as much.

'Were you in London on the day of the Armistice, Miss Hill?'

'Yes.' Violet nods. Who will ever forget that strange day? It had felt as though at every turn she would come across a party, with everyone as welcoming as if they'd always known each other, but it didn't happen, no matter how far she walked.

'That afternoon I was sitting in the lobby of the Savoy Hotel in the Strand – do you know it?' She nods. 'I was waiting for James. He had some papers he needed me to sign urgently. My son Kingsley was dead, ten days dead. When I sat down I couldn't be sure how I had done so, how my legs had brought me to the hotel, though I knew where I was. Every movement was made automatically, as though I was being guided to where I needed to go. I was sitting there and a woman came through the revolving doors. She went around twice, in fact, before entering the hotel. She had a flag in each hand and waltzed around the lobby alone, slowly, then spun herself back out into the street. I didn't know her, nor have I seen her since. That's what the world is now, for me. My very essence is out of time with everyone else's. I am turning in a contrary direction, with no ability to right myself. Spiritualism reduces that. It makes the clock strike in harmony.'

He sounds so sad. And though he refuses to accept that her concerns have any validity, it's impossible not to believe that this poor man, made vulnerable by pain and despair, is being duped. And not just by Selbarre – who knows what other cruel-spun webs he's fallen into, fooled by the loom and shadow of another man's greed?

'In twelve years I lost my first wife, my brother, two brothers-in-law, two nephews and then my Kingsley. The coldness that brings, it's almost unbearable. That loss in the noumenal world cannot be borne without a gain, surely. And the profit is in the world of the spirit, which returns some of the missing warmth. My family has been broken, but with the world of the spirit it can be remade. Imagine looking through a dirty window and just for a second there is a clean patch of glass and you see something – never enough to make out the whole picture, but just enough to convince you that what you're looking at is the *right* picture. That's how I felt. I still do.'

Is it awful to be impatient with the ways grief is manifest in others? Is she cruel even to think it? The way he talks about it makes grief sound like a disease. And for those who, like him, didn't want to share the burden of their grief, who actively tried to contain the disease, well, who's to know how deep it can take hold?

They stand on the pavement in silence for a moment. The nursemaid and child Violet spotted earlier are walking towards them, hand in hand. With her free hand the little girl is clutching a couple of primroses. The creamy heads are already wilting, despite being so fresh as to have soil still adhering to the stalks.

'Goodbye, Miss Hill,' he says. 'I appreciate your attempt to prevent what you saw as my being taken advantage of, but I have no need of your assistance.'

Selbarre was as equally real and fake as a priest in a pulpit. Truth exists, but Sir Arthur Conan Doyle wants only shades of it. He is no different from the child ahead on the path: being led by another's grip. And in his hands he thinks he's clutching life but he's not: it's death.

Violet's old *ABC* is still lying on the desk from the day before. She puts her head on it and closes her eyes. She is exhausted. London whispers to her from its tattered pages. Tales of promises and betrayal, of pain and glory. She's been a fool, she thinks. Not foolish because she fell for Selbarre's con. No, she will forgive herself that. She can't forgive herself for what she never understood until today: facts don't create truth, they shadow it. Life as it plays out is impossibly different, more alien, than anything a single human mind could conceive. Clients didn't hire her to uncover some necessary, vital truth: they hired her to correct imbalances in their lives. To right temporary wrongs in loss and gain.

Her fingers touch the worn cover of the book under her head. She imagines its pages coming to life around her, suddenly animate. She watches herself swoop winglessly around thousands of city streets. The map of London lies below her, at once perfectly familiar and entirely new when seen from the air. The scar of the Thames cuts the city; roads curve and loop. Peeping in and out of windows, high and low, her drop and rise are that of invisible currents. Roofs are as easy to lift as those on a doll's house. Gently, gently, she can prise them back one by one and peer inside, her breath that of a zephyr, and see the people of the city going about their lives. And everything playing out on those private stages – the improbable, the curious, the coincidental, the deliberate cross-purposes – makes a mockery of facts.

The door slams. 'Look at this!' It's Chrissie, a newspaper held high in her right hand. Her hat is pushed back, her round face flushed. She waggles the paper even more furiously and leans over, panting, her left hand on her knee.

'How can I when you're waving it around like that?' Violet grabs it from her and reads the headline aloud. '"Church Figures Fear for the Peace." What of it?'

'Not that! *Here.*' Chrissie flips the paper around to the bottom of the front page. *Leading Society Spiritualist Accused of Fakery! Gathering at London Spiritualist Association Thrown into Confusion!* 'That's a bit much, surely,' Violet mutters. And underneath that, in – thankfully – smaller type: *Woman Identified by Onlookers as Miss Chrissie Bullman.*

'Ah.'

'*Ah*? Is that all you got, Violet Hill?'

'I have an explanation, Chrissie!'

'How'm I meant to find a new position with my name all over the papers like this?'

'You don't have to.' It's only as she hears herself say the words that she realises this life is *her* truth, and what else can she do but continue with it? She, too, has losses and gains to balance if she is to live in a way that's honest to herself. 'Not if you don't want to, that is.'

'But the money?'

'I don't know. I'll think of something. Your typewriter's not been collected yet?'

'No.'

'Good. First, send James Forrester a note, telling him that his account has twenty guineas owing and he's to pay up double-quick.'

Chrissie giggles. It's a ha'penny wasted, Violet knows, but the price of a stamp buys her the right to imagine his face when he opens the letter.

February 2018

1

'Some people say they miss the cast when it's removed.' The doctor raised her voice over the whirr of the small electric saw. 'You'd be surprised how used to them you get.'

'Not me,' I said, watching my left arm appear from its grubby cocoon. My skin was the pinky-white of a newborn animal. Tiny flecks of white dust stuck to invisible hairs, creating an oddly furry effect. I flexed my fingers and watched the uncertain pull of tendons as far as my elbow. It felt as though it belonged to someone else. When I stood up to leave, the world was lop-sided. I could feel myself listing slightly to the right, as though unaccustomed to a new weightlessness on the other side. I let my left arm drop to my side, but it felt odd, just swinging there, so I bent my elbow and tucked my fist up near my chin, as though I still had a sling on. Then I realised how daft that was, and stuck my hand into my pocket instead.

'See what I mean?' she said.

I looked at myself in the disorienting blue lights of the outpatient toilets. My face was thin, and because I hadn't done more to my hair for weeks than run a brush through it, my natural brown had grown out through the bright red colour I usually dyed it. I looked ghoulish, a stranger to myself. My arm was pale, the skin still puckered as though I'd fallen asleep in the bath and the water had gone cold around me.

On the evening we'd arrived back from France, Colin had phoned with news that my attacker had been identified as John Kirk, a thirty-four-year-old from St Albans. He didn't have a record. No cautions, not even a traffic violation. The previous week JD had been tracking Eric Alnez, a man with a seriously impressive sleight of hand in high-end technology shops. In the background of a shot, JD spotted my attacker. On a hunch, he re-examined all the Alnez footage, and snapped Kirk in three frames. When Alnez had been arrested the previous day, he had given up Kirk's name as an accomplice but claimed not to have any idea where we might find him. 'It won't be long now.' Colin sounded positively chirpy. 'You'll be at an ID parade before you know it. In the meantime, you know we're looking out for you just as hard as we're searching for him, okay?'

'Okay,' I told him, trying to sound equally positive. 'Thanks.'

Anytime I'd been outside the flat alone since we'd got back from France, I'd been careful to stay in busy, well-lit places, so instead of walking home I got a bus from the hospital. My next stop was the hairdresser. I would be back at work on Monday and I wanted it to be as though I was just returning from the Christmas break. As though everything that had happened hadn't happened. It was a need I always had whenever something unexpected occurred: a desperate urge to right the ship, to reset the previous course, no matter how large or small the enforced shift in direction, rather than just accept it as part of the normal to and fro of living and allow myself to change with it. My mother attributed it to those months spent in hospital as a child followed by 'your terrible experience' – her phrase for 'the event' – less than a year later. How else was a little girl to cope, was her theory, unless she could insist that the world around her reverted to what was knowable and familiar?

Whatever the reason, as I sat in the hairdresser's, watching my hair return to its false red, I realised how much I needed my job in order to be myself. There were new cases waiting for me, new faces to learn and follow. I sat and flicked through back issues of gossipy magazines, sipped coffee, pretending I was someone who did this sort of thing on a weekday morning. Various Kardashians skimmed past in a blur of boobs and bums, and identikit women in bodycon dresses stood awkwardly in their pristine kitchens announcing how happy, sad, loved-up, how determined to put his cheating behind them they were. Kylie's engagement was over, but in the next magazine there she was, with a chap, newly loved-up. That was quick, I thought. Then I saw the magazines were in the wrong order – Kylie's new man *was* the heartbreaker. Life, back to front. It was how I felt about myself: no matter how much I wanted otherwise, I knew it would be different, that my job would never be quite the same again. How could it be, now that I had watched myself fall and rise in the shadows?

Walking home, the assistant in Claire Voyante's opticians spotted me and waved, her face framed in the giant lens sticker on the window. I thought of Phyllida and the one-woman crime spree she'd been on the day I met her, and mentally retraced her steps from that morning: Claire Voyante's, Camille's, the Primrose Pharmacy, Pavement Books. I didn't walk up as far as Gordon's Kitchen, the café where I'd thought I was having a word with Phyllida about her habits, but realised afterwards that she had been having a word with me about mine. How many times had she done that circuit, or some equivalent of it? Much as her life story fascinated me, I didn't want to learn more than I already knew about her pilfering habits, especially now the local station had my phone number as a contact for her. I seriously doubted whether she was going to change her ways simply because Gary Cook and I had both asked her to, so it was best I wasn't involved. There had been a recklessness to her, a disregard for authority that was the result of having once cared very deeply, rather than never having cared at all.

In the post-lunch lull, Regent's Park Road wasn't particularly busy. The local worker bees who'd buzzed out for sandwiches were back at their desks; the babies were napping; the school kids who clustered outside the shops every afternoon hadn't appeared yet. Two young lads wandering up the road caught my eye. As they passed a bike tied to a railing, without breaking their conversation they both kicked the lock. My shout of 'Hey, stop that!' was acknowledged with a single finger.

On a whim I decided to go to Winterson's and see if Alec could knock off early. I sat in the shelter and flicked through the news while I waited for a bus. Across the road was a Victorian pub, the Five Lamps, one of the few local boozers to escape the gentrification of the street. One night shortly after I'd moved in with Alec I was on the top deck as the bus pulled up to the stop closest to the pub. I had a perfect view of the pool room on the first floor. A couple were sitting beside the window, alone, one on either side of a wide table. He put his glass down, leaned across and punched her hard in the face. She fell backwards, out of sight. The bus shuddered and moved on.

A van pulled in to the bus stop beside me, the open passenger window framing my view of the pub door. The driver fiddled with his GPS and ignored me. Through the van windows I noticed a man wearing jeans and a wax jacket leave the pub, slamming the door behind him. Quickly I turned my back as if reading the timetable posted on the bus shelter, though I was watching his reflection in the Plexiglass. From where he stood, John Kirk wasn't in a position to get a good look at me, but I tugged my scarf up just in case. He stood outside the pub, smoking, scrolling his phone.

My fingers shook as I speed-dialled the station. 'Gary? Susanna Tenant,' I said quietly, desperately willing the tremble out of my voice. Then, while I waited for the sound of a squad car, I called Leon. A dog with three legs loped down the far side of the road, its gait loose and uneven. It stopped to piss against a black SUV parked a few feet away from the Five Lamps. Kirk threw his cigarette at the dog, took a car fob from his pocket and pointed it at the car. *Shit*, I thought. It was probably the same car that had frightened me the day I'd first met Phyllida.

He got into his car just as the van that had been shielding me from view drove off. I heard the sudden shriek of a siren. As the squad car rounded the corner I stepped off the pavement and gestured towards the SUV awkwardly manoeuvring out of the parking space. Kirk looked out the window. He saw me. Stared at me. I remembered every time I had seen those eyes. How I had watched them over and over, frozen on a screen. And now they were looking back at me. Blinking, alive. There could never have been a more familiar stranger. He put a hand to the car door, as if about to get out again, but suddenly clocked the squad car. Instead, he revved up and sped off down the middle of the road, just as a red BMW made a fast turn out of a narrow mews entrance. The BMW drove directly into his path. The speed Kirk was going at, he lost control immediately. As his car bucked and thrashed, the scene seemed to pause, turned into a piece of footage. But at work I was in charge, I could pause, rewind, fast forward, make strangers dance to the whim of my finger. On the street, all I could do was watch as his car rose like a shining black monster and lurched forward, disappearing with an ocean's roar of breaking glass.

Then: sirens, screaming, a shrieking chorus of alarms. And over them all, my voice, shouting as I ran to where the car protruded from the front window of Gordon's Kitchen. A buggy lay on its side just inside what remained of the front window frame. A ripped blanket embroidered with the name *Tom* was knotted around its mangled wheels. In a piece of luck that would surely haunt Tom's parents for life, the buggy had been empty at the time of impact because Tom had been hiding under a table at the back of the café, persistently ignoring his childminder's requests to come out.

There was a single fatality.

She had been sitting alone, in her usual seat behind the door, beside the window.

Phyllida's death by dangerous driving would soon be joining three sexual assaults, a single charge of assaulting a police officer and, because of his newly found connection to Eric Alnez, three accessory charges, on John Kirk's charge sheet.

2

I'd been only home ten minutes but was already draining my second large glass of wine when Alec walked through the door.

'Celebrating?' he asked, looking curiously at the open bottle on the table in front of me. 'I bet it feels good to be rid of that cast.'

'I saw him. On Regent's Park Road.' My hand shook as I topped up my drink. 'I saw him, John Kirk. I called the local guys and Leon to come and get him and—'

And then, then I began to cry.

'Are you hurt?' He dropped onto the sofa and put his arms around me. He sounded frightened. 'What happened? Jesus, Susanna, why didn't you call me?'

I had wanted to phone him, of course I had, but Leon and Colin arrived on the scene just minutes after the crash, and if I'd spoken to Alec in front of them I would have broken down, just as I had on the evening Kirk tried to assault me. In the footage of my attack I had looked so vulnerable, breakable, and I couldn't bear the idea of my colleagues, my friends (in Leon's case at least) thinking of me as a victim. 'I'm sorry but, honestly, I'm fine. He didn't touch me. Didn't even get close. He's in custody and won't get bail. But his car . . . It went out of control and into a café window.'

'Oh, Christ, *that* was John Kirk? The accident at Gordon's Kitchen?' He lifted the glass from my hand, took a long drink and gave it back. 'The crash was all over my timelines this afternoon, but not his name.' He looked upset, and I hated myself for putting him through this again.

'The details will be released later or in the morning. Colin wanted to contact the next of kin and the assault victims first. The woman who died, she was . . .' I wondered how best to describe Phyllida, which words could capture her capricious oddness, her strange beauty. 'She was the woman in the mink coat.'

'I know. We're getting her.'

'What do you mean?'

'Someone from Dunease Court phoned Winterson's just before I left. Mrs Hartigan was a client, a pre-pay. But I'd no idea it was Kirk who caused the accident.'

'Wait – *you* knew Phyllida?'

He appeared momentarily nonplussed at my casual use of her first name, but nodded. 'I'd met her, yeah. She organised everything in one visit, just a few weeks ago. You'd mentioned seeing her on the street only a few days earlier. I remember thinking it was a coincidence. She was terminally ill.'

What? 'No, she wasn't!' I could hear anger in my voice. Not only did he know her, but he knew more about her than I did. I wasn't having that. 'She can't have been!'

He looked confused. 'Why do you say that? The first responders wouldn't have access to her medical history. She was very sick, love. Actually,' he smiled, 'at the time I wished she hadn't insisted on confidentiality, because I wanted to tell you about her. She had such a cool attitude. She said she had to arrange her own funeral because the director of Dunease Court would put her body out on bin day otherwise.'

A few weeks earlier Phyllida had sat where Alec was now and told me her story. Told me how she was tired of protecting Margaret's memory. I remembered that she described keeping Margaret's secret as being in servitude to her. *That's no way to live*, she'd said. But now it appeared that she had actually been telling me, *That's no way to die.*

3

Winterson's Traditional Simplicity Plan and its exhortation to *enjoy ease of mind thanks to essentials-only arrangements* didn't include flowers, so I gave Alec money to get a wreath, insisting he get something bright, flashy. He didn't query why I was so insistent on buying her flowers. I suppose he thought I felt it appropriate, given that I was on the scene at her death, even in a tangential way. But it didn't feel tangential to me. Over and over I'd wondered what would have happened if John Kirk hadn't spotted me. Perhaps he'd have noticed the BMW sooner, in which case Phyllida would still be alive – for a while longer at least. I'd said as much to Colin but he didn't agree. Kirk was more than three times over the limit, he said. Distracted by seeing me or not, he simply wouldn't have had the reaction time when the BMW turned the corner so fast.

Phyllida's funeral was the first time I had seen Alec at work since the day we'd met. It was strange to see the Winterson's version of him – serious, watchful, quiet – and know that a few hours later he'd be back home, bare feet on the table, listening to music, drinking a beer, his head free of the day's grief. There were only a handful of people at the service and most of them I recognised as Dunease Court staff. I noticed Ron the receptionist, and the residents who'd been on the New Year's Day walk. 'Hello, there,' I said to one of them.

'Have we met?' he replied, bewildered.

'Sorry.' Sometimes I forgot to pretend I didn't recognise people. 'My mistake.'

Alec introduced me to the director of Dunease Court as a police officer, one of the first at the scene of the crash. Robert Grain had a plump, oven-ready look to him, and when we shook hands I noticed his were perfectly manicured, far more so than my own. At one point, he and I stood alone together, Phyllida's coffin just a few feet away.

'The poor woman,' he said, his over-hushed tones making me want to snap, *She can't hear you, you know.* 'And after all she'd already been through. Just imagine the agony she had already suffered! Boiling oil!' He gave a theatrical shudder.

'What do you mean?'

'I beg your pardon, Detective Constable Tenant. I forgot that you wouldn't have known her history. She worked in a commercial kitchen for years. Close on twenty, I believe. One of those places that makes pre-packed dinners for supermarkets, you know the sort of thing. She had an accident – slipped and fell, knocking a vat of cooking oil all down one side of her. She was in hospital for months. That was long before she came to live with us at Dunease Court. She confided in me, but I'm sure she'd understand my sharing her history with you. Phyllida had been very well compensated for her injuries, which enabled her to live out her days in such wonderful comfort as Dunease Court provides.' The ponderous way in which he readjusted

his features when he said her name was as if an internal
monologue had supplied the stage direction *He smiles fondly.*

'What are you talking about?' I could hear how rude, even
aggressive, I sounded. I didn't care. The police officer in me
wanted to assert and refute and argue. To challenge his
unctuous 'confided'. To defend her with photos, with studios
and stardom. *Her history!* 'How do you know that?'

He looked at me strangely. 'She told me, naturally. Dunease
Court has a comprehensive interview process. The first thing
she bought with her compensation was a fur coat. She had
always wanted one, she said, since she was a child. Though she
told my colleague Ron that it was a gift from a former, ahem,
lover.' Again, that *faux*-indulgent smile. 'Who knows? Phyllida
was quite the character. So . . . whimsical, I suppose you might
say.' This patronising description made me hot with anger.
No, no, no, I wanted to shout. *You're wrong.* It was nonsense.
Wasn't it? But . . . what if she was not the woman I believed
her to be? In which case, who was she? And Jack? Everyone,
in fact, every character in the story of her life as she'd told it
to me. I recalled using the word 'legends' to describe Margaret
Warner and Philip Harrison, and she had corrected me; to her it
suggested a story that had no basis in reality. Surely someone
so particular must have been telling the truth. But what reason
would Robert Grain have to lie? I tried another tack.

'What about her family?'

'She was divorced, and we haven't been able to make
contact with the next of kin listed in our files. The phone
number she gave us appears to be incorrect. I hope it doesn't
cause any complications, when it comes to claiming her
ashes.' He nodded towards the coffin, his voice dropping

again. 'Dunease Court has no provision to store that sort of, eh, material. Health and safety, you understand.'

Was my version of Phyllida the true one, or was his? Or neither? Phyllida's life as she'd related it to me sounded like memories revealed, not a fantasy shared. I would have seen it on her face had she been lying, I was sure of it. It made no sense. Okay, so I hadn't known she was terminally ill, but why should she tell a near-stranger something so profound? The prospect of untethering from the world made more sense of the shoplifting and her complete disregard for getting caught.

Finding the truth would be easy for a police officer: adding one fact to another, as a necklace is strung, bead by bead. Put everything in a line and tug until it gave. But my impulse to investigate fizzled out almost immediately. I wasn't prepared to take the risk that the trail might lead to Robert Grain's version of her. Whoever she was, she had been real to me. More real, in fact, than many of the lives I watched playing out on screen every day.

There was a simple reason I'd never told Alec I knew her: her story wasn't mine to shade or dilute. It would have been over so quickly had I retold it: every minute of each decade of her existence reduced to the length of time it took me to stumble forward and back through the years. I would have forced a form on something shapeless. How can we frame a life until it ends? Only when it stops being an unending sequence of present moments, one tumbling after the other, only then is it visible. Knowable. The story of a person doesn't exist until life is over. Perhaps we are all just memes, waiting to be followed.

If the *real* past is in living memory, then the history Phyllida told me was true because it was alive inside me. Her story would end when mine did. Until then, I could hold tight the myth of Mrs Jack Hartigan, of Phyllida Hartigan. Of Violet Dockery, too: the woman I had never really encountered at all, even though I had sat with her, heard her speak. Of everyone Phyllida had been, Violet Dockery was the most long-lost of them all.

Well, let Robert Grain keep his version of her, I decided. I would keep mine. That's how the world works, isn't it? There is no heart in what's real. Truth is momentary, fleeting. It has become what we claim for it.

I said a quick goodbye to Alec and turned to go. I'd only been back at work for three days before needing to take leave for the funeral, but because Winterson's Traditional Simplicity Plan was so traditionally simple it was barely noon, so I decided to go in after all. Colin had assigned me a case of eight unidentified dead following a fire in a homeless hostel a fortnight earlier, and I was itching to get back to my screen.

'Wait! You're Susanna, aren't you?' Ron stopped me at the door.

'What?' I nodded, still distracted. 'Sorry, yes.'

'We found this in Mrs Hartigan's room. It's addressed to you. I brought it in case I saw you here.' He passed me a Pavement Books bag containing *German Poets of the Great War* and an old ledger. Its marbled cover was faded and scratched, and the cloth binding down the spine had frayed. There was a yellow Post-it stuck to the front: *From one detective to another. You will discover a familiar name here. PH.*

I waited until I was on the Tube to have a proper look. *Case Notes, 1913. Private* was handwritten in ink on the flyleaf and a small card was glued inside the front cover, *Violet Hill Investigations. 12 Cleveland Street, WC. TN Regent 2820. Specialists in private enquiries of a personal or delicate nature.* The book was about two-thirds full, and each page appeared to be a densely written account of an investigation. I'd never heard of Violet Hill, so she couldn't have been the familiar name Phyllida's note referred to. I flicked at random through a series of petty crimes, a litany of faithless husbands, of dog snatchings and domestic pilferings. Then I saw it.

Case number 17. Gareth Slatten. Commencement date: 27 October 1913.
£1 deposit paid at commencement.
Name: Hannah Slatten, 38 Harmon Terrace, NW5.

Hannah's husband Gareth Slatten is footman to Henry Gardiner, the Marquess of Denismore, 33 Cranford Crescent, NW1. My estimate of Hannah is that she is approx. 30 years. Tall, thin build, rough hands. Very pale. Bright copper hair, which makes her skin even paler. Intelligent, but nervy, restless. Has the bewildered hardness of a woman who understands what happiness is, yet has none, nor the means to achieve it. She was in service as nursery maid in the same household as her husband until marriage in 1905, and had cared for the Gardiner daughters as though they were from her own flesh, she said. Has three children herself, the youngest (a boy) was with her. She did not offer the child's name. Her husband was taken in charge 4 days ago & remains on remand in Brixton Prison. She offered £2, or as close to it as she said she could borrow, to clear her husband of the charges of theft alleged by his employer, who is adamant that Gareth stole money & personal items, referred to in the charge documents as 'significant family heirlooms.'

As two of my last four cases involved missing pets, I tried not to betray my excitement at such an important commission. I wanted her to believe her request was the sort of everyday investigation I could sleuth in my sleep, and said as much (which I regretted immediately). 'You're the cheapest I could find,' she replied.

29 October. I asked Hannah to describe the household & she referred to the cook Mrs Keily as 'a drinker and a fool'. Excellent news. Today I watched outside 33 Cd. Cres. until Keily left on her half-day out. Followed her 2 miles to Avery's pawnbroker's on Winton St., & then to the Five Lamps public house, where she remained for one hour, twelve minutes. From there, to Regent's Park to watch the band. She was in drink by then. It was easy to engage her in conversation by purporting to be a governess. I enquired if her household was in need & she said not, & would not 'recommend her master's name, not even to her worst enemy'. (Tho' the smell of port & brandy on her breath would have been enough to deter anyone wishing her harm.) I encouraged her to talk about the household, & she offered that the footman is 'a vain, stupid man' – but didn't mention his current predicament, which, surely, is curious? – and the maids are 'thick as doorsteps only not as useful'. If only every case had a Mrs Keily! I bumped her arm to ensure she dropped her bag, & palmed the Avery pawn chit while fussing around her to restore its contents. Chit redeemed a cut glass & gold-leaf bird, clearly of value. There are two large pawnbrokers' shops between Cd. Cres. & Winton St. so

I feel it a safe assumption the ornament was one she did not want to be seen with by anyone who might know her household or situation.

30 October. Morning: Hannah confirmed the ornament is the property of her husband's employer the marquess: a wedding gift, she says.

Afternoon: waited until the butler was out on an errand. Called at the kitchen door & insisted on speaking with Mrs Keily in private. Showed her the ornament. Transpires that she was stealing from a thief – if stealing one's own possessions lays one open to such a charge. Initially she claimed to have found the bird while looking for some mislaid serving spoons. When pressed, she admitted coming across the items allegedly stolen by Slatten hidden in a trunk in an unused attic room & decided to take one for herself. The master himself placed the items there – she was adamant she saw him do so (which made a mockery of her claim to have merely come across them. Hannah Slatten was right; the woman is a fool). How much cash did you find? I asked. What cash? she said. There was no money in the trunk. The master would never leave a penny down without a reason, she said. He manages the household expenses himself, and holds every farthing prisoner. She did not – and will not – go to the police: she & her husband would both lose their places immediately & without a character. Her husband has dependent family she said, but did not elaborate. Yet it still made no sense. Why would the Marquess of Denismore trump up this charge against his footman, a man in his employ for well over a decade, and whose wife – as Keily herself told me – had been so favoured by Gardiner's daughters? She had no idea, she said. Nonsense, of course. Household staff always have an idea. I wasn't satisfied with her explanation, I told her, & would be taking the ornament to her master after all. I turned to go, taking a risk on the woman's fear & greed.

She called me back: if I returned the ornament to her, & promised to cut her name out of the entire business, she would tell me. I agreed.

Keily's story is that Slatten had taken a most terrible advantage of Beatrice Gardiner, the younger of the two Gardiner girls. She is fifteen. The circumstances are now such that both Henry Gardiner and his wife are aware of the girl's unfortunate situation. The master flew into a ferocious rage, and threatened all manner of ruin for Slatten, until Lady Virginia, fearful that gossip would ruin whatever was left of Beatrice's chances for the future, halted him.

Mrs Keily's opinion is that the Gardiners' daughter is 'a terrible, forward piece, sniffing for trouble since she left the nursery & now she's found it'. But I was not there to argue the rights & wrongs of the matter. I wanted only the truth Hannah was paying for.

They are all thieves in that house. The theft charge was Henry Gardiner's revenge: it ensured prison, ignominy, a ruined family, yet his child's name would never be mentioned. Presumably there was never so much as a penny in cash stolen: as the master, he could claim anything was gone & be sure that no one would call him a liar, least of all the police. Slatten was a thief too, but what he stole was virtue. As for Keily, she viewed her own thieving as fair wages for silence.

31 October. Hannah called at the office with gaol visiting order for 2 Nov. for me. She had begged one for herself too, for the following day. I'm nervous. I have never been to Brixton Prison before.

2 November. What a truly frightening place! Dirty and exhaustingly noisy, without a screed of privacy. Everyone packed in together, yet each prisoner entirely, pathetically, alone. A man could go mad from the unending clatter. Slatten blustered initially: he had done nothing wrong, the charges were false, etc., etc. Without mentioning her name, I relayed what Keily had told me & said I would go to the marquess to corroborate the story if I needed to. He admitted it & begged me not to tell Hannah, that it would destroy her. The girl wouldn't leave him be, he said. Not for a year or more. He would change his plea, he said, admit guilt to the thefts & accept his sentence.

Evening: called to see Hannah. Her small parlour was very cold and damp & I could hear children shrieking & squabbling in the kitchen. One of them has a loud, croupy cough. Did Gareth Slatten truly think I would agree to wilfully cheat his wife of the truth she was paying for? That she deserved & I promised? Hannah stayed very silent and still while I told her what I had discovered. So quiet, in fact, that I repeated myself, unsure she had understood what I was telling her.

4 November. Gareth Slatten is dead. I hardly know how to write it. He killed himself yesterday, shortly after Hannah's visit. I have read her note over and over, yet it remains a jumble of words.

5 November. Visited Hannah, but she would not let me into the house. She is distraught, and I do not know her well enough to tell whether his death or his actions in life are making the larger contribution to her grief. She has very little money left, she says, & without Gareth's income will be evicted by Christmas. She had no intention of paying me, she said, because it was my 'vicious meddling' that left her with a dead husband.

14 December. Newspaper report of inquest. Verdict is that he ripped his shirt for a noose & hanged himself while the balance of his mind was disturbed. The coroner didn't mention my name or enquiries, merely Slatten himself and the Gardiner family.

16 December. After much deliberation, I called on the marquess at Cd. Cres. He was reluctant to see me until I said I would go to the police if he did not make financial restitution to Slatten's family. Hannah was his daughters' nursery maid once, I reminded him, but mention of her name made him angrier & he accused her of being 'a party to the whole sordid business'. He turned me out of the house, swearing he will ruin me too if I ever make a word of it public. The police will not take my word over his, he told me, and before he'd even finished his sentence, I knew he was right. I knew my threats were hollow ones, not even worth the breath

carrying them. Noreen Keily will deny everything for fear of dismissal. It is a risk I cannot take.

20 December. Wrote to Hannah. Related my visit to her erstwhile employer & his refusal to listen to the dire situation she is left with. There is nothing else to be done.

21 December. From attic to cellar, Cranford Crescent is a house of thieves. Between them, they have stolen Hannah Slatten's future & that of her children. My letter was returned, opened.& resealed, with the words 'May he rot in hell for eternity' scribbled on the envelope. But whether it was Henry Gardiner or Gareth Slatten she meant, I don't know.

The last words Hannah spoke as she shut her door on me last month are chasing each other inside my head. I cannot seem to shake them off. 'She is the age,' she said, her voice low, 'of his own child.'

Bar a few ink splodges, the remaining pages were blank. So the 'familiar name' to which Phyllida's note referred was Henry Gardiner's. She must have recognised it when I pointed out the plaque on our house. But this man, so heartless in his power, was completely different from the character I had conjured up . . . and to think that the man I had cast as a tragic, ill-treated servant had abused Gardiner's child. Gardiner had been so cruel to Slatten's family, but could I blame him for wishing ill on the man who brought such pain to his own?

From one detective to another, I thought. I double-checked the date on the ledger: 1913. There were no women serving in the police in 1913. It was tough enough being a female detective now, so what must it have been like a hundred years earlier? And a private one at that: a woman without a regular wage, dependent on the mistakes or distress of others for her living.

Alec once told me that the dead don't let you down. But in giving me Violet Hill's notebook, Phyllida had proved him wrong. How had she come across it? It was a handwritten diary, so though it would be entirely in keeping with her personality to give me a stolen book, she hadn't nicked it from a shop. How typical of her to leave a riddle behind. Phyllida's original name was Violet: perhaps there was some connection. I quickly googled *Violet Hill Investigator 1913* but found nothing. I turned the book over in my hands, examining it as intently as if it were evidence. It appeared perfectly authentic: handwritten in ink, the paper faded, the card covers spotted with damp. Tucked inside the back cover was a piece of paper, folded into four: *A fee earned is a fee deserved. Yrs. ACD.* It looked old but was undated, so I couldn't tell which entry in the journal it related to or who ACD might be. I leafed through the pages again, inhaling its musty smell, picking out words – *governess, mite, errant* – from another world.

The train screeched and shook. It was time to get off, to where my life was waiting for me, just minutes ahead. Being shunted back into myself had been exhausting. I had gone back to work more tired than I had been before Christmas. But at least I was *me* again, narrator and witness of my own existence.

I closed Violet Hill's case notes. In the sudden gloom of a tunnel the lights flickered and I glanced up. In the train window, a shadowy blue-eyed woman holding a book was looking back at me.

NOVEMBER 1919

'Lemon or orange?' Chrissie's fingers are dangling hooks on lines. She hovers over the candied lemon then swerves off to one side and lands an orange instead. 'Mmm.' She pops it into her mouth and speaks while she chews. 'Will Major Gillies hold up your operation during the minute's silence?'

'I didn't want to ask.'

'It's odd, isn't it, to think of the country – everyone all together – just stopping like that?'

He knows she's picturing the world as a game of musical chairs, the sudden freeze in mid-action as the tune falls still: dogs stopped in their bark; postmen with one hand raised to the letterbox; cooks at open oven doors, roasting trays searing their meaty hands. 'I think it's intended to be more of a pause,' he says, imagining a surgeon slicing open a chin or cheek or cartilage, the slim steel blade sunk fast in the flesh for a count of sixty, 'so lots of people will have planned where they'll be and what they'll be doing.' She's right, though. It *is* hard to imagine ships forced to hold course and trains halting in the middle of nowhere, ignoring their devout allegiance to the timetable. Everyone united in a mourning that is supposed to feed the nation's soul, but to him feels maudlin and stagey. What's wrong with grieving in your own private way? Why does it have to be collective, a national spectacle? There's already talk in the newspapers of holding a silence ceremony every year. What a terrible idea, he thinks. Because what will happen when no one is left alive who lost someone to the war? Silence is of no use to history. How are generations as yet unborn to learn from the absence of sound?

'Did I tell you I got a letter yesterday from a woman who used to be a client?' she says. 'Tanner forwarded it. Settling an account a full two and a half years late. Imagine!' She leans forward, suddenly animated.

'Why did she pay up after all this time?'

Chrissie is always eager to talk about Violet's cases. If only she could get a book made out of them, she has told him often, 'so that they won't get lost'.

'This woman took Violet on to find out if her husband had,' she flushes, 'a mistress. And when it turned out he did and, guess what, a kiddie too, she – Mrs Johnson her name is – took up nasty and said she wasn't going to pay. Well, he's only dropped the woman and the kiddie and gone back to her after all this time! With his tail well tucked between his legs, Mrs Johnson said in her letter. She decided it would be a bad omen not to pay up, now that he's home again. What should I do?' Chrissie says. 'Should I return the money?'

'Keep it,' Will says. 'You deserve it. So, what are you going to do on Tuesday? Will you go to the Cenotaph?'

'No. I can't stand the stink of all those flowers piled up and left to rot.' She shudders. 'Remember in July?' Of course he does. They had gone for a walk there, on one of his day trips to London. It was the hottest summer in eight years and the stench of the wilting, stinking mounds had turned his stomach. New flowers delivered daily were piled on top of the old, the soon-to-be-dead heaped upon the already-dead. All those country meadows and gardens and fancy flower shops giving up their harvest, just as their fields and villages and streets once yielded their men.

'Anyway, I'll be at work.' Chrissie is a typist at the Ministry of Pensions. 'A minute's silence in that room will be nice. I wish we had one every hour.' There are thirty girls in the room and the incessant clacking of typewriters drives her dotty. He hasn't had the courage to say it to her yet, but soon he will be out, and earning, and then she'll never have to hear another typewriter again if she doesn't want to. That day in London at the Cenotaph, she'd called him a hero, but he'd asked her not to say that again. He hates the word. What horrible impossible standard does that place on a clay-footed man to be believed a hero by a woman? Some hero he is anyway, he thinks, that he doesn't yet have the courage to tell Chrissie he loves her, that he can't bear the thought of going through the rest of his life without her near him. After his next operation, he's decided. He'll tell her then, for sure. The last one didn't go well and had to be redone, which meant an additional two months in hospital. But the next one? If he comes through that all right, then yes. He'll tell her.

She tucks the lid back onto the box and stashes the sweets in the drawer of the little cabinet next to his bed. 'I suppose unless Major Gillies changes the time of your operation, you'll be asleep and miss the whole thing.'

'Me and the babies of England all having our naps.'

She smiles. Chrissie doesn't laugh as much as she did when he first met her nine months earlier. She just appeared in the ward one day: a woman he'd never heard of, clutching a parcel from Davey. She had been sweet on his brother, it was obvious, but then so were all women, if Davey wanted them to be. She'd stood nearby as he unwrapped the package. There wasn't much to it. A note, saying *I'm away. Look after yourself. D.* It was wrapped around a horribly familiar green lozenge-shaped disc. He turned it over in his hand. Harry's identity tag, still on its cord. Will hadn't known Davey had it in his possession, or how he'd got hold of it. The only other thing in the envelope was yet another pawnbroker's chit for Davey's Star Medal.

Look after yourself. How was he to interpret that? A sign of brotherly affection ('Take care now, won't you'); a callous statement ('Look after yourself because, believe me, I won't'); a knowing life lesson ('Our duty is to mind ourselves, each and every one')? He shrugged. It hadn't mattered which way he looked at it, Davey was gone and would come back only if or when it suited him.

Chrissie hadn't said much about Davey that first day. It had taken a while for the full story about his brother's connection to her and her employer to come out. He could tell his brother had let Chrissie down in some way, which made it doubly kind that she had taken the trouble of coming to Sidcup. It would be months before she told him that she had peeped inside the parcel and decided it would be bringing all manner of bad luck down on herself not to ensure the safe return of a dead man's identity disc to his family. Will had written to her the day after her visit, to thank her for fulfilling Davey's commission. Unexpectedly, she had replied, offering to redeem Metcalfe's chit for him. Within a month, she was visiting regularly. Every Sunday she appears, the answer to a prayer he didn't know he'd made. She comes on her half-day too, when she doesn't have errands to run for her mother. They usually walk in the grounds, or into Sidcup, but Gillies told him he's to rest before the next operation, so today they are confined to the ward.

He takes Neville's metal straw from his breast pocket and twists it between his fingers. He's taken to doing this almost without noticing, twirling it like a miniature baton. Chrissie teases him sometimes, says he's like a child with a pretend thermometer, playing at being a doctor. Neville's mother had visited Will when she and her husband came to collect their son's body. She told him that all those months while Neville was in hospital she had felt as though she was hardly breathing. The entire time, she felt as though she was standing at her own front door, with a War Office telegram just put into her hand, which she refused to open: while it was still sealed, there was a dim comfort to be had in the not-knowing. 'But now it's open,' she said, 'and everything's over.' She had taken Will's hand. 'Thank you for your kindness to my son. I won't forget it.' But he hopes she will. He doesn't want her to feel a forced connection to him, a gossamer thread tying his existence to Neville's. He doesn't want her to think of him, and what he is doing, and feel forced to compare it to her son's stunted life.

'I got a letter yesterday too. From Davey.' He takes an envelope from the drawer and passes it to her.

'He's in *Ypres*? She pronounces it the soldiers' way, *Wipers*. 'He's gone back to where the fighting was?'

'And where Harry died. Sounds like him and his boss are

doing a roaring trade, organising séances for touring visitors. He says there's plenty of people want to go there, to get close to their dead.'

'But why? It's not as though folk have graves to visit.'

'That doesn't seem to matter. In fact, it probably makes it easier. They can conjure up whoever, wherever, and can't get caught out. Look at this. The new *Michelin Tyre Guide*. He sent it with the letter.'

'What's that say?'

'*Ypres: un guide, un panorama, une histoire.*'

'Do you understand it?'

He nods. His French is excellent; he can read it perfectly. But *understand*? No. The book is full of before and after photographs and drawings. Cathedrals and grand civic buildings and beautiful countryside, next to empty fields and ruined homes. For the life of him, Will can't imagine why anyone would want it.

'Pickford's are doing tours of the battlefields. There's a poster on the Underground,' she says. 'Thirty-six pounds all found for ten days. Luxurious accommodation, it said! Imagine that.'

Davey had tucked a note into the book:

Am I the last of the soldiers or the first of the tourists, who's to know? Apart from being good at doing voices, that medium we were using was a dead loss. Selbarre sent her packing a while back. We've got a new one, a Belgian piece, and we're making plenty. New York next, so Selbarre says, though he's been promising that for a long while. Hope this catches up with you, if you have left Queen Mary's.

To be a visiting spectator, a guest in the place where he once thought he'd end his days? No, he can't imagine it. It makes him uncomfortable, the thought of tourists exploring absence. Spectators of nothing. Rushing around the vanished churches, honking their new motor cars around the jagged, rusting chaos of the fields. He imagines an empty place, a countryside without a bird to be heard or an animal to be seen, yet crowds of people wandering around, each and every one treading over grave after grave, trampling the hidden dead – Harry! – further and further into the ground. And his brother in the thick of it, greedily harvesting money from grief.

'War doesn't change people at all, does it?' he says.

She shakes her head. 'Some folk, well, some folk are just no good and that's all there is to it.'

He likes the unquestioning certainty in her. It's not a lack of curiosity, more an assumption that the world isn't all hers to know. She doesn't ask him much about his war. She doesn't believe she should insist on trying to understand what he experienced. She knows she never can, and rather than chase that ache, instead she is practical. And kind and honest. What better way to live can there be?

Will had spotted an article in the *Sunday Pictorial* a few weeks before: a spirit photograph of Kingsley Conan Doyle, which was, according to his grieving father, definitely supernormal and not remotely fraudulent. The article reported that Sir Arthur Conan Doyle was planning more tours, and at each place would give lectures on spiritualism and spirit photography, illustrated by lantern slides. Will had thrown away the newspaper. While the world continued to be distraught, there would always be a place for men like Davey, willing to supply comfort at a cost.

The bell for visiting time rings. It used to mean nothing to him, that sound, but now he jumps to it, like a dog sighting its lead. The bell brings her and it takes her away. He times the weeks to her visits now, feels the crescendo of his week build to them. His life is again, finally, tidal. He now trusts it to return when it leaves.

Since her third visit, Chrissie has always kissed him hello and goodbye. That visit was soon after he'd had a dressing changed so he hadn't been wearing the mask. She had kissed his cheek, so gently as barely to touch a patch of new, exposed skin. She had never seen his face before, yet she smiled, and he was grateful to her for doing so. Today, the mask sits on the table next to him. She leans over and gives it a peck on the tip of its tin nose. 'It's like kissing the side of a tram,' she says, and he surprises himself by laughing. She touches his cheek, then leans back again and stares at his face. 'There's definitely been a big improvement,' she says. 'Since last month, I can really see it. You'll be out of here before you know it!'

'Then what?'

'You know what! You should be a teacher again. Major Gillies says so too, and you've told me yourself that you want to. You're young, Will. Think of all the lucky little kiddies out there just waiting to learn what you've got to tell them!' Chrissie lifts her hand to her lips to lick the last traces of sugar from her fingers, then wipes them on her handkerchief. The white square is a diminutive flag of surrender against the dense black of her dress. She lifts a fold of the black crêpe between two fingers.

'I never had use of mourning during the war.' She drops the fabric and puts the handkerchief back into her handbag. 'I never thought the person I'd be wearing it for would be her.'

Her voice is low and sad as she stands up. 'No. Not Violet.'

Pneumonia had taken Violet from healthy to ill to recovering to relapsed in little more than a week. Chrissie was by her side the entire time. She'd fallen so very ill so quickly that, for the first few hours, Chrissie was sure it was the Spanish flu, and sat there, waiting for her skin to turn that horrible amethyst colour. But, no, the doctor told them. It wasn't that. And the relief! Lord, the joy Chrissie had felt at hearing those words, forgetting that other, ordinary, illnesses could slaughter a person too, just as they always had before the plague of peacetime attacked the country. But can any death be ordinary? he wonders. Won't we each wish a different wish in that moment, pray on a different star, finally admit and atone for a different misdeed?

Chrissie had organised Violet's funeral. Two weeks later, at the end of June, Chrissie closed Violet Hill Investigations. She boxed up all the calling cards, ledgers and notebooks and keeps them safely, along with the suit. The first time she took the jacket from the peg, it rustled. Sheets of newspaper from December were still pressed into the lining. She took them out, pressed them again, and put them back where they belonged. She told him about finding a cashier's cheque in Violet's desk, with a note pinned to it: A fee earned is a fee deserved. Yrs. ACD. The cheque was for twenty guineas, yet Chrissie had so far resisted his suggestion that she cash it and keep the money, which is surely what Violet would have wanted. But Violet had had a reason for keeping it, Chrissie thought, so why should she be any different?

Nurse Goodfellow signals from the door. She's holding it open, her customary encouragement to the last straggling visitors to be on their way. 'Wait!' Will says, suddenly nervous, desperate not to watch her walk away. He tugs her arm so that she has to sit down beside him again. What does he want to say? I'm frightened. I love you. I'm sorry you lost her.

'What is it?'

'Nothing. See you next Sunday.' He doesn't know where the edges of his love for her are. Perhaps there are none. He pictures love as a magic carpet, forever unfurling with each step they take. Moving them forward, ever forward.

'That all?' Chrissie asks, but doesn't stand up again. She stays perfectly still, so they are side by side, both facing forward. Then she turns her face to the window over his bed.

'Look,' she says. The panes are perfectly clear and polished and suddenly full of the low winter sunshine that Violet loved. 'It wasn't her time, Will, it just wasn't. It's so unfair.'

Nor was it Harry's or Neville's, or the dozens of comrades' Will lost. Or the hundreds of thousands of others just like him and everyone they lost . . . each individual pain swelling, multiplying. Echoing to the ends of the earth. To where there must be no time, no way of making sense of it. It will never happen again, that's for sure. How could it? The world has been washed clean, and children – his and Chrissie's children, he desperately hopes – must grow up strong and wise and true, untainted by cruelty. 'Death is unfair. There's no use holding it to account.'

'I talk to her sometimes,' she says. 'As though she'd just popped into another room. Out of sight, but still there, around the corner.'

'I know,' he says.

'And every time she doesn't answer, it cuts me. Every time!'

He says nothing. Because what is there to say, when there is no single word in any language in the world that could ever be the balm for her loss?

Will takes Chrissie's hand into his own, covering his palm. Her fingertips rest on the pulse in his wrist, rough and warm, as though it had always been just the two of them. As though they would always be there.